The Unusual Second Life of Thomas Weaver

by

Shawn Inmon

The Unusual Second Life of Thomas Weaver

by Shawn Inmon

Copyright © 2016 Shawn Inmon

All rights reserved.

No part of this book may be reproduced or transmitted in any form or by any means without written permission from the publisher, with the exception of brief quotations in a review.

This book is a work of fiction. Any resemblance to events or persons living or dead is purely coincidental.

ISBN: 1535239492

Also in ebook publication

Printed in the United States of America

Dedication

For Tommy, Eric, and Carl

I hope I did you justice

Chapter One
August 1976

"C'mon, Zack. You promised."

This was true. For Tommy's fifteenth birthday, in a moment of guilty weakness, Zack had promised to take him to one of the lake parties. He had evaded keeping that promise, but tonight was the last party before Zack left for Oregon State, and Tommy knew it.

"Okay, you can come tonight, but don't make me regret it. If you tell Mom anything, I'll kill you. Understand?" Zack waited for Tommy to meet his eyes.

Tommy looked up at his big brother, five inches taller than him, even after he'd had what was going to pass for his growth spurt. He gave him what he hoped was a confidence-inspiring grin.

"Do I look like a narc to you?" In light of their history, that was a poor choice of words. Tommy had ratted Zack out more times than he could remember.

Zack's eyes narrowed. "No, you don't, at least not lately." Lightning quick, Zack punched him in the side. Tommy winced, but didn't say a word. "That's why I'm bringing you along. Well, that and you make a good cover story with Mom. She'd never believe I'd take you to a kegger."

I can't really believe it either, but...heck yeah!

"As far as she knows, we're just going to the lake for a bonfire. Got it?"

"Got it."

Zack's gaze lingered for two seconds longer, looking for weakness. "Good. We're leaving in fifteen minutes. Get changed and grab a towel."

Anything Tommy said could endanger his chances of going, so he shut up and went to their bedroom at the back of the house, the one that would soon be all his. He shimmied out of his gym shorts and fished his blue and gold swim trunks out of the bottom drawer. When Tommy reappeared in the living room, Zack shook his head. Skinny legs, Mom-approved swimsuit. "Oh, hell no. Not going to cut it. You look like you're auditioning for the Osmonds."

Zack and Tommy were as different as brothers could be. Zack was a younger version of their father, six feet tall with wavy brown hair that he wore in a long, careless shag. He was a natural athlete, an excellent middle distance runner with a full ride track scholarship at Oregon State. Zack got good grades and managed to stay out of serious trouble, due more to his ability to charm his way out of consequences than to his behavior. Zack had every girl he was ever interested in, and he had been interested in a lot.

Tommy was not handsome, athletic, academically gifted, charismatic, or popular. He studied hard to get lower grades than Zack got without effort. He had a few good friends, but none of them were the popular kids who ran the school. Zack reigned over the popular clique. Seeing the brothers together, people sometimes wondered if the milkman had made an extra delivery on his early morning run, sixteen years earlier.

For Tommy, therefore, this debut with Zack's friends felt important. If he had any chance to move up the hipness scale at Middle Falls High, it would start at this party.

"Man, don't you ever go outside?" Zack stared pointedly at Tommy's pale legs.

Tommy didn't go outside much. He was fair-skinned, and long exposure to the sun turned him into a giant freckle. Or roasted him like a lobster.

"Okay. Never mind. Too late to do anything about that, but that swimsuit has got to go. It looks like something Mom picked out for you."

Tommy opened his mouth to say, "She did," but wisely closed it.

"You must have a pair of old jeans in there that you won't need for school this year, don't you?"

Tommy ran a quick mental inventory of his pants and said, "Yeah, but—"

"No buts. Go get 'em. Hurry."

When Tommy returned with the jeans, Zack brandished a pair of scissors. The jeans were well-worn, faded and soft with wear. Zack chopped at the legs with abandon, then held out his masterpiece with a devilish smile.

Zack had cut the jeans off so short that the pockets on both sides hung down below the cut. "Holy shit, Zack! You cut 'em off too short! My ass will hang out." Tommy's voice sounded high and squeaky in his own ears, so he shut up.

"Man up. Don't be a baby. Look at mine."

Zack's own cutoffs were the same, at least in theory. Of course, the style wouldn't look the same on Tommy. *Screw it. If I have to let my ass hang out of my cutoffs in order to get into this party, so be it.* "Change your shirt, too. Don't you have something cool to wear? Wait, what am I thinking? Of course you don't. Look under my bed, my Foghat shirt is under there. You can wear it tonight."

"Yes!" Tommy turned and almost stepped on Amy, their dachshund. Amy had a knack for standing where she was most likely to be in the way. He jumped over her, yelled, "Sorry, Amy!" over his shoulder, then nearly barreled over his mother, Anne, half hidden behind a towering laundry basket. "Sorry, Mom!"

"Those better not be the jeans I got you for Easter. Those have to last you until Christmas!" The words echoed off the bedroom door, which Tommy had shut behind him. He pulled off the cutoffs and considered a new dilemma. He held the cutoffs against him. *Do I need underwear with this? I don't want to be a complete dork, but I don't want my dingle berries hanging out, either.* He tried the cutoffs on commando, but he was convinced he would be making his big debut in more ways than one.

Underwear it is.

Tommy rummaged under Zack's bed, pushing aside a stack of *Penthouses* and *Playboys*, until he found the black Foghat T-shirt. It was slightly rank, but no doubt cooler than a clean white shirt. He pulled it on and examined his look in the half-mirror over the dresser. His hair stuck out at many angles, as it always had. *Nothing ever helps, so why bother?* He gave up and headed for the front room.

Chapter Two

Zack jumped and slid gracefully across the hood of the '69 Camaro. He had seen Starsky and Hutch do the same thing a few weeks before and he'd been doing it ever since. Tommy opened the passenger door, clambered in and rolled down the window. The V-8 rumbled to life with its hoarse feline growl. The 8-track stereo clicked on and the rolling intro to Led Zeppelin's *Kashmir* blared from the speakers. Zack nodded his head in rhythm to the music, looked at Tommy, smiled his Pepsodent smile, and winked.

Man, I wish I could hate him. No one can hate Zack, though. The bastard.

"You can ride shotgun unless we see some foxy girl walking down the road, then you're in the back. Got it?"

"Got it." Tommy pursed his lips and squinted out toward the horizon, going for his best 'I'm cool' pose. He had practiced it in the mirror that afternoon.

Twenty minutes later, Zack turned the Camaro off the highway onto a stretch of country road. A few miles later, he slowed and turned left onto a gravel road. This deteriorated into a dirt road, which soon gave way to a meadow marked by half a dozen sets of tire tracks. A campfire crackled in a crudely rocked fire pit, loosely surrounded by large logs. Around the perimeter sat three old pickup trucks, a Pinto, an old Dodge, and a '63 Impala. On the far side of the meadow was what Zack and his friends termed The Beach. It was just a muddy lake shore, but the name had stuck.

Zack rolled up and parked beside the Pinto. "Listen, Squirt. Try to find somebody that's not too cool and hang out with them. Just don't draw attention to yourself and you'll be fine. You're my brother, after all." He got out of the Camaro and walked up to a 300-pound behemoth lounging on a truck tailgate. "Beer me, Tiny."

Jim "Tiny" Patterson had a lumberjack beard that merged with the black thatch on his chest. Zack claimed that Tiny had hit puberty in kindergarten. Tiny pulled a clear plastic cup off a stack, held it under the tap of the keg sitting next to him, and handed it over. Zack poured the entire cup down his gullet, smacked his lips, and held the cup out again. "I dub thee 'Sir Tiny, Keeper of the Keg.' Beer me again, Sir Tiny."

When Zack had his refill, he looked around the party for feminine companionship. Tommy watched as Zack's eyes fixed on a pretty brunette with long, tanned legs and a white halter top. A moment later, Zack's arm was around her, whispering something in her ear. The girl giggled.

Tommy sighed. *What's it like to be good at every damned thing you do?* He slipped out of the Camaro, trying to be inconspicuous. He considered walking up to Tiny and confidently saying, "Beer me, dude," but knew he would never be able to pull it off. He settled for eye contact and a nod. *The less I say, the less chances for me to make an ass of myself.*

"Baby Weaver," Tiny rumbled, but smiled as he said it. His paw deftly plucked another cup, filled it, then held it out.

"Thanks, man."

Tiny moved his hand back a fraction of an inch. The smile disappeared. "That'll be a buck, Baby Weaver."

Tommy flushed. The sum total of his earthly wealth amounted to less than the requested buck, and none of it was on him. He glanced around for Zack, but his brother was already gone. "Uhhh…"

Tiny smirked. "Just shittin' ya, man. You're covered."

"Oh, ha. Good one."

With Tiny's limited attention span exhausted, he began humming along to *Gimme Three Steps* by Lynyrd Skynyrd blasting out of the truck's speakers. Tommy wandered the edges of the party, flitting around like a moth at various groups, but moving away when someone looked at him. Eventually he came to rest against the side of the Camaro.

After ninety minutes, his first beer was warm and only half gone. Olympia beer was weak to begin with; as Zack always said, *It's the water, and nothing more.*

Zack had snuck out to parties like this for years, and Tommy could see why. The whole party revolved around him. Tommy had always imagined these parties to be exotic, grownup affairs. The reality fell far short. There was a lot of casual flirting, and some couples wandered off into the woods. Massive amounts of beer and marijuana were consumed, much of both by Zack, who was already looking unsteady.

Never mind. I'm at a party with the cool kids, and I haven't humiliated myself yet. Here's to me. He took a swig of the warm, flat beer, then tried to pour out the remainder without anyone noticing, lest he be revealed as a lightweight. Just then, he felt something soft and warm brush against his arm, and a feminine voice say "Hey."

He turned and looked straight into the bottle-green, stoned-drowsy, dilated eyes of Amanda Jarvis. Tommy froze. He had never been so close to a goddess before and didn't know how to act in her divine presence.

Admittedly, Amanda wasn't a goddess in the technical sense. Just like Tommy, she was a sophomore at Middle Falls High. Beyond that, they lived in different circles. She was tall and lean, with strawberry blonde hair that feathered back from her heart-shaped face and fell straight down her back. She had dated college men since eighth grade. The Amandas of Tommy's world dated Zacks, not Tommies. She was wearing cutoffs and a burnt orange halter top that showed off her dark tan. The mixture of weed, tanning lotion, and perfume that wafted from her made his knees feel a little weak.

For one dizzying moment, Tommy thought she was going to kiss him. She didn't, but she flashed her dazzling white teeth at him and said, "Hey," again. Her voice was distant, as cool as the other side of the pillow. "Uh, hey." Tommy felt the telltale burn on his cheeks. If Amanda noticed, she gave no sign.

"I had to bring my cousin tonight, and she hasn't found anyone to hang out with. She's bugging me to leave, but I'm not ready to go yet. Would you talk to her?" She ran the tips of her fingers across Tommy's neck, causing gooseflesh to erupt down his arms. He fought the urge to shiver with delight. If he'd had a tail, it would have been wagging vigorously.

Whatever minimal effort Amanda was spending to persuade Tommy to do her bidding was unnecessary. He would strip naked and run through the center of the party if she so much as asked.

"Okay!" *Too much.* "I mean, yeah, sure. Where is she?"

Amanda inclined her head toward a short, heavyset redhead sitting alone on a log, staring into the fire, heaving a long sigh of boredom.

The universe aligns.

"Yeah, sure, Amanda. I'll hang out with her. Do you know what she's interested in?"

Amanda ignored the question. She had transferred ownership of the problem to a minion, and that was all that mattered. "Her name's Georgia. That's her name, though, not where she's from." Amanda laughed.

Tommy smiled as though that were funny. "I'll talk to her."

"Thanks." Amanda vanished like a genie, leaving behind that intoxicating mix of Fabergé shampoo, dope, and Babe perfume.

Tommy looked one way, then the other, trying to be inconspicuous about his mission. Tiny had abandoned his post at the keg and was passed out, a large mound of human in the grass. Tommy refilled his cup, then wandered toward the fire.

As he approached, Georgia looked up from the flames. "I know she sent you over here. If she had the sense God gave crabapples, she'd be dangerous."

Tommy smiled. "Amanda? Yeah, she asked me to come and talk to you, but I've been spending all night trying to work up the nerve to come talk to you anyway. She just gave me an excuse." Tommy paused, waiting to see if his nose might grow.

Georgia finally looked away from the fire and sized Tommy up. She said, "Whatever, doofus," and scooched over on the log. It was a little after ten, and the sky had clouded over. The evening felt cool.

"I'm Tommy." He sat down, a reasonable distance away.

"Georgia," she said, turning to look back into the dancing flames.

"I've never seen you around town. Where do you go to school?"

"Hawaii. My Dad took a job over there a few years ago."

"Hawaii? Awesome!" Tommy eyed her copy-paper complexion, tried to imagine her laying out on a sandy beach, and imagined her roasted to magenta. Her narrowed eyes and sour expression finally delivered the message: *I don't suffer fools gladly. Wise up, or begone.*

Tommy could not wise up, but he could and did shut up.

Without looking at him, she said, "Yeah, I get it. I thought it would be cool to live in Hawaii, too, but after a few weeks, I just figured out high school is high school, wherever you are." She nodded her head absently at Amanda, now cuddled up to an older-looking guy wearing a wife beater that showed off his workout biceps. "Well, whatever. Two more years, then I'll be off to college and I can leave all that petty high school bull behind."

I wonder if college isn't just more high school on a bigger scale, Tommy thought. "What do you want to study in college?"

"What are you, my guidance counselor?" She glanced at Tommy. "Ah, forget it. I want to study Astronomy," she said, pointing up at the sky. Starless, thanks to the clouds. As she did, a huge, warm raindrop splashed against her pale skin, as if the very stars she wanted to study had spat on her. There hadn't been any rain in the forecast. More warm drops splattered down, then became a sudden sheet of water. The bonfire hissed as people scattered for cover.

Tommy yelled "See ya!" to Georgia, ran to the Camaro, and jumped into the shotgun seat. Zack did not show up; he was probably off in the woods with that foxy girl. After five minutes, when Zack did not materialize, Tommy looked in the ignition and saw that Zack had left the keys in. He turned the key a click, then flipped the wipers on. They could barely keep up with the deluge.

The party was obviously over. Engines started all around him. As the Pinto beside him backed up and turned away, the headlights flashed across the bank where a small group had been just a few minutes before. He thought he saw Zack lying on his back on The Beach, rain pounding down on him. *What the hell?*

Tommy opened the door and ran to the general vicinity. Sure enough, there Zack was, laying stretched out, mumbling something incoherent. "Zack!" Tommy shouted over the storm. "Zack, come on, let's go!"

Zack's head turned in Tommy's direction, but his eyes didn't focus. "No, I'm good right here."

"It's raining!"

"No shit," Zack seemed content in spite of the weather.

"Come on, let's get out of here."

Zack lifted his head, focused on Tommy for a moment. "Hey, that's my shirt." He didn't seem inclined to move more than that, so Tommy tried to pull him up into a sitting position. He got him bent almost to 90 degrees, then his hand slipped. Zack fell back, banged his head and laughed.

"Zack, come on, we've gotta get out of here. Everyone else is gone."

"Chickenshits. What, are they gonna melt?"

"C'mon. You're too heavy, I can't lift you all by myself."

"That's because I'm a grown ass man and you are but a boy."

Tommy sighed. He could not carry Zack, so Zack would have to cooperate. Tommy considered the problem, then did what he usually did under pressure: fib.

Zack's eyes were closed and his mouth was open, making him look like a fish that had washed up out of the river. Tommy slapped Zack's cheek. "Wake up! Hey, you know Amanda? She said her parents weren't home and that the party was moving to her house. Let's go. We can catch up with them." *If that doesn't get him moving, I'm screwed.*

Zack rolled over on his stomach. Tommy was afraid that he had passed out face down in the muddy grass, but he was just gathering his strength. He pushed himself up on all fours, like a baby getting ready to crawl. With Tommy lifting and guiding, they did a drunken tango to the Camaro. Zack slid behind the wheel and Tommy ran around to the passenger side. Once inside, Tommy looked and saw that Zack lacked the wherewithal even to shut the driver's door. Tommy cursed, got out, ran around, glanced to make sure none of Zack's extremities were in the way, and slammed the driver's door.

Before Tommy got back around to his side, Zack leaned across the passenger seat and vomited. "Dude," Tommy said. "That is so gross. You're probably going to blame me for that in the morning." He stripped off Zack's Foghat t-shirt and used it to scoop as much of the mess onto the grass as possible. He threw the shirt into the back seat.

Zack did not vomit again, nor did he do anything else. Tommy's heart sank. There was no way that Zack could drive them anywhere. Unless Tommy were prepared to drive the Camaro home, they'd be spending the night right here. *I only have my learner's permit, but I do have a licensed driver with me, even if he's out cold. I'll worry about sneaking Zack into our bedroom once we're home. One crisis at a time.*

Tommy pulled and tugged Zack's dead weight across the bucket seat to the passenger side. As he slammed the door, Zack's head lolled toward the window. *Bonk*.

Mental note: Do not drink yourself blind like this. It's a pain in the ass for everyone else.

The downpour had eased into a more normal summer rain, but Tommy still shivered as he ran around to the driver's side and clambered in. Under his breath, Tommy whispered, "Okay. Okay, okay, okay. It's okay." He scooted the driver's seat forward, adjusted the mirror and seatbelt, but neglected to buckle Zack in. "Okay." He turned the key, and the motor growled to life.

Tommy had often imagined swiping the Camaro for a moonlight run. In his imagination, it had never gone like this. He put the gearshift into reverse, took a deep breath and let out the clutch. It was stiffer than he expected, and he popped it out too fast. The Camaro lurched backward a few yards, then died. Tommy winced in expectation of ritual ridicule, but Zack was beyond noticing anything.

C'mon, Weaver. You can do this.

This time he let the clutch out slowly, backing up in a curve until the headlights picked up the muddy tracks in the field. He pointed the nose of the car toward it and shifted into first. Too fast; the car jerked forward.

Tommy drove the Camaro old-lady style—back straight, nose pressed forward toward the windshield, every ounce of his being focused on the road ahead. The muddy field gave way to a muddy dirt road, then a straight gravel road. The Led Zep 8-track clicked over to *Trampled Underfoot*, keeping time nicely with the windshield wipers. Tommy relaxed a little and shifted into third, not too awkwardly, nosing the Camaro up to thirty.

When the gravel road T-intersected with County Highway 13, Tommy came to a complete stop. After looking both ways, he turned on his blinker, shifted into first and pulled onto the road. He managed to shift into second and third again without incident. Visibility was lousy, but no one else was on the road.

This isn't so tough. I got this. Next stop: home.

Tommy couldn't resist goosing the Camaro up to fifty, then sixty, enjoying the feel of the acceleration. The RPMs registered at 4000 and he felt alive and powerful. He pushed the clutch in to shift, but couldn't find fourth gear. He took his eyes off the road, looked down, shifted into fourth, and let the clutch out.

When he looked up, he saw the reflected eyes of a small doe, frozen in the middle of his lane.

"Shit!"

Tommy slammed on the brakes, pushed in the clutch, and cranked the wheel hard to the left. The Camaro swerved violently, tires screeching as the momentum carried the muscle car into the oncoming lane. The back bumper passed the doe close enough to riffle the small hairs on her face.

The first hard rain in a month had brought up all the oil embedded in the pavement. The minute Tommy braked and swerved, momentum and force gained more control of the vehicle than the soaked, nervous boy behind the wheel. When the Camaro began to roll, Tommy's head hit the driver's side window hard enough to feel no more.

The car rolled over violently once, twice, three times. Finally, it slammed down right side up, the front end crushing a blackberry bush, the rear end hanging into the oncoming lane.

When Tommy came to, he couldn't see. *Am I blinded?* The warmth on his face finally explained the cause as blood running into his eyes from a cut on his forehead. He squinted, wiped the blood away, then unbuckled his seat belt. His left arm wouldn't move. It felt like shoulder damage, and was starting to hurt like hell.

The engine had died, but the 8-track and wipers were still going. The surviving headlight pointed into the bramble tangle on what had been the left side of the road. The end of *Trampled Underfoot* sounded ghostly as it faded out. Tommy reached down and clicked off the key. A nauseating wave of pain emanated from his left arm. He bit his lip to keep from crying out.

The commingled reek of blood, puke and gasoline assaulted his nostrils.

Oh, shit, oh shit, oh shit. What have I done? Mom's going to kill us, if Zack doesn't kill me first for wrecking his car. "Oh, no, no, no. Zack, I'm so sorry. I wrecked your car. Zack, I'm sorry...."

Answered only by silence, Tommy wiped more blood out of his eyes, then looked at the passenger seat.

It was empty, the door hanging open at a crazy angle from one mutilated hinge.

"Zack!" He looked wildly over his shoulder into the back seat. Nothing there but a vomit-stained Foghat t-shirt. He reached across to throw his door open and flew outside, cursing as he banged his left arm. There was a still, crumpled form in the path of the roll, several yards back in the left lane.

"Zack!" Tommy's scream tore at his throat. He sprinted forward, then slowed as he approached the body. "Zack, Zack, Zack..." His voice faded to a whisper.

Zack lay inert, one arm tucked grotesquely backward behind his head. The angle of his neck looked improbable. His handsome face, washed clean by the continuing rain, was unmarked and peaceful. He had never seen it coming.

Tommy sat gingerly beside him, all urgency gone.

"Zack?" A whisper, nothing more. "Please. Please don't leave. Zack? Oh, Zack, I'm so damn sorry."

Chapter Three
May, 2016

Darkness.

Thomas Weaver bolted upright. He turned his head violently from side to side, He was bathed in sour sweat. The old dream, dreamt so often it had worn a groove in his psyche.

Okay. Okay, okay, okay. Come on, Thomas. Everything's okay.

His heart still trip-hammered in his chest, but that would fade with waking. He reached toward his nightstand, found a tumbler with half an inch of whiskey still in it, and drained it. "Hair of the dog," he grumbled.

Thomas squinted, trying to focus on the digital clock beside his bed. 6:15. The alarm would have gone off in ten more minutes. He clicked the button to turn the alarm off, untangled his legs and swung them over the edge of the bed. He leaned forward, put his head in his hands. He rubbed his face, took as deep a breath as he could manage and shuffled off toward the bathroom, the bus, work.

***

"Thomas, we have to let you go."

Thomas's shoulders slumped. He looked at the dirty tiled floor between his feet. When he raised his head, his eyes pleaded along with his voice. "C'mon, Harry. Really? I know I've been in a little slump, but I'm doing the best I can." He wasn't, but the lie slipped easily off his tongue. "I know I'll pull out of it. I've got that guy coming back in this afternoon. I know he's gonna go on that Escalade."

"We're not letting you go because of performance, Thomas. We're shaking up the whole department. Unfortunately, your position has been eliminated."

Thomas leaned back in the uncomfortable, straight-backed chair. "Ah. Dammit, that sucks. I know business has been off. Who else?"

"Who else?" Harry puffed out his cheeks. He blew the air out in a steady stream of futility. "Well, actually, the way it worked out...no one else. Just you."

Thomas turned his head away and stared out onto the used car lot. The weather threatened to piss rain at any moment. A cheerful rainbow of cars bearing window stickers that said things like WON'T LAST AT THIS PRICE!!! fanned out toward the edge of the lot. Barkley Ford wasn't hard to find, thanks to the twenty-foot-high blow-up gorilla holding a sign that said: "I go APE for the deals at Barkley Ford!" Strings of red, green, and yellow pennants hung limply between light posts.

Thomas lifted his chin. "Just me, huh?" He glanced at Harry, whose pinched face always had the look of a man caught in a lie. Harry flushed, then looked away.

Thomas's hands shook with sudden anger. His voice rose in both octave and volume. "If you had the balls your old man had, you would be straight with me. Give me my dignity, at least."

The barb hit home, but Harry lowered his voice. "Come on, Thomas." His smile was obsequious, but held a hint of triumph. "Tommy boy. It's been a good run. Let's not ruin it at the end."

Thomas brought his anger under control. His eyes softened. "It *was* good. When your dad was here, everything was great. We got demos to drive, we had benefits, the dealership wasn't chopping us off at the ankles every time we turned around." Thomas's eye strayed to the framed picture that hung above Junior's desk: Harold Barkley Sr., ten-gallon hat perched at a jaunty angle, a sincere smile on his homely face. "But that was before. You don't have the cajones he did." He stood up, wanting to be anywhere else, and caught a look of relief on Harold Barkley, Jr.'s face. That did it. He whirled around, grabbed Harry's tie, and yanked. He had meant to bang Harry's face into the desk, but the tie came off with an ineffectual whisper of plastic against cloth.

"Seriously?" Thomas looked at the tie, lying limp in his fist. "A clip-on? What are you, twelve? Did your mom pick this out for you because you can't tie your own tie?"

Harry's face turned red. *That stung the son of a bitch.* Thomas laughed scornfully, and his anger dissipated. Harry reached for the phone on his desk.

"Gonna call security on me now? Who exactly would that be? Old Vern down in the oil change bay? Julie out front? Do you really think anyone's going to run me out of here for you, you little chickenshit?"

The familiar throbbing in his temples took over. A powerful thought took hold. *I can walk out of here, get drunk, and stay drunk for as long as I want. No hangover if you just stay drunk.*

Thomas drew back his right arm, making a fist. Then he giggled, and stuck the hand out to shake. Harold Barkley, Jr. stood up in haste and backed away.

"Pussy." Thomas shrugged, walked out of the office, and tipped a wink at Julie, the pretty young receptionist. "See you in another life, kid."

An hour later, Thomas walked into the apartment he shared with his mom. They effectively divided the apartment in half. The upstairs—a large bedroom and a full bath—was his, the downstairs hers. Her half included the kitchen, but that was of little concern to Thomas most nights. He found most of his nutrition in the hops and yeast of forty-ounce Rainier beers.

Forties were fine for nights when he had to get up and go to work the next day, but now that he was no longer burdened by employment, he could get to serious drinking straight away. He had gotten off the bus two stops early so he could stop at the liquor store, where he picked up two fifths of Jim Beam. Next was a trip into Daylight Donuts, where he picked up two cream-filled Bismarcks for his mother. By the time he finished the short walk home, he'd already had a nip or three and was feeling toasty.

No one greeted Thomas as he entered. His mother was probably in her bedroom, watching TV. Unlike Thomas, who had an entire buffet of bad habits to choose from, Anne had quit smoking ten years ago. Sweets were her only remaining addiction. He set the small donut box on the counter, reached into the cupboard, took down a saucer. Through the glow of a nicely-started drunk, he delicately plucked the two donuts out and placed them on the small plate, pulled a paper towel off the roll and placed it over them. He sucked the little bits of chocolate off his fingertips.

There. My good deed for the day, complete.

He had a sudden thought of himself in a Boy Scout uniform, giving the three-fingered Scout salute, and laughed. Then he got a glass, filled it with ice, and poured the Beam over it. That mellow chug was the sweetest sound in Thomas's world. He took a swig and headed upstairs to his bedroom, closing the door behind him.

He looked around at his private fortress. He was fifty-four years old, but his room was indistinguishable from a teenage boy's.

In the far corner was his bed, a crumpled mess of sheets, pillows and blankets. *Guess I'll have plenty of time to make my bed, now.* A clothes basket sat in the other corner, a stray sock and pair of underwear dangling over the side. Against the near wall was his desk. A computer with a 27" monitor gleamed darkly, dominating the flat surface, but on a lower shelf, he saw the green blinking light of his Xbox One. It beckoned him: *Come on, big boy. One NASCAR race. Just one.* Thomas had answered that siren call too many times, though. One game, one race, inevitably led to another, and another and another, until the sun came up. Tonight, the possibility of beating Jeff Gordon and Jimmy Johnson in a season-long sprint for The Cup held no charm for him.

Instead, he nudged the mouse to awaken the monitor. The background showed a blue sky and green rolling hills. He double-clicked the icon for Google Chrome and it brought up his home page: Facebook. The little world icon was grayed out, indicating that he had no new messages. This was not unusual. He had joined six years earlier, methodically friending most of the people from his teen years on. For six years, their lives rolled by on his feed. Aside from his birthday, when he got a few perfunctory 'Happy Birthday!' posts from the people who did that for everyone on their friend lists, hardly anyone ever contacted him. Thomas mostly scrolled, read, and watched other people live their lives.

He drained the tumbler of bourbon, refilled it from the now half-empty fifth, and set it down beside the turntable. He looked owlishly at the tone arm. It took three passes before he picked up the arm, then dropped the needle on the spinning record. The familiar static came from the speakers, then fell into silence as the needle found the groove. The quiet was replaced by the opening double bass notes of Charles Mingus's *Better Git it in Your Soul*. He picked up the oversized headphones, slipped them over his ears, then turned the volume knob hard to the right. The music vibrated into his very being. For the first time that day, he smiled with authentic pleasure.

He closed his eyes and swayed slightly from side to side as the music enveloped him. After a while, and a good deal more drinking, the sway grew more pronounced and threatened to topple him. He tumbled heavily into the old overstuffed chair.

By the time the record segued into *Goodbye Porkpie Hat,* he had drained the last of his drink, refilled it, and emptied half of it again in two gulps. Before the song was over, he finally found what he was looking for: the merciful blankness of a near-blackout drunk.

Chapter Four

Ten hours later, Thomas pried his eyes half open to see where that infernal knocking was coming from. He closed them again. Morning sunshine filtered in through the curtains.

It is awfully fucking bright in here. He closed his eyes, correcting his first mistake of the day. He wanted to slip back into the beckoning oblivion, but the pain in his bladder, the worse pain in his neck, and that goddamned knocking wouldn't allow it.

"What?" he shouted at the woodpecker-at-the-door. Ten seconds awake, and yelling already marked mistake number two. His head throbbed and waves of nausea started low inside him. His mouth tasted like a litter box. He coughed to clear the phlegm and said, in a somewhat more normal voice, "What?"

"Tommy? Honey? It's after nine. It's Thursday. Aren't you supposed to be at work? Did you oversleep? Can I make you breakfast?"

Just the thought of food nearly brought his stomach up. He fought down the nausea. Mustering a little strength, he called out: "No. I don't have to go in today. Please. I don't feel good. Just go away."

That was all he wanted. To be left alone, forever alone.

Anne was not stupid. She was used to him *not feeling good* in the mornings, but she wasn't used to him not going to work. He had always managed to answer the bell.

"Tommy? Everything all right?"

Mom, I can't remember the last time everything was all right. Has it ever been? I can't imagine everything ever being all right again.

He squinted against what felt like the oppressive brightness of the semi-darkened room. The small desk lamp burned like a little sun. He had slept mostly sitting up in the chair all night, which explained the pain in his neck. He spotted the leaded glass tumbler, upside down in his lap, his slacks damp beneath it. He had an overpowering urge to throw the glass through the door. He shouldn't, but as with most things he shouldn't do, Thomas was helpless to stop himself. He curled his fingers around the heavy glass and hurled it with everything he had.

He hoped for a satisfying explosion of glass and a startled scream, but the glass just bounced off, leaving a chip mark in the door frame.

Shit. Can't even make a scene any more.

Silence from the other side of the door, then the sound of her slippered feet retreating, a rebuke in every step.

He tried to stand, but his body didn't respond. After an awkward tumble, he ended up face down on the carpet.

Fuck it. This is just fine.

He nestled his face down into the green and orange shag carpeting and mercifully passed out again.

Seven hours later, he pried his eyelids open again. The room was darker now.

Good.

He lifted his face and felt stray carpet strands on his tongue. He tried to spit them out, but one clung stubbornly to his tongue. He performed the gymnastics necessary to wipe it off on his bicep. He managed to sit up, happy to find that he could move all his parts. Two questions ran through his brain simultaneously: *What's that smell?* and *Why don't I have to piss anymore?* Both questions had a single answer, and Thomas drew as deep a breath as he could, then let it hiss out through his teeth. It wasn't the first time he had passed out and wet himself, but repeating the process didn't add to the charm of the experience.

He crawled to the edge of his bed and used the bedpost to pull himself most of the way up. He tried to take off his shoes, but they were too tight. *Why do my feet always swell up when I pass out?* He finally managed to wedge them off, then peeled off his wet pants and boxers. He caught a glimpse of himself in the mirror. His mom had written, "Be the best you there is!" across the top of the mirror in lipstick two years earlier. *Evidently, the best me there is, is a paunchy, skinny-legged slob with no pants on. And I feel at least as lousy as I look.*

Then it came: the sudden inevitability of onrushing vomit. He barely made it to the metal trash can before throwing up a long, ribbony cord of puke. He held his face in the can, inhaling the dueling odors of pizza crust, stale beer, and bile. He held that position for thirty seconds, waiting for Round Two, but it didn't come.

That's better. Stage One of Dr. Thomas's hangover cure works again. I should patent it.

Thomas stripped off his shirt, pitched it somewhere near the hamper, and tottered down the hall to his bathroom. He climbed into the shower, turned the water as hot as he could stand it, and stood underneath the spray until the water grew cold. He didn't bother with soap or shampoo. This wasn't about hygiene; it was about regaining some form of humanity.

Dripping wet, he stood in front of the medicine cabinet and reached for the aspirin bottle. There was no cap on the bottle. *Good plan, Thomas. Way to think ahead.* He tipped six aspirin out into his palm, slapped his hand to his mouth, and crunched the pills between his teeth. They tasted nasty, of course, but he had learned that this helped speed the relief.

He pulled his right eyelid wide apart and peered at his bloodshot eye. *Yellow. Jaundiced. That's not good, if I gave a shit, which I don't.*

He walked back to his room, naked except for the towel around his neck, somewhat further along the evolutionary scale than before. He plucked a pair of neatly folded pajama bottoms and a t-shirt from his dresser. *Thanks, Mom. Nothing like being fifty-four years old and still having your mom doing your laundry. On the humiliation scale, that's got to register right up there with naked public speaking.* He pulled the t-shirt over his thinning wet hair, slipped on the PJ bottoms, and sat down on the floor to work on the urine stain. The damp bath towel only went so far, so he tossed it into the basket and stood up. His mother had gotten him a bottle of Stetson cologne for Christmas, and it was on top of his dresser. He opened it, steadied himself against the dresser with one hand, and poured a liberal dose of cologne onto the dark stain.

Good as new. Why is it called toilet water, if not for this?

He should, he knew, go downstairs and make things right with his mother, but couldn't summon the will. Instead, he sat in the chair and watched the second hand of the clock sweep his life away. His eyes fell on a small photograph of two teenage boys. It leaned against the lamp on his bedside table, its edges worn smooth by decades of handling. The colors had faded over the years. In the photo, the taller boy had the younger in a headlock. Both were smiling, though the smaller boy's smile was a little forced.

Thomas heaved himself up with a grunt, picked up the picture and held it close. He did this most days of his life, had done so for nearly forty years. Had he possessed the slightest degree of art talent, he could have painted it from memory. Behind the boys, a lake beckoned and a breeze ruffled their sun-kissed hair. They squinted into the sun. A good day.

For the ten thousandth time, Thomas said, "I'm sorry, Zack. So damn sorry." Tears glistened in his eyes.

Thomas put the picture down on the bedside table. The two boys smiled eternally back at him. For just a moment, the ghost of a smile tugged at his own lips in answer, then faded.

When Zack's Camaro had spun out of control, it had taken Thomas's life with it. A sense of numb inevitability had settled into him that night. He'd sleepwalked through his last three years at Middle Falls High, his one sodden, underachieving year at Western Oregon State, and six years of marriage. Mercifully, the failed union had produced no children.

Years blurred together after the divorce. In 2004, just before the real estate market took off, it had seemed natural for his Mom to sell her home and move in with him. It wasn't like he had a social life she could interfere with. By his mid-forties, a series of bad jobs had led him to begin selling cars at Barkley Ford. Early on, it had been the perfect job for him. It had camaraderie, hundreds of wasted hours talking sports, stupid bets, and thousands of gallons of bad coffee. It was the closest he'd ever felt to being at home.

Then Harold Barkley's physician had diagnosed his abdominal pain and leg numbness as spinal cancer. Less than six weeks later, he was gone. So, soon, was Thomas.

And now here he was, in his mid-fifties, unemployed and, if he was honest with himself, unemployable. His checking account contained a robust $849.36, and rent was due in less than a week. There was no savings account. His mom had a few thousand dollars put away for a rainy day, but that wouldn't last long. Then what?

I've really tried. I tried to pick up the pieces and move on. I tried to find my center, but I don't think I have a center anymore. I tried everything, but every day, the pain is a little worse.

I'm even lying to myself. I haven't tried. If it wasn't a quick fix, I gave up and got drunk.

A gaping eternity of darkness opened in front of him, beckoning him, welcoming him. The blackness had a gravity of its own, and it pulled him down, down, down. Finally, he knew what he needed to do. Tears ran down his face. He took a deep breath to steady himself, but it came out in a series of small shuddering sobs. He ran the back of his hand across his eyes. *Okay. Okay. First things first. Let's try to do at least this one thing right. I've done little enough right in my days.*

He fished around in his desk drawer, found a clean sheet of college-ruled paper, uncapped one of his blue Bic pens, and started to write.

Mom —

I suppose I should start by saying I'm sorry, but I've been saying that all my life. I don't know if it means anything anymore. It feels like I've been running away from this decision ever since the night I killed Zack.

"*I killed Zack.*" He had never written or spoken those words before, but they had hung over his head since that night, an eternal, unspoken accusation. The few times he had come close, he had backed away, lest the words gain even more terrible power over his life. Now, too late, he found that putting them on paper brought a bit of perspective.

I wish it had been me, that night, instead of Zack. If I'd had the sense to buckle him in, if I hadn't been so rattled, if I hadn't been so eager to hang out with kids playing kid status games, Zack would probably still be alive. He would have made you proud. I haven't.

I know you would have been sad about me dying, too, but at least I would have done it to myself. I really do love you, Mom. I've done a crappy job of showing it, but I hope you know that. I don't think there's anything on the other side, but if I'm wrong, then I'll see you there eventually. Zack and I will be waiting for you.

Tommy

He looked at the short note. His handwriting still looked like a grade schooler's. He folded the single page and left it on top of his keyboard where she couldn't miss it. He went to the bathroom, poured a glass of water, then carried it back to his bedroom. He sat the water on the nightstand, then frowned down at the crumpled bed sheets and blankets. The corner of his mouth twitched in disapproval.

Nothing else for it, then.

He stripped and remade the bed. Five minutes later, it was an island of perfection in the sea of crap and chaos that was his room.

He reached into the nightstand drawer and pulled out a small plastic bag containing several dozen small white pills.

As he had stolen them from his mother's medication cabinet, he had told himself they were in case he ever had trouble sleeping.

The time for lies had passed. *I've known this was coming for a long time now. Glad it's finally here. Let's be honest, this one last chance: my life has been a gradual trip to the bottom, and I'm there.*

He emptied the pills onto the smooth coverlet and divided them up into groups of three. He had never been able to swallow more than three pills at a time unless he chewed them first. He was afraid that these might taste horrible and make him throw up again, so he wanted to swallow them whole.

The last swallow from the glass finished off the last little group of pills.

'Tis done.

He looked down at the freshly made bed. *That's too nice to mess up, Thomas Weaver.* So, he lay down on his side on the floor, pulled his legs up, and tucked his hands between his knees.

In five minutes, he fell into a barbiturate sleep.

Twenty minutes later, he was gone.

Chapter Five

Sunshine.
Sunshine? What the hell?

Before Thomas came fully awake, part of his brain tried to make sense of that. He had fallen asleep, theoretically forever, in a dark bedroom, with the blinds shut tight. Where in the hell was sunshine coming from?

Wait. What? Where am I?

Thomas opened his eyes. Everything was surreal. At first glimpse, his surroundings bore an astonishing resemblance to the bedroom he had shared with Zack. He closed his eyes tight.

Nope. No way. Don't know where I was heading, but I'm sure it's not here. Gotta still be alive, and this is my brain playing This is Your Life, Thomas Weaver.

He rubbed his fists into closed eyes, then opened them slowly, squinting against both the light and the impossible reality.

It was still there. A perfect replica of his teenage bedroom.

Thomas sat straight up with a start, expecting it to dissolve into the specter of another phase in his life, but it remained.

He was no longer on his side on the floor, but on his back in bed. *His* bed, a twin, from his high school years, the one topped with a bright orange cotton spread that had symmetrical raised ridges across it. He remembered laying under that bedspread, pulling off little pieces of the ridges and rolling them into little orange balls. He hadn't thought of doing that in decades.

The bedroom walls were covered in fake wood grain paneling. To celebrate the bicentennial, Zack had painted each individual stripe red, white and blue. It looked as perfectly garish in this dream as it had in real life. Farrah Fawcett and her impossibly white teeth beamed down from the poster above Zack's bed. A round night table sat just to the right of his bed. Against the other wall was an empty twin bed, *Zack's*. Zack's cheap old stereo sat on the night stand between the beds.

It was the most lifelike dream he could imagine. Sunlight flowed in through the window above his head, warm and gentle. He thought he might get up, and see if the darkest recesses of his dying brain had created the rest of his childhood house in such intricate detail. Or, was it a typical dream, and he would step outside the bedroom into a funhouse collage of other memories? He just smiled a little at the memory-visit, laid down, and closed his eyes once more.

He gathered his thoughts. He had never killed himself before, so he had no idea what was supposed to happen. This all felt so real...

He cracked his left eye open.

Sunshine. Orange bedspread. Record player. Thomas folded the covers back and swung his legs out of bed. His bare feet landed on what passed for carpet in their old bedroom. It was thin, a horrible amalgam of browns, oranges, and reds, and seemed to have no padding underneath. *Why did anyone make a carpet so ugly? Was it intentionally manufactured to be sold as a remnant?*

He glanced down at himself and almost choked.

When he had committed suicide, he had weighed around 220 pounds. Now he looked down at stick-thin legs with bones jutting every which way. He was wearing tighty whiteys and a plain white t-shirt. Thomas stood up, noticed the old swivel mirror atop the dresser at the foot of his bed, and walked toward it. *I am pretty sure of what I'm going to see, though I'm not sure how to handle it.*

He was skinny. More shockingly, he was young. His teenage face stared back at him. *No. Was I ever that young?* The wrinkles, the bags under his eyes, the jowliness—all gone. When he raised his eyebrows, so did the reflection. Tommy leaned a little closer into the mirror. There was a hint of an old acne breakout at the lower left side of his mouth, and a new pimple graced his nose. His hair was sticking out at all angles. He hadn't worn it long in many years.

His bladder was full.

Shit. If you pee in a dream, or whatever this is, you pee in the bed, right? I can't let that happen. I don't want Mom to find me laying in my own piss.

His bladder insisted.

I need to wake up. Or move on to whatever fresh hell might be waiting for me next.

In the meantime, pissing is going to happen, somewhere. Maybe if I do it in the toilet in my dream, I'll have sleepwalked there, and will not completely miss the toilet, or forget and piss with the lid down. He flung open the door and scrambled down the hall toward the only bathroom in the house.

He made it, if barely. No morning leak had ever felt so good, even if tinged with worry that he was wetting the bed back in the apartment. He took a look around the bathroom as he flushed; *in real estate, they would call it 'dated.' Very dated.* The toilet and bathtub in matching pale mustard yellow, yellow daisy appliqués on the mirror, a straw laundry hamper in the corner with a forest green top: Vietnam era all the way. He saw a scale on the floor beside it.

Over the years, Thomas had avoided scales, unless starting a new diet or being forced to get on one at a doctor's office. Would it show his hallucination-weight, or his real weight? The dial came to rest on 148.

One hundred forty-eight pounds! The most successful diet of all time. "*Congratulations, Mr. Weaver, you just lost seventy pounds. Can you tell us your secret?*" "*Well, Dr. Oz. First I got really depressed. Then I tried to kill myself and woke up weighing seventy pounds less. It's both easy and fun.*"

Thomas put the lid down on the cushioned toilet seat and sat on it to collect himself. Whatever this was, it showed no signs of ending. He stood, opened the bathroom door as quietly as he could, and slipped out into the living room. A small brown dachshund stared up at him, brown eyes like beacons of curiosity. He kneeled in the hallway and extended his hand. "Amy? Is that you?" His mom had named her "Amiable," after her easygoing personality, but they had always called her "Amy." The little dog waddled forward, sniffed his outstretched hand, then gave a little chuff and backed away. She didn't bark or growl, but something wasn't what she had expected.

"I don't blame you, Amy. I'm a little weirded out by this whole thing too." Thomas walked into the living room. The first thing he noticed was the lingering rankness of stale cigarette smoke, the residue of his mother's Viceroys. He had forgotten she had smoked in the house.

Restaurants had smoking sections, airplanes allowed smoking, and everyone who smoked, smoked in the house. Hell, doctors smoked while they were examining you in the hospital.

The living room was just as he remembered it. The heavy lined burgundy curtains kept the room dark in spite of the bright sunshine outside. School pictures of Zack and Tommy decorated the walls, comprising a time capsule of their school years and ending with Zack's junior picture. Sculptured gold carpet covered the floor. To his left were the stereo cabinet and a 27" Curtis Mathes color TV. He remembered the day it had been delivered. He had been so excited to watch his cartoons in color on Saturday morning that he had barely been able to sleep the night before. Across from the TV sat a tan couch festooned with red, orange and green flowers, and the La-Z-Boy recliner that had once been his dad's. Now, it was his mom's to sit in and read the paper.

The paper.

A rolled-up newspaper stuck out of the magazine rack. With growing trepidation, he walked across the living room and collected the rolled-up *Oregonian*.

Under the masthead, the date was displayed as Friday, April 16, 1976. The headline was about Good Friday services. Thomas sat down in the La-Z-Boy and began to read.

A metallic click broke the silence, one Thomas remembered as the latch on his mother's room door. He heard the soft shuffling of slippered feet approaching, peppered with excited canine footfalls.

Mom.

Anne's hair was askew, and still dishwater blonde. She wore an old housecoat over her dressing gown. She walked past Thomas as if he were invisible, started coffee, then lit a Viceroy. He peered over to watch as she got a cup from the cupboard, poured some milk in it, and stood by the pot to smoke while the pot percolated.

My God. She's so young. And pretty. I don't remember her ever looking that way.

Hey. She walked by me like I was invisible. Maybe I am invisible. Maybe I'm not really here after all—just visiting like one of the ghosts in A Christmas Carol.

Tommy stood up from her chair and took three tentative steps toward the kitchen. "Mom?"

His voice sounded high-pitched and slightly strangled. He put his hand to his throat. She didn't look. "What?"

Can you see me?

Don't be ridiculous. If she heard me, she can see me.

"Nothing. Just wondering...how you are?"

"I'm being talked to before my coffee. You know not to do that." She turned to face him.

Thomas's face fell. "Uhh, sorry. Never mind."

She forced a bit of a smile. "Just teasing you, sweetie. I'm fine. At least I will be once the coffee is ready."

Tommy heard gravel crunch in the driveway outside. They both looked out the kitchen window at the green '69 Camaro that rolled into the driveway.

"I'd better start some breakfast," his mom said.

That's Zack.

ZACK!

Jesus H. Christ!

He had an idle thought that perhaps he shouldn't swear, even mentally, in what might be the afterlife. Tommy's palms went slick and he felt an odd tingling at the base of his neck. He was holding his breath, waiting to see if Zack, dead for nearly forty years, would climb out of the Camaro.

The car sat there. The door didn't open. Tommy strained to see who was behind the wheel, but from this angle, he couldn't see. Finally, after two minutes of interminable waiting, Zack emerged, unaware that he was a living miracle.

Tommy grew dizzy. He groped for a kitchen chair and sat down. He felt tears start, and hoped he would not have to talk.

Come on, Thomas. Get a grip. You're not going to pass out.

Zack slid open the door and walked into the kitchen. "Hey, Mom. Squirt." As if it were the most natural thing in the world.

Thomas remembered Zack as a full-grown man. Now Zack looked to him like a boy in a man's body. His face was smooth, unlined, whiskerless. His good-humored eyes showed the sort of innocence found in very few adult eyes. 'Handsome devil' described him well.

Their mom smiled at Zack. "Hi, sweetie. How was practice?"

"Okay. Coach ran me hard this morning. I'm gonna go take a shower."

"Hurry. Breakfast won't take long."

Zack turned to look at Tommy, sitting slack-mouthed and motionless. He nudged his mother. "I think maybe

Tommy's had a stroke or somethin'. He looks goofier than usual."

She turned her attention to Tommy. "Tommy? Honey, are you all right?"

Tommy shut his mouth, tried to smile, then nodded. Zack let out a quick laugh. "You get a little weirder every day," he said, heading in the direction of the bathroom.

"Tommy, set the table for breakfast. I'm going to make us some bacon and eggs." She pulled a carton of eggs and a package of bacon out of the avocado-green refrigerator, and started cracking the eggs into a large bowl.

This is all too real. This is no dream. I'm really here.

Tears ran down his face, and he turned away from his mother so she wouldn't see them. He wiped his eyes, remembered he was still in his underwear, and said, "Gonna go get dressed real quick. Then I'll come set the table." His voice was thick, but she didn't notice. On his way past her, he wrapped his arms around her waist, laid his head against her, and said, "I love you, Mom. I'm so glad to see you."

She leaned her head against his for a moment, patted the top of his head, and said, "You're sweet, Tommy. I love you too. Go get dressed now."

Tommy walked down the hall to the boys' bedroom and sat down on the bed. He turned the knob on the Kenmore stereo and watched the tone arm drop into place. The rat-a-tat-tat snare drum of Charles Mingus's *Solo Dancer* came through the tiny speakers on either side of the turntable.

With the audio camouflage of '50s jazz, Tommy let the tide of emotions wash over him. He sat on the edge of the bed, put his head in his hands, and began to shake. Tears ran down his face. He let everything go in a cascade of wracking sobs. *Solo Dancer* gave way to the next song as forty years of survivor's guilt, sorrow, regret, anger, and mourning poured out of him.

Zack walked in, wearing only a towel. Seeing his younger brother bawl in hysterics, for no apparent reason, overwhelmed even his immense reservoir of cool. Shifting from one foot to another, he stared at Tommy for a long moment. Then he walked over and laid a hand across his brother's shoulder. "See. I told you that if you listened to that godawful music long enough, you would go totally fruit loops."

Tommy jumped, embarrassed, but Zack turned his back without waiting for a reaction. He dropped the towel, showing his bare ass.

Tommy took a deep, shuddering breath, then laughed a little. He found it difficult to sustain a cathartic breakdown while looking at his brother's behind. Zack bent over and shoved his posterior further into Tommy's face, moving it from side to side, daring him.

Tommy reached out, intending just to push him away, but he had never had any impulse control. He slapped Zack's ass hard enough to leave a red imprint. Zack jumped, whirled around, and smiled, back on the more comfortable ground. "Oh, think you can take me on, big boy?"

No. First he rises from the grave, and now he will kick my ass. Tommy backed away. As Zack took one step toward him, a feminine voice called from the kitchen. "Boys! Come on! Food's on!"

"Saved by the Mom again, Squirt." Zack grabbed a pair of jeans draped across the end of the bed and put them on without bothering with underwear. He picked a grey t-shirt emblazoned with "Disco Sucks" off the floor and donned it. "You better hurry and get dressed, or it'll all be gone when you get there."

Tommy smiled at him, a silent thank you for not beating him up, for not really making fun of him for crying, but mostly for being alive.

His clothes were just where he remembered. Leaving the white t-shirt on, he pulled up an old pair of Levi's that were a little high water, then some socks and his Adidas. By the time he got to the table, Zack and his mom were sitting, waiting. His mother had set the table without waiting for him. Zack sat at the table's head to the left, where he had sat since their dad's departure five years before. Tommy's place was between Zack and his mother, with a wrapped present sitting on his plate. There was a smaller package on Zack's plate.

"We waited for you. Mom made me."

"Come sit down, Honey. You can open your present, then we can eat before it gets cold."

Tommy felt a little lost. He didn't remember starting each day off with a full breakfast and presents waiting on a plate.

"Present?" Tommy said.

"I know you two were too old for Easter baskets, but I still wanted to get you something. Yours is a little practical, I'm afraid."

Easter. Holy crap. Today is Easter, and I am risen.

Tommy shook his head, but the surreal fog didn't clear. He sat down and picked up the package. It was wrapped in yellow paper with blue and gold stars, and folded slightly in his hands. The feel of it snapped a memory into place.

He tore open the wrapping and pulled out a pair of Levi's. "I noticed that your growth spurt this winter has made your school jeans a little short, so I thought this could help you get through the end of the school year."

Tommy smiled, rubbing the jeans against his face. "That's great, Mom. Thanks."

"All right, Zachary David. Your turn."

Zack's present was wrapped in the same paper but was smaller—a hard little rectangle. He tore one end of the wrapping open, tipped it upside down and gave it a little shake. Two 8-track tapes fell out. Led Zeppelin's double album, *Physical Graffiti*. His smile lit up. "You are the coolest. Most moms would have picked out Bread, or The Starland Vocal Band. This is boss." He stood up, walked around to the other end of the table and enveloped her in a bear hug.

"Still a rock 'n roll girl at heart, I guess," she said, dimpling.

Tommy stared at the box. *Trampled Underfoot* played in his head. A deer. The Camaro spinning through the air. Color drained from his face.

"Okay, let's eat," Anne said. She put a mound of scrambled eggs on her plate, did the same for Tommy, then handed the bowl to Zack. Zack scooped the rest of the eggs onto his plate. She served herself two pieces of bacon, put three on Tommy's plate, then passed it across to Zack as well. The two of them started talking about their plans for the rest of the day, oblivious to the fact that Tommy was frozen in place.

Tommy stared straight ahead for thirty seconds. He glanced at Zack, then at his mother, then smiled a little to himself. He was famished.

He dug into the bacon and eggs.

Chapter Six

Temporal Relocation Assignment Department, Earth Division

The tall, white-clad figure walked the narrow aisle. On either side, identical desks extended beyond where the human eye would have expected them to disappear over the horizon. She lingered a moment at each desk, glanced at the individual's work, tapped a manicured finger lightly against the desk, then moved on.

At one desk, she stopped and spent several moments examining the scrolling information flow. She lowered her chin to gaze over the tops of her half-rim glasses. "Thomas Weaver, Middle Falls, Oregon, United States, North America?"

The worker, a round-faced, unruly-haired female, kept her eyes glued to her work. "Yes, Margenta."

"Emillion, how many cycles are you watching over?"

"Forty-nine."

"And how many souls?"

"Three hundred forty-three, of course."

The tall woman nodded, as if that were the expected answer. "It is policy, is it not, to give equal attention to all clients?"

"It is."

"Then why, pray tell, is your mind so often preoccupied with this single cycle?" Margenta tapped a whirling display, bringing up an image of a teenaged Thomas Weaver. "Why this particular client?"

"Are my reports not up to snuff, ma'am? Am I falling behind?"

"No, you are meeting your quotas. You are feeding the machine."

"Then?"

"Then, I can't help but wonder why you are so interested in this singularly uninteresting life? Enlighten me."

Emillion reached out, touched the image of Thomas Weaver's worried face. "He is so human, ma'am."

"By definition, all your clients are human. Is there an additional metric of which I am unaware?"

"He has qualities I admire."

Margenta reached into the scrolling words and images, pulled a section close to her. She tilted her head back to view them through the spectacles, then looked a wordless query at Emillion.

"Certain qualities cannot be quantified, don't you agree, ma'am?"

"I do not. Everything can be quantified. That is why we are here." Margenta continued on, pausing briefly at each desk, tapping a finger before moving on to the next.

Chapter Seven

After the disorienting breakfast and Easter gifts, the rest of Easter Sunday stretched before Thomas like an unexpected vacation from a lifeless existence. He was again fifteen. Zack was alive. All outcomes were still possible.

Armed with grease rags, wrenches, chamois, Armor All, and Windex, Zack spent the day babying his Camaro. Anne cleaned the house, did laundry, and made a few casseroles they could pop in the oven and eat during the week.

Thomas spent the afternoon on a long walk through the old neighborhood, reveling in its odd familiarity. In his mind, this place and time had begun to lose its color and fade into the sepia tone of memory. Here it was, though, in living color. He unconsciously reached into his jacket pocket for his iPhone to listen to his music, then remembered.

Going to be a few things I'm going to have to get used to.

The sun occasionally broke through the clouds, and the temperatures were in the low fifties—about as pleasant as March could be in western Oregon. As he wandered, he took stock of his new surroundings. *This part of town doesn't look much different now than it will in 2016. Satellite dishes the size of an RV might come and go, but everything else looks pretty much the same.*

Except for the kids.

Everywhere Thomas looked, there were kids—drawing with chalk on the sidewalk or driveway, throwing balls, riding bikes, roller skates, or skateboards. *This is what we did before video games.*

He walked half a dozen blocks, past rows of small single-story houses, until he reached the edge of the business district. The Pickwick Theater's marquee was advertising *The Bad News Bears,* but the sign and lobby were dark. *No matinees on Easter Sunday in 1976, I guess.* He walked past the Shell station, advertising regular gas for $0.579 a gallon. Premium was a nickel more. Just past the gas station was a rundown little bar called *The Do Si Do.* The dilapidated marquee in front read: "One night only—The loudest bar band in the world—Jimmy Velvet and the Black Velvets."

At the edge of the neighborhood, Sammy's Corner Grocery brought a new rush of memories. The worn wooden floorboards, the hanging fluorescent lights, the odd mixed scent of stale packaging and fresh food, brought him up short by its long-forgotten familiarity.

He didn't need to ask where anything was, because the layout was suddenly in his mind. His feet carried him to a spinning metal rack of comic books. At eye level, superhero comics, then, lower, *Little Lulu* and *Betty and Veronica.* He leafed through issues of *The Mighty Avengers, The Amazing Spiderman,* and *Marvel Team Up.* He reached into his pocket, but found only two dimes; not enough to buy a comic book even in 1976, but not completely useless. He wandered over to the small candy section and saw the familiar Hershey bars and Reese's cups, but his eye fell on the bright red packaging of a Marathon candy bar. *Can't remember the last time I had a Marathon. When did they stop making them?* He went to the front counter, and Sammy rang him up on an old-fashioned register with actual push keys. Thomas put the twenty cents on the counter. Sammy swept them off in one smooth motion, caught them in his other hand and tossed them in the tray. It was all very cool and retro, but it also left him broke.

Guess it doesn't matter how cheap something is if you have no money.

He ate the Marathon on the way home, letting the chocolate and caramel stir long-buried memories back into reality. Thomas got home just before dark and sat down to a dinner of ham, au gratin potatoes, and salad.

Between the late breakfast, the Marathon, and this, it's more than I've eaten in a single day in years. Most of my calories of late have been the liquid variety. Funny, I don't feel the need for a beer, which is probably good. No idea how I'd get my hands on one—walk down and steal one from Sammy's? Don't think I could do that, either.

The conversation at the dinner table wasn't much, but Thomas found it soothing and homey. Zack talked about track team politics, then Anne vented a bit about a horrible patient and an even more horrible doctor. At seven o'clock, they all sat down in the living room and watched *Walt Disney's Wonderful World of Color* and *McMillan & Wife* on *NBC's Sunday Night Mystery Movie*. The dialogue was a little stilted, and Thomas solved the mystery before the second commercial break, but the scenes playing out in the dark on the low-definition screen were secondary to the simple comfort of being there.

Although I keep wanting to pause the DVR, or fast-forward through commercials. Not only is there no DVR, there's no remote. If we want to change the channel to one of the three others, including the one that doesn't come in too well, someone has to get up and turn the dial. Me, naturally, as the youngest. In the meantime, we either make a trip to the bathroom during commercials, or learn what corporations want us to know about Anacin and Tide.

When the Eleven O'clock News came on, Anne said, "Okay, boyos, bedtime. Off to bed with you."

A bedtime. Haven't had one in decades. But it's fine; this day has worn me out, at least emotionally. He kissed his mom goodnight, laid his head against her shoulder, held it there a moment, told her again that he loved her, and headed to bed.

Thomas took his clothes off and climbed into bed, but his mind wouldn't stop. *How long does it take to adjust to some-*

thing like this? How can it be 1976 if I remember everything that comes after it? Reagan will come up short in his run for the presidency this year, but beat Carter next time around. The shuttle's going to explode. The Berlin Wall will fall. The Trade Center's also going to fall. Isn't it? Is that something that already happened, or is gonna happen, or what?

Everything here could disappear when I close my damn eyes. That's how I got here in the first place, just closed my eyes and went to sleep, but I don't want that to happen again. Life felt completely disposable until today. Now it's precious again.

Even so, I can't stay awake forever. I saw how that turned out in the Nightmare on Elm Street *movies.* "Eventually, you gotta sleep, even if Freddy is coming to get you," he mumbled.

A few minutes later, he lay on his back, staring up at the ceiling and wondering whether it had asbestos in it, when Zack padded into the room, undressed, and crawled into his bed.

Zack. He's going to die in less than four months, and I'm going to be the one to kill him. Or am I? Now that I'm here again, can I change things? If I do, will it change everything going forward? How could it not? What will happen if I just don't go to that kegger with him?

Zack said, "Hey, Squirt?"

"Yeah?"

"Aren't you going to play one of your awful records?"

"You don't care?"

"Nah. I've kinda gotten used to them. Don't know if I can go to sleep without it."

"Okay."

Thomas rolled over, pushed the lever on the stereo, and heard the same Mingus song that had played during his nervous breakdown that morning. He turned the volume knob until the music was barely audible.

"That okay?"

"Turn it up a little, like it usually is."

Like it usually is.

For Zack, for this Zack, there had been a Tommy in this same bed the night before, listening to the same Mingus record. In relative terms, that was about when Thomas had taken enough sleeping pills to kill himself three times over.

So where did that Tommy go? Is he still here? Am I him? Shit. I am never gonna figure this out. Maybe I'll check some Isaac Asimov or Ray Bradbury out of the library, since I can't just Google 'theories of time travel' any more. In fact, unless I wake up somewhere else, I guess I won't be Googling anything for twenty-five years or so. No more PCs, smart phones, search engines or social media. But you can still smoke almost wherever you want, you don't have to take your shoes off to get on a plane and gas is cheap. The whole world feels slower.

Then it slipped out. "That's a pretty good tradeoff for not being able to Google something."

"What? What did you say? Goo-what? What the hell is that?"

"Sorry. Think I was already asleep and dreaming about something."

A few moments passed in silence.

"Zack?"

"Yeah?"

"'Night. See you in the morning."

"'Night, Squirt."

Chapter Eight

Thomas swam through layers of consciousness, sorting out a swirl of dreams from reality. He opened one eye. Red, white, and blue walls.

Yes! Still here!

He put his feet on the threadbare carpet and looked at the clock. 6:45. Zack's bed was empty, sheets and blankets thrown back in a careless heap. Thomas made a quick pit stop in the bathroom, then wandered out to the kitchen.

Mom's Chrysler is gone. Must be at work already.

Thomas laid his hand against the coffee pot. *Still warm.* He poured himself a cup and took a sip.

The caffeinated bitterness made him wince. *Whoa! That'll put hair on my chest. Does everything taste stronger in the seventies, or are my taste buds just young again?*

"Since when do you drink coffee?"

Thomas jumped. "Damn, Zack! Are you part cat? You're gonna give me a heart attack."

"Well?"

"Well, what?"

"Well, when did you start to drink coffee?"

Almost forty years ago, but that's not a good answer. "I dunno. It just smelled good, so I thought I would try it. Tastes pretty awful."

"Yeah, and it'll stunt your growth." Zack bent at the waist so his eyes and Thomas's were at the same level. "You can't afford any more stunting."

"Smartass."

"Get moving, I'm leaving in fifteen."

"Leaving?"

"You know, school? It's a place where they teach things. Didn't school even teach you what school does?"

School?

Oh, shit, School! His stomach dropped. I don't like this at all. A large building crawling with hormonal teenagers, with bodies like adults but brains like kids, doesn't sound fun. "Um, I don't know if I'm going to school today."

"Hell you aren't. You know Mom's rule: if you aren't in the hospital or the morgue, you go to school. Get your ass in gear. I don't want to be late. Your backpack's by the door. Hope you got your homework done."

That would depend on how diligent Tommy was before I arrived on the scene, which I have no idea. Thomas scarfed a bowl of Cap'n Crunch, slammed another cup of coffee, and was in the Camaro fifteen minutes later. It was a warm spring morning, and Zack rolled down his window, put on his sunglasses, leaned back, and started blasting his new Led Zeppelin 8-track from the speakers. Mercifully, it was *Kashmir* playing, not *Trampled Underfoot*.

The drive to Middle Falls High was short. Zack pulled the Camaro into a spot at the far end of the parking lot behind the main building, then was up and out of the car without a backward glance. Tommy got out and looked in the old Ford pickup parked next to them. It had a gun rack and rifle across the back window.

"It's okay to bring guns to school? Holy crap."

Thomas realized he was talking to Zack's retreating back, too far away to hear. "All righty then. See ya. Good talk."

Thomas shouldered his orange and brown Oregon State backpack and walked slowly toward the high school, wondering where he was supposed to go. *Second semester, sophomore year. What the hell classes did I have? Who were my teachers that year? Who is the President, anyway? Jimmy Carter, or is it still Gerald Ford? Maybe there's a schedule in the backpack.*

He unslung the pack and riffled through it as he walked. Biology textbook, American History, Algebra II. *Oh, crap. I don't remember Algebra I. How am I going to fake my way through Algebra II?* At the back of the pack, he found a tatty Pee-Chee folder, soft with wear, covered in doodles that were no doubt his. Inside was page after page of graded homework, but no schedule.

Well, duh. I wouldn't have written it down, any more than I'd write down our phone number and address. Maybe I can go into the office and make some kind of excuse and they'll tell me where I need to go.

A sharp whistle broke through his fog. "Weaver! Wait up!"

Thomas turned and saw a lanky teenager running toward him. *Oh my God. That's Billy Steadman.*

Billy had been Tommy's best friend from seventh grade until the summer after their sophomore year, when his parents had moved to Maine. They hadn't stayed in touch. *Kids didn't make long distance calls in the seventies; long distance was expensive, even if you waited until evening rates kicked in. Only girls wrote letters to their friends. I remember trying to hunt him up on Facebook, but never had any luck.*

Thomas started to reach out for a big bro hug, then caught himself. *How do I act? Shit. I don't remember how I talked, or how I did anything when I was a kid.* "Billy! Man, you look great!"

How dumb was that? I'd have said that in 2016. I sound like a middle aged man. He'll think I'm a weirdo.

Billy looked like every other teenager streaming into the school—jeans, a sweatshirt and Chuck Taylors. He was a few inches taller than Tommy, with straight dark hair that hung down in his eyes and a complexion overrun with acne.

Billy squinted. "Oh…kay. Whatever. Did you get the essay done for Burns?"

Burns. Burns. Mr. Burns. History. Almost forgot about him. But then, he's kind of forgettable. "Honestly, I don't know."

"Yeah, me too. I got something down on paper, but I don't know if it's what I need or not."

I wish I knew that much. "I don't know if I even wrote anything" would sound nuts.

Thomas and Billy walked into the school and merged into the flow of teenagers. There were so many. Middle Falls only had an official population of 45,126, but the school district drew from smaller surrounding communities, so there were more than a thousand kids enrolled.

Halfway down the hall, Thomas realized he had lost Billy. He looked over his shoulder. Billy had veered off and was bent over, spinning the combination lock on a locker.

Christ! My locker combination. No idea what that is. There are so damn many things I don't know. How in the hell am I going to pull this off?

Billy opened his locker and threw his backpack inside. He retrieved his American History textbook and a blue three-ring notebook. Thomas stood, uncertain where his locker was. *Think fast. Teen vocabulary.* "Man, the weirdest thing happened this weekend. I was wrestling around with Zack and I hit my head pretty hard. The doc said I've got a concussion or somethin'. I'm having a hard time focusing and remembering anything today. I know it sounds weird, but I am drawing a complete blank about which locker is mine, or what my combination is."

Billy glanced sideways at him. "Must have been a pretty hard hit." He reached over two lockers and spun the dial. "7-40-22. Remember?"

"Ha! Oh, yeah, of course. Good thing you knew it."

7, 40, 22. 7, 40, 22. 7, 40, 22. And I think part of that sounded like adult me. I'll have to watch that. Billy smelled bullshit.

Billy shrugged, then returned to messing around inside his own locker.

Thomas looked inside his own locker. The odor of sweaty gym clothes, forgotten brown bag lunches, and old textbooks wafted out. A picture of Bruce Jenner throwing the javelin adorned the door. On the top shelf were an old homework assignment and a blue Bic pen. He tore off a corner of the paper, wrote "7-40-22" and stuffed it in his front pocket.

What's the worst that can happen if I don't pull this off? It's not like I'm scamming anyone. They might put me in the nuthouse up in Portland, I guess. That probably wouldn't be great.

He pulled his copy of the history book out, grabbed his Pee-Chee and hung the pack up on the hook in his locker.

"Ready?" Thomas said.

"Ready."

"Lead on, Macduff." *Because I sure as hell can't.*

Thomas followed Billy through the teenage throng, recognizing no one outright. Some faces looked familiar, but he couldn't match names to most of them. With a small jolt of recognition, he saw Amanda Jarvis, dressed in a tight white top and denim miniskirt. He remembered her as a goddess-like figure, fixed forever in his mind due to the kegger. Now she just looked like a skinny kid, trying to act more important than she was.

Down the hall, up a flight of stairs, then down another hall, Billy finally turned into a room marked 222. The room was already half full, and they slipped into two half-desks at the back of the room. Thomas inhaled the long-forgotten smells: pencil shavings, mimeographed papers, and teenage pheromones, all mixed together.

These kids looked much more familiar. Names came into sharper focus, such as the girl with long red hair beside him. *Alicia Holcroft. She got married a few years out of high school. Two kids. Opened her own bakery,* Cravin' Cupcakes. The boy in the corner, bent over a copy of Dune; Ben Jenkins. *Went to U of O, then finished up at Stanford Law. He's gay, but I didn't know that until I caught up with him on FB. He told me then that he didn't have a single comfortable day in high school.*

In the back row, with empty seats around her like a moat, *Carrie Copeland. Cooty Carrie. When we wanted to insult each other, it was always with her. "Oh, yeah? Well, you'd screw Cooty Carrie." She attempted suicide her senior year. Did it again, two years later, but got the job done that time. I wonder if she started over somewhere in time, like me, or did she make the cut and pass on to whatever's next?*

I guess I can thank Facebook for how many of these people I recognize. All those Throwback Thursday pictures.

Two seats to his left, one tall, thin, dapper boy stood out. He had short hair and wore what Thomas thought of as business casual: grey sport coat, blue button-up shirt, and khakis. The boy turned, looked at Tommy, and smiled. Tommy returned the smile, then felt his face freeze as he made the connection.

Michael Hollister. Holy shit. Michael friggin' Hollister. Middle Falls' most famous graduate. He didn't become a politician, or an athlete, and he didn't invent Post-It notes. The world would come to know Michael as the West Coast Strangler. Between 1978 and 2002, he had murdered twenty-nine men and women up and down the I-5 corridor. His signature had been a red and gold tie, done in a perfect Windsor, around each victim's neck. Until some ambitious new killer came along, Michael would hold the record as Oregon's most prolific serial killer.

That was all in the future. At that moment, Michael Hollister was a seventeen-year-old boy smiling at Tommy, whose blood ran cold as he remembered more of what he'd read at serialkillers.com.

Michael had varied his abduction methods, locations, and victim profiles, confounding the police and FBI for many years. Travelers or state maintenance workers had found his earliest victims at rest areas along I-5, where Michael had seated them on a toilet, pulled their pants down, then arranged the necktie. In the early 1990s, Oregon had installed security cameras at all rest stops, forcing Michael to dump the bodies in rural areas.

In 1983, Michael sent an anonymous letter to *The Oregonian* stating that he preferred to be known as "The Necktie Killer," instead of "The West Coast Strangler." It didn't matter. The 'West Coast Strangler' handle stuck. In 2002, he achieved serial killer hall of fame status: Ann Rule wrote a book about him.

If not for a couple of missteps, Michael might have gone on killing until he got too old to strangle people. In 1984, Detective Harold Carmichael of the Oregon State Police stored a scarf worn by Allison Anderson, the Strangler's sixth victim. He kept the scarf in evidence because it had a single smear of blood on it that appeared inconsistent with the more profound bloodstains. Upon testing, this blood was a different type than Alison's. Michael had scraped his arm while manhandling Allison's rather curvy form into position. He had left a bit of the blood on her scarf, where he mistook it for hers.

Then, in 1995, Michael Hollister nearly killed a man in a fight that broke out in, of all places, a wine bar. As part of the booking procedure, the police had taken a DNA sample, which went into the state and national database. Michael hired the sort of attorney the Michael Hollisters of the world could afford, and the prosecutor dropped the assault charges. Even though he escaped consequences at the time, the arrest ended up costing him dearly.

In early 2001, the state of Oregon received a federal grant that allowed them to DNA-test hundreds of pieces of cold case evidence. The stray bloodstain on Allison Anderson's scarf matched all thirteen data points of the sample Michael Hollister had provided in 1993.

Detective Carmichael, sixty-one years old and less than a year from retirement, was given the job of leading the dozen officers that were dispatched to arrest Michael at his well-appointed home. When Detective Carmichael rang his doorbell, Michael answered by saying, "Collecting for the Policemen's Ball?" He did not resist arrest.

On the ride to the station, Michael asked how they had caught him. When Carmichael told him about the scarf, Michael nodded. "I knew it. A little bit of blood. Should have just walked away from that idiot at the wine bar."

Thomas felt suddenly ill. *Serialkillers.com* had featured pictures of a number of Michael's victims. Their faces swam through his memory.

There are twenty-nine people, going about their lives at this very moment, whose destiny is to be killed by that scrawny little teenager.

Chapter Nine

Thomas somehow faked his way through the rest of the school day. Only two of his classes included Billy, but he managed to get to the rest of his schedule by asking questions of harried teachers, and on one occasion, the janitor. Sitting through each class was not quite the dull eternity he remembered; *either my mind has matured, or more likely, I was too busy worrying about being called on.* When school finally let out, Thomas ran into Billy at his locker. "See ya in the morning."

"Nah, I've got an appointment to get fitted for braces first thing."

"Hey, braces might suck right now, but eventually you'll be glad you got them."

Billy had knelt to fish something from the bottom of his locker, and he gave Thomas a sidelong upward look. "Yeah, and I should get a job and start saving for my college education. What are you, Weaver, my dad?"

Oops. My middle-aged man is showing. Come on, Weaver, you're supposed to be a teenager. "Ah, just trying to make you feel better, brace face."

"With friends like you, not sure I need enemies."

Thomas slapped Billy on the back, said, "Good luck, man," gathered up his homework, and jogged to Zack's

Camaro for the ride home. Fifteen minutes later, the parking lot was mostly empty, but no Zack.

Shit. Of course. Track practice. He has track practice every damn day. I should have taken the bus home.

He shouldered his backpack and ran to the loading area, but the buses were already gone. *How long did his practices last? Hell if I remember.* He slung his backpack over his shoulder and trudged back to the Camaro. To his relief, the passenger door wasn't locked.

Of course it's open. Who locked their doors in a school parking lot in 1976?

Thomas settled into the bucket seat and dug a notebook out of his backpack. Mr. Burns had cut him a break, giving him an extra day to produce five hundred words "Analyzing the ways in which technology, government policy, and economic conditions changed American agriculture in the period 1865-1900." *My god. He couldn't have picked a more mind-numbing topic if he'd had Google to hunt up a list of them.* Thomas thumbed through the history book until he found a chapter that looked relevant, then laid it open on the dashboard and began to write.

First thing I've written in forty years. Well, other than my suicide note.

An hour later, with his hand cramping up, he had one essay page finished with no sign of Zack. Thomas slid the notebook back in his pack and took out Truman Capote's In Cold Blood, his assignment for English. "Could be worse. Could be Shakespeare."

Midway through the first chapter, a bit of movement caught Thomas's eye. It was a lone male figure, perhaps a teacher, cutting across the parking lot toward the deep woods that framed the back of the school. Then Thomas recognized the herringbone sport coat and lean frame. *Michael Hollister. He had—he has—an odd, herky-jerky way of walking, long strides without moving his upper body much. And why isn't he carrying any books, or a bag? He's got his hands in his pockets, walking like a man on a mission.*

Was Michael Hollister a closet stoner back in the day? If so, maybe he should have stuck with the weed. Never heard of a stoner half killing someone in a wine bar fight.

Thomas tracked Michael's progress without moving, hoping to remain unnoticed. It seemed to be working, even as Michael passed within about thirty yards of the Camaro. As quietly as he could, Thomas let In Cold Blood slip to the floor of the car.

When Michael was a football-field-length away, near the edge of the woods, Thomas opened the car door and stepped out.

What the hell am I doing? Following the serial killer into the deep, dark woods? Come on, Weaver. You've seen this movie before, and it ends up with you being skewered to a tree by a sharp metal object.

Even with that thought echoing in his mind, Thomas walked toward the woods.

Michael Hollister's first reported kill wasn't until 1978. Of course, if I followed him into the woods and he killed me, I wouldn't have been around to read about him on serialkillers.com. So, does that mean I'm safe? Or what? I'm never gonna figure this stuff out.

What I know for sure is, I'm here. Everything else is guesswork. The stoners went to the woods to get high during lunch. Maybe that's what he's doing, going out to the woods to smoke a doobie with some friends.

Yeah, sure, a guy who dresses like a Young Republican is going out to light up with the stoners. I'm thinking not. And friends? Never seemed to have or want any.

Once Michael disappeared into the foliage, Thomas set out to follow him at a safe-seeming distance.

This is stupid, this is stupid, this is stupid. Is that the final thought that went through the empty heads of all those dead teenagers in slasher movies?

When he was twenty yards away from where the path cut into the deeper woods, Thomas dropped to one knee and pretended to tie his shoe while looking around, then proceeded as quietly as he could manage. The woods filtered out much of the sunlight. A few yards past the entrance was a small clearing cluttered with pop cans, hundreds of cigarette butts, roaches, and Cheetos bags. There was even an old bench, listing but still upright. *Ah. Home of the stoners. It's a wonder they haven't set fire to the whole forest.* Thomas slowed his pace even more, especially when he came to a bend in the path, lest he stumble upon Michael in full stride.

After ten minutes of steady walking, Thomas realized the brush and trees dampened any sound. Deep in the woods, it was quiet as a cathedral on a Tuesday afternoon. The path, wide and worn at the entrance, had shrunk to a small footpath.

Very peaceful, if I wasn't on the path of a serial killer in his natural habitat.

After another couple of hundred yards, Thomas paused, listened. A few birds flitting through the branches. A frog croaking somewhere in the distance. *My footsteps have to be echoing through the whole forest, no matter how quiet I try to be. What am I doing? I need to get the hell out of here, get back to the car.*

Thomas turned on his heel and walked back toward the school. When he had taken three steps, a distant, echoing caterwaul sounded. He froze in mid-step.

The wail continued. It started low, then climbed: a sound of anger, frustration, pain. The odd echoing quality made it sound even creepier, not-quite-of-this-world. As quickly as it started, it quit, choked off in an instant. *Off to my right. Can't tell how far.*

Thomas held his breath, his pulse loud in his ears. Every instinct told him to run back down the path until he reached open daylight. He turned his head, listening and watching. The cry came again. Definitely to his right.

Shit. If you hear a scary cry in the woods, do you do the right thing and see if you can help, or do the smart thing and run like hell? Thomas sighed, cursed inwardly, then left the path to his right. *I can't walk quietly though this, damn it*, he thought, feeling a blackberry vine drag across the cuff of his jeans. He pushed on.

After he had gone far enough to feel lost, he heard the cry a third time. *Closer. Much closer.* Thomas slowed his pace, which was a good thing, because he stumbled upon the edge of a moss-covered cliff that dropped down to a small clearing. On the opposite side of the clearing was another mossy cliff that rose, then plateaued, creating a small valley. In the middle of the open space was an old, rusted-out flatbed truck that looked like it might be abandoned from a decades-old logging operation. One door hung open. There was no sign of whatever was making that unnerving sound, much less of Michael.

Thomas saw a movement against the far cliff wall. He cocked his head and squinted. *What the hell? Michael's emerging out of solid rock. What kind of witchcraft bullshit is this?*

Michael took two steps out into the clearing, reached up, put his jaw in his left hand, wrapped his right around the back of his head and gave a sudden tug. The violence in the action gave Thomas a shudder. He took two slow steps back away from the cliff's edge and blended behind a tree. Michael swung his arms around his head in a weird callisthenic, ran his fingers through his hair, turned, and walked down the canyon bed, toward what Thomas thought was the school.

He was whistling the theme from *The Good, The Bad, and The Ugly*.

When Michael was well out of sight, Thomas remained still for several minutes, letting his heartbeat return to normal. He picked his way along the edge of the drop-off until he found a spot where the cliff gentled to more of a rocky bluff, with the neglected remnants of a trail leading downward. At the bottom, he crossed to the spot where it had looked like Michael had emerged from the cliff wall. A trick of light and shadow made it look like there was nothing behind the ivy and whatever else that hung down. He pushed the foliage aside to reveal a small opening in the cliff.

Oh, that's just great. A freaking scary-ass cave where the serial killer likes to hang out after school. He glanced at his watch, realized he'd been away from the Camaro for almost half an hour. *I need to get back. Zack's gonna be done with practice soon. If he leaves for home, I'll have to walk, Mom will be worried, and life will suck. How the hell did we survive the seventies without cell phones?*

Discretion is the better part of valor, right? I can always come check this place out some other time, right? Bring torches and villagers to investigate, right?

Sure. What other justifications can I come up with?

The wail sounded again, but this time it wasn't far away, and the reason for the echo was clear.

Something is trapped in there.

Thomas took a deep breath and stepped into the opening. The thick, green tendrils fell in place behind him, shutting out the exterior light. He paused for a moment to let his eyes adjust to the near-darkness. He reached his hands out and felt cold, damp walls on all sides. The only sound was the buzz of a few flies.

Shit. I knew giving up smoking was a bad idea. I don't even have a lighter on me. And something stinks in here. With my luck, I'll step right into it.

The opening narrowed, slowing Thomas's progress as he tried to feel for both sides and possible low ceiling obstacles. His toe kicked something small, sending whatever it was clattering ahead of him. He dropped to a knee and groped ahead, hoping not to grab something gross or dangerous. Instead, his fingers touched what felt like a flashlight. He felt for the switch on the side. When he pushed it up, a beam of light pierced the darkness, pointed directly at a ceiling only a few feet above his head. He saw a narrow opening ahead, turned sideways, sucked in his non-existent gut and squeezed through. Thomas leveled the beam and saw a small, tight, corridor run a few feet ahead, then bend out of sight. He stepped ahead, went around the corner and gasped.

The light revealed a small animal staked spread-eagle to a square of plywood on the cave floor. There was no way to tell what the unfortunate creature was, or what it had once been. Small finishing nails secured each foot to the plywood. Whatever it was, it was split down the middle and laid open. Pink flesh and loops of intestines showed bright color in the flashlight beam. Drops of blood dotted its fur and pooled beneath it, with flies already gathering.

Shit.

Thomas took a step forward for a closer look. The little creature's head was missing. He scanned the cave with the light, locating a small natural shelf. On it rested a macabre array of skulls, mostly picked clean of any identifying flesh. Thomas's lips pulled back in a grimace of disgust.

It's the laboratory of the damned in here. But how did he get the skulls so clean? Is he boiling the flesh off, then bringing them back here?

Talk about questions I didn't wake up today expecting to ask myself.

A skittering movement near one of the heads answered his question. Thomas leaned forward and focused the light without getting any closer.

Beetles. Flesh-eating beetles, eating whatever's left. I think I'm about to puke. Thomas clamped a hand across his mouth and looked away. His first instinct was to turn and run for something resembling normal civilization. After the urge faded, he flashed the light around the cave some more. Then, at last, he saw what had made the sound that had brought him there.

A pet carrier and a small tool box sat in a corner. Inside the cage was a cat, snarling a low, threatening growl at Thomas. He took two steps toward the cage, mumbling softly, "It's okay, it's okay, everything is all right." The cat wasn't buying it. It made itself small against the back of the cage, growling louder.

"Poor thing. It's okay. It's all right. I'm going to get you out of there." Thomas paused. *Am I going to get that cat out of there? Is that smart? When Michael comes back, he'll know someone's been here.*

Screw it. I am not leaving this cat to suffer the same fate as...as that. He didn't take another look at the small, disemboweled body on the plywood.

Thomas approached the cage and noticed a small mound of dry cat food in the front of the cage.

He came to feed it. He'd only do that if he was thinking long term. Serial killers don't just wake up one morning and say, "I think I'll kill someone today." This is his training ground. Worse, his playground.

He looked closer at the tool box. Most of the original red was faded and rusty. The words "Property of Ed Gein" were scratched across the top. *The madman who inspired Norman Bates and Leatherface. Great. A serial killer with a sense of humor.*

I hate to think what's inside, but I have to look.

To his immense relief, the box contained no tiny bodies or bones. He found an old pair of leather gloves, a pair of pliers, a small hacksaw, and a box cutter. Only the box cutter looked newish. The other tools looked like something picked up off a junk heap.

Okay. Let's get you out of there, Morris.

Thomas reached out and fidgeted with the cage door mechanism. The cat leaped forward and slashed at his hand, catching his middle finger.

"Son of a bitch!" Thomas pulled his hand back. He put the finger in his mouth and sucked, tasting his own blood. The cat retreated to the back of the cage, eyes flashing.

"I guess I can't blame you. Not gonna give you the chance to do that again, though." Thomas thought of the gloves inside the toolbox. The idea of putting them on—sharing a second skin with Michael Hollister—revolted him. The thought of getting his fingers ripped up was worse, but worst of all would be to leave the cat to death by torture. Grimacing, Thomas slipped the gloves on.

As he squeezed and twisted the lock mechanism, the cat slashed at the gloves. This time, no damage. Finally, Thomas pinched, then turned the metal the right way. The door sprung open, but the cat didn't move.

"I don't blame you for being freaked out, but let's get you out of there."

The cat flattened itself against the bottom of the cage, eyes locked on him. Thomas reached in, intending to pluck it out and free it. Instead, it sprang forward and bit through the thin leather glove and into the meat of Thomas's palm.

"Goddamn it!" Thomas roared. He yanked his hand out and peeled off the glove, shining the light to inspect the damage. The cat sprang forward in a grey blur and vanished toward the mouth of the cave.

Thomas took a deep breath and let it out slowly. Two small puncture wounds were seeping blood. He cursed again under his breath. *No good deed goes unpunished. Now what? Now, what the hell do I do?*

The cage sat empty on the ground. Thomas nudged it onto its side with his toe, hoping that Michael would think a predator—a coyote, maybe—had come and eaten the cat. He laid the gloves carefully inside the tool box, then returned it to what he hoped was its original position. *As for you, little fella,* he thought, looking down at the mutilated animal on the plywood, *there's nothing I can do for you. Wish there was.*

He turned away from the death cave and used the flashlight to pick his way back to the entrance. Now that his eyes had adjusted somewhat to the darkness, the entrance was easy to see. He set the flashlight down near where he'd first kicked it, or so he hoped, and emerged, blinking, into the fading light of day. *Holy shit. It's getting dark. Zack's going to leave without me, for sure.* Thomas set off at a steady jog in what he hoped was the right direction.

It feels good to be able to run and not be out of breath after two steps. If I ever pick up another cigarette, I hope God strikes me dead. Unless I'm already dead, and this is one big existential mind game. In which case, carry on, God, carry on.

I should have left the flashlight on. Crap. That would use up the batteries, and next time he comes back to play sicko, he wouldn't be able to see until he brought some more.

A five-minute run carried Thomas to the nearly-empty parking lot, breathing hard, where Zack was pacing beside the Camaro.

"What the hell are you doing, twerp? What were you doing out in the woods? Are you out there getting stoned?"

"No, no, no." Huff, puff. "I missed the bus, so I decided to go for a walk, then lost track of the time. Sorry I made you wait."

Zack gave his brother a doubting look. "Sure you did. Okay, you don't want to tell me what you and your little friends are doing out in the woods, fine. You're lucky I saw your homework on the seat, or I would have left without you. I almost did anyway."

"Thanks for waiting for me, Zack. It's been a bad day. Walking all the way home wouldn't have made it any better."

"Just get in. We're going to be late for dinner."

Chapter Ten

I know I'm glad to be here when I'm even happy to sit down to tuna noodle casserole with my brother and my mom, thought Thomas. After Zack's death, Anne had quit cooking regularly, and sit-down dinners had become things of the distant past.

"So...why were you boys late?" Anne said, scooping tuna and noodles onto a plate and passing it to Thomas.

Zack and Thomas exchanged a quick glance. Zack: "Oh, coach kept us after practice for a few minutes to go over assignments for the meet this Friday. Can you make it?"

"Friday afternoon? Probably not. I'm on the schedule then. If someone can switch with me, I'll be there. Is it a big meet?"

"Nah, not really. Just a couple left before Districts, though. I'm going to push myself in the 880. I think I can get the best time in the state this year. That guy from Pendleton is two tenths of a second ahead of me, and he's already committed to going to Oregon. Can't let a friggin' Duck have the best time, can I?"

"Oh, no, that would be disastrous." She couldn't quite keep a straight face. "And don't say 'frigging', especially at the dinner table."

Zack rolled his eyes, but said, "Yes, Mom. I'll remember not to say, 'friggin'.'" He looked at his plate and whispered to himself, "At least, not when Mom's around".

"That's right. At least not when Mom's around."

"Nothin' wrong with your hearing, is there, Mom?"

"And don't you forget it," Anne said, but with a smile.

Thirty minutes later, dinner was done, the dishes were done, and Thomas lay across his bed trying to finish his American History essay. *This is killing me. What in God's name do they think I'm going to learn from an assignment like this? How to be a corporate drone that completes the most boring assignments without a complaint? Probably. I'm already seeing how much of what they're pitching me in school is propaganda.*

No amount of brain-numbing reading, though, could cleanse the cave's images from his mind. *If he's already torturing and killing animals, can people be far behind? Maybe he didn't become the West Coast Strangler until 1978, but what if he made a few practice runs first? Most every town has unsolved murders. Any of them could be Michael Hollister's.*

He slammed his history book shut and chewed on the end of his Bic.

This is beyond my problem-solving abilities. What can I do?

If I were Bruce Willis or Arnold Schwarzenegger, I'd just blurt out a little quip, then blow the future serial killer away, saving the world the bother. But I'm not, and I don't have it in me to kill someone, even if they need killing. There isn't anyone I can talk to about this. I can see it now: "Hey, Billy? I'm really from the future, and that weirdo Michael Hollister is going to grow up to be a mass killer. Wanna help me take him out?"

For the first time since waking up to find himself in 1976, Thomas thought it might be nice to have a drink. Just one, to soothe his nerves.

Mom's gotta have a bottle somewhere. What would one drink hurt?

He rubbed his hand across his mouth, an old gesture from his previous life. He shook his head.

Nope. Been down that path. That will soothe me all right. Soothe me back into oblivion.

Thomas rolled off his bed and meandered out into the kitchen. *Maybe a Coke. Not a rum and Coke. Just a Coke.* He opened the refrigerator and poked around inside. There was no Coke, just his mom's Tab. *Gotta be better than nothing, right?*

He popped the can open and took a long drink. The hideous chemical taste of saccharin awoke from wherever his mind had buried it. *Oh, God. I was wrong. That is definitely worse than nothing. How does she drink that shit?*

"Oh, ho, so you're the one that's been sneaking my Tab, huh?"

Thomas jumped, a guilty expression replacing the revulsion. "Doesn't anyone in this house make noise when they walk? Jesus!"

"Just teasing, Honey, and don't take the Lord's name in vain. You can have one once in a while. Just don't make a habit out of it. I don't want you addicted to them, or," she said, taking a Viceroy out of the pack and lighting it, blowing smoke toward the ceiling, "these. I don't want to pass on my bad habits, understand?"

Right. Aside from almost forty years of alcoholism, no bad habits here.

"Right, Mom. You got it. Can I talk to you about something?"

"Of course, Honey. Come on, come sit down on the couch. Talk to me."

Shit. Now I've done it. Why don't I ever think before I speak?

"Here," he said, handing her the almost-full Tab. "You better take this. I don't want to get hooked."

"It's kind of awful, I know, but you get used to it."

"I'm gonna let you be the one that's used to it."

She flicked off some ashes, sat down on the couch, and patted the cushion beside her. "Okay, what's on your mind?"

Thomas looked around. "Where's Zack?"

"He said he was going over to Jimmy's. Where he actually went, I have no idea."

He tried to look shocked at the implication, but couldn't pull it off. "Okay, I've got this English assignment, and I need a little help."

"Hmm. Okay; that was more up your father's alley than mine, but he's not around, so I'll do what I can."

I'm already regretting this, but it's too late now.

"Well, I got an assignment from Mr. Graves today," he lied. "We have to write a short story to turn in on Friday. I got the idea to write about a guy that travels back in time from the future. But, instead of traveling way back to when dinosaurs were around, he just goes back to when he was a kid."

His mother nodded. "Interesting idea. Okay…"

"But, I'm a little stuck on it. So far, I've got him going back and missing all the things that he had in the future, like computers that you carry around in your pocket and flying cars and stuff. But, then, I was wondering…what if, when he went back, he saw things that were wrong?"

"Wrong, how?"

"You know, just wrong. Like, people being mean to people, and he knew it was going to turn out bad, like maybe someone teases some girl, then she kills herself because of it."

"That's a little over-dramatic, but go ahead."

If you only knew. "Then, in the story, he runs into a guy that he knows will eventually become a serial killer."

"A what?"

"A serial killer? You know, like…" Thomas paused. *Who would she know in 1976? Ted Bundy? Later. Son of Sam? Almost, but not yet. Wait…* "Like the Zodiac Killer in California. Do you remember that?"

She shook her head. "No, not really. Maybe I read something about it in *Redbook*? It's not all housekeeping tips and recipes in my magazines, you know."

"Anyway, he sees someone who is still a kid, but is going to grow up and kill a bunch of people. So, what would he do? I know it would be easy to say that this kid would just kill him, but I don't think this kid's got the guts for that. But, he wouldn't want this guy to grow up and kill a bunch of people either. So, what would he do?"

Anne took a long drag on her cigarette, then blew it out the side of her mouth.

Damn. That cigarette looks good, but I don't feel the physical pull, just an emotional one. This younger me isn't an addict. Wonder what she'd say if I asked to bum one?

"I don't know, Honey. I think that maybe he would try and make things better for people. Isn't that what you would do? If you can't figure out how to do that, maybe you should write a different story?"

That's my chance. "You're probably right, Mom. It's kind of a stupid idea, I know."

"No, it's not stupid," Anne said. "You just might need to work on it a little more."

"Okay. Thanks, Mom. I'm gonna go write my History essay."

Chapter Eleven

The next morning, Thomas's eyes flew open before Zack's alarm went off. *Still here.* He rolled on his side, watched Zack's even breathing and sleeping face. *Alive. He's alive.* He rubbed a hand across his eyes.

I have no idea how I got here, or why I've got this chance, but I'm not going to blow it. I will not let him die again. I am going to change things. Problem is, I don't remember much about what's supposed to happen. What the hell happened in 1976? Did Elvis die? No. I think that was '77. Jimmy Carter's going to be elected President in November, unless I've changed everything already, and Gerald Ford wins instead. The Bicentennial happens this summer, with the fireworks and tall ships sailing into New York harbor, but what else? I need to figure out a way to test how much I can change things. Other than keeping Zack alive, how much do I want to change things?

An hour later, after a shower and a cup of his mom's leftover coffee, Zack and Thomas pulled into the Middle Falls High parking lot. *Billy's getting his braces on, so I'm on my own today. I think I can survive the day without him.*

Thomas shouldered his backpack and walked into the teeming mass of teenagery that was Middle Falls High before first period. He skipped going to his locker and went straight to homeroom, so he could watch as everyone filed in. Carrie

Copeland was next to arrive. She walked with her head down, looking at the floor.

Thomas turned and looked at her. In his memory, she had been ugly, but now she just looked carelessly groomed. Dishwater blonde hair hung limply down to the middle of her back. Her bangs curtained her eyes. Her red sweater covered a shapeless blouse tucked into a long brown skirt.

If Carrie noticed he was looking at her, she didn't let on. Her eyes didn't move from the book in front of her.

Why did we make fun of her? If you got her hair done, and dressed her like everyone else, she'd look like any other girl in school. Did we pick on her just because she's quiet, or because every ecosystem needs someone to pick on? Whatever it is, it's bullshit. I'm gonna do something about it.

Thomas glanced at the clock, then stood and walked over. He sat in one of the empty desks surrounding her. "Hi, Carrie."

Her eyes widened, but she didn't look or answer. "I'm Thomas. Sorry, I mean, Tommy Weaver." He paused. Still nothing. Some other students had arrived, and he felt their eyes on him. *Because no one ever talks to Carrie. I'm being a weirdo.*

Yeah, fuck all of you. I didn't make this rule, that Carrie was an outcast, and I don't have to obey it. Whether he did or not, Carrie did, so Thomas forged on. "Hey, I know we don't know each other very well, but we have a couple of classes together, and I was wondering if...maybe it would be all right if I called you at home some time, so we could talk?"

Her eyes widened again, unable to contain her surprise that someone was talking to her. She gave an almost imperceptible shake of her head.

"No? It's not all right if I call you at home?"

She cleared her throat, blushed a bit. In a voice so quiet Thomas had to lean forward to hear, she said, "My Dad." She cleared her throat again. "My Dad won't let me talk on the phone." For just a moment, she raised her eyes and met his before looking down again.

"Oh, okay. That's cool." Thomas glanced over his shoulder. His conversation with Carrie looked to be the most interesting thing likely to happen in class that day. "Uhh…" *Hadn't really planned on her not wanting to talk to me. But, why would she? Aside from the fact that I am breathing, what exactly do I bring to the table?* Thomas swallowed hard. "Well, how about I talk to you at lunch, then. Would that be okay?"

Carrie's eyes flitted off the floor. She glanced quickly over her left shoulder, then back down. Her cheeks had blushed up to a blotchy red.

C'mon, Thomas. You want to help this girl, not make her die of embarrassment. Just give up and move on. Thomas pressed his lips together in a failed attempt at a smile. Anthony Massey mock-whispered "Shot down in flames!" as Thomas slunk by. The room, suddenly full, burst out in laughter.

Anthony was always a horse's ass. Still is. Still was, anyway. Or still will be? God.

Mr. Burns strode into class and laid his black briefcase down on the desk at the front of the room. "Nice to see everyone so full of good humor on a Tuesday morning. Let's keep that excitement going with a pop quiz." The laughter immediately changed to groans of protest.

Thomas slunk back to his own desk. When he glanced back at Carrie, she was looking directly at him. The unexpected eye contact gave him a small frisson, bringing goose-bumps to his arms. The tiniest of smiles passed her lips, then vanished.

Chapter Twelve

Two hours later, Thomas stood outside the lunchroom, looking at the day's menu. *Chili and cinnamon rolls?* The memory of thick, meaty chili and gooey cinnamon rolls caused his stomach to grumble. *Those were so damn good. Why does everything taste better here, now?*

He opened the heavy door, and the smell of warm cinnamon rolls enveloped him. Thomas found a card with his name on it on the wall, filed under "Class of '78," and handed it to the lunch lady. Two minutes later, he had a bowl of steaming chili topped with grated cheddar and a huge sweet roll. *Must not have been so concerned with Type II diabetes and childhood obesity in 1976.*

No, because we got outside and burned all that off. We explored, scuffled, competed, and acted like kids.

Middle Falls High was large enough to require two lunch periods. In the far corner of the room, next to the window that looked out on the student parking lot, sat Carrie Copeland. A fair percentage of the limited number of open seats in the lunchroom surrounded her.

What the hell would that feel like? To be constantly quarantined by social pressure? To be cut off from all human contact? No wonder she killed herself.

Thomas took a deep breath, picked his way through the crowd of teenagers, and set his tray down directly across from her. Instead of a tray, she had a bologna sandwich and an apple sitting on top of a worn and creased brown bag. She had taken two small bites of the sandwich.

Jesus. She even eats timidly. What is going on with this girl? He slid in along the bench across from her. "Hey. Mind if I sit down?"

She didn't answer, but glanced out the window at the parking lot. No one seemed to notice that Thomas was talking to Carrie.

"Listen. Carrie. I don't want to bother you. If you don't want to talk to me, that's cool, I'll leave. I'd just like to get to know you a little bit."

"Aren't you afraid you'll get cooties?" The lunchroom din nearly drowned out her voice.

Ah. She knows. Of course she knows. If your nickname is Cootie Carrie, you probably know it. A shy smile crossed Thomas's face. He shook his head. "Here's the truth. A lot of the kids in this school are just assholes. Most of the other kids figure that the assholes are going to pick on somebody, and as long as it's you, it probably won't be them."

Without lifting her eyes off her lunch, Carrie said, "And, which are you?"

"Me? Oh, I'm in that tiny third group that doesn't give a crap what anyone thinks. It's very freeing. They can make fun of me if they want to."

Carrie took another delicate bite of her bologna sandwich. "Mmm-hm."

"What? You're not buying it?"

Carrie looked down at her sandwich. "Easy enough to say when you're not an outcast, I suppose. Anyway, you've done your good deed for the day." Her eyes met his for a brief moment and he saw fire there, but she didn't say anything else. She pulled a piece of waxed paper out of the bag, wrapped the sandwich, and dropped both it and the apple into the bag. She folded the top over twice, stood up, and walked out of the lunchroom, eyes on the floor.

Thomas watched her walk away. A skinny, stringy-haired kid in a Pablo Cruise t-shirt stopped on his way by. "Man, that's a bitch, You try to score with the grossest girl in school and she won't have anything to do with you? That's the worst, man."

Without a thought, Thomas threw an elbow straight out behind him. He intended to hit the guy in the leg, maybe give him a Charlie horse. Instead, he caught him square in the balls. The wisecracker fell to the ground like a string-cut marionette, writhing with both fists tucked into his crotch. He groaned. "Why'd you do that, man?"

Thomas stood, looked down, said, "Don't be an asshole. Oh, and Pablo Cruise sucks. Ten years from now, no one will know who they are."

Thomas left his tray behind and hustled out of the cafeteria, hoping to catch up with Carrie. He flung the door to the hallway open and dashed through it—and smack into Seth Berman. Seth wasn't a man-mountain like Tiny Patterson, but he was an athlete—not just big, but solidly built. His sloped brow and slightly agape jaw indicated membership at the far left end of the evolutionary chart. His expression might have been worn by the first dinosaur who wandered into a tar pit. Surprise gave way to anger. He looked down, saw Thomas, and pushed him back into the cafeteria.

"Hey, homo, watch where you're goin'."

Homo? Seriously? I guess that was the go-to insult in 1976. The worst thing one man could call another. Thomas glanced over Seth's shoulder and saw Ben Jenkins, avoiding eye contact.

"Sorry. It was an accident."

Thomas moved to step around Seth, but a single Neanderthal finger against his chest pushed him a step and a half backwards. Looking past Seth, he saw Carrie turn the corner toward the ladies' restroom.

"I said, 'Watch where you're going, homo." Seth emphasized the last word. For the second time that day, a crowd gathered to enjoy Thomas's embarrassment.

Come on, Weaver. Get the hell out of here. Leave Cro-Magnon Man to his ancient prejudices and live to fight another day. Seeing the crowd, Seth smiled. He pushed his finger against Thomas's chest again.

Goddamn it, that hurts. Screw this.

"I don't know what your problem is, man. I bumped into you by accident. I guess you need to accuse other people of things you think are embarrassing to make yourself feel better. Whatever. That says a lot more about you than it does anyone else."

"Wha?" Seth cocked his head, like a dog hearing a sharp whistle. He said it again. "Wha?"

Seth's friend Jamie Myers, who had been watching the proceedings from the sidelines, leaned over and said, helpfully, "He's saying he thinks *you're* the homo, Seth."

Seth's expression changed from confusion to anger. He pulled his finger away from Thomas's chest, bunched his fist and swung. Any trained fighter could have ducked the blow. Thomas was not a trained fighter. The ham hock fist connected with his forehead.

Stars exploded in Thomas's head as he pitched over backwards and landed near the trash cans.

***

When Thomas finally came around, he raised his head to look around and saw the back of Zack, with Seth and Jamie on the other side. Seth was half a head taller than Zack, but he looked uncomfortable, like a recalcitrant child scuffing at the ground.

"I'm gonna give you a pass this time, Seth," Zack said. "I'm going to assume that you didn't know that this was my little brother. If you had known that, I'm positive you never would have done something so stupid. Right, Seth?"

Jamie Myers said, "Right. Right, Zack. Sorry." He reached up, grabbed Seth by the shoulder and led him away.

Zack turned, reached down, and helped Thomas sit up straight.

"Oh, man. Thanks, Zack. That guy kicked—"

"Yeah. He kicked your ass. What did you do to make him so mad?"

"I bumped into him. Then he called me a homo."

"So you took a swing at him?"

"Oh *hell* no. I told him he was accusing me to make himself feel better."

Zack laughed. "In other words, you called him a homo. Yep, that's probably enough with Seth. He's an idiot. You're not a homo, are you? I know you keep stealing my Playboys."

Thomas flushed, but said, "No, I'm not, but what if someone around here is? How does that make him feel? It's just not right."

"I suppose so, but getting your ass kicked by Seth Berman probably isn't going to fix that, is it? If you're on a mission to stick up for homos, fine, but your technique isn't working." He gently touched the bump around Thomas's forehead. "Hey. I can see his class ring imprinted in your forehead. Cool."

Chapter Thirteen

Thomas shifted on the cold metal bench. The sky overhead was a dozen different shades of gray and black. *Or, as we like to call it, another beautiful spring day in western Oregon.* The organized chaos of a high school track meet spread out before him.

I get why track meets don't draw the big crowds that football and basketball do. It's too scattered, too much going on at one time.

At the southern end of the track, a dozen athletes from four different schools stood in a ring around a sand pit, watching a knobby-kneed boy awkwardly attempt the triple jump. Another group of boys, in shorts so small they would have been laughed at in 2016, stood balancing long poles on their shoulders, waiting for the pole vault to start. On the northern end, Tiny Patterson whirled around and around, and with a bestial howl audible in the bleachers, put the shot almost forty-five feet.

Zack stood near the start/finish line, bent at the waist, stretching in preparation for the 880 yard race. He had already won the 440 by three strides, coasting the last quarter lap. He was his own toughest competition today, and he had saved his best for the 880.

A high school track meet is one of the few things that didn't change much. Aside from the races being run in meters instead of yards, a meet like this would look almost the same in 2016. Well, except for all the parents in the stands videoing their kids on their iPhones, of course.

Zack stood at the starting line, hands on hips, and surveyed the crowd in the bleachers.

He's looking for Mom or Dad.

Thomas half stood and waved to catch Zack's eye. Zack nodded, scanned the immediate area, then refocused on his stretches. *I know who he was looking for. My teenage brain wouldn't have taken it in, but somewhere in Zack's heart, it kills him that Dad isn't here.* He shook his head. Their dad hadn't been back to the house to visit them for five years, since moving out in the middle of the night, but he had twice been spotted at the edge of the crowd as Zack ran. Today, though, that ghost of family past was not present, and Anne had been unable to get out of her scheduled shift at the hospital. Not that Zack was short on people to root for him. It seemed like every eye in the sparse crowd was on him.

Zack dropped down into his starting stance, fingertips on the ground, head up, eyes forward. The starter's gun rang out and all eight runners leaped forward. By the first turn, it was obvious the only race was for second place. Zack was already six strides ahead, gliding comfortably, focused only on his own form, his breathing, and his internal clock. Coach Manfred stood at a spot on the other side of the track from the starting line, stopwatch extended. When Zack went by, he checked the time, scribbled on a small chalkboard, and hustled back across the track. As Zack loped by at the end of the first lap, the coach held the chalkboard up for him to see. Zack flashed the smallest of grins and seemed to pick up his pace.

He's going to do it. I don't remember him having the best time in the state his senior year, but unless his shoelaces come untied, he's going to do it.

Thomas jumped to his feet, cupping his hands around his mouth, shouting "Go, Zack! Go!" before sitting back down.

How is it possible that he's outrunning everybody when it doesn't even look like he's trying?

By the time he hit the final turn, Zack finally started to flag. His perfect form picked up a slight jerkiness. Most in the crowd didn't notice or interpret the change, but his teammates did. They ran along the inside of the track, shouting encouragement.

Turning his head from side to side, face flushed, Zack opened up his stride to gobble up the distance. He broke the tape at the finish line, stumbled, and would have fallen onto the cinder track if Coach Manfred hadn't been there to catch him. He hugged Zack, pounded him on the back, and yelled something in his ear.

Zack looked up at Tommy from beneath his shock of hair and gave a quick nod of his head. Thomas jumped to his feet again, screaming, "That's my brother! Yessss!"

The track announcer, carrying an oversized microphone and trailing a long black cord, conferred briefly with the official timer, then clicked on the mic and intoned: "Ladies and gentlemen, if I can have your attention, please." He paused. "It will be some time before the results of the Boys 880 Yard race are official, but if the preliminary results hold, Zack Weaver's time of 1:51.2 is the fastest 880 time in the state this year."

Thomas sat down on the bench, exhilarated.

"Hello, Tommy."

The unfamiliar voice came from behind him. He half-turned to see who it was.

Michael Hollister.

Thomas froze. His heart raced.

Shit! "Umm...hey?"

"I know you probably don't know me. I'm Michael Hollister. I'm a senior, like your brother."

"Oh, um, hey." *Shit, shit, shit.*

83

"I went for a walk in the woods behind the school the other day after school and I saw you come out just a few minutes behind me. You don't look like the pothead type." Michael paused and looked at Thomas, who shook his head, agreeing that he didn't look like the pot head type. "But those are the only people I ever see out there."

"Oh." Thomas chuckled. *Lame. Come on, Weaver, get it together.* "I missed the bus home on Monday and had to wait for Zack to get done with track practice. I...just went for a walk in the woods, something to do." *Lame, lame, lame.*

Michael's eyes said: *I hear you, but I do not believe you for one damned minute.* He squinted into the setting sun, looking over Thomas's shoulder. "Yeah, no big deal. I just never see anyone out there, other than the stoners. So, big race for your brother, huh?"

"Yeah. I think so." *What the hell do you want?*

"Best in the state this year, maybe?"

Thomas just nodded. *And you care...why, exactly? Where the hell is this going, you animal torturer and future serial killer?*

"Not going to be valedictorian in our class, but not too far off, either, right?" Michael shaded his eyes with his right hand, stared at Zack. His eyes met Thomas's for a brief moment, took his measure, then flitted away. "Must be tough, having a brother that's so damn good at everything."

"Lucky for me, he's cool about it."

The single nod again. "Even worse." Michael said, smiling and tapping a two finger salute against his forehead as he stood up and walked down the bleacher aisle. Thomas watched his retreating back, his characteristic walk. When Michael got to the parking lot, he scissored his long, lean frame into a deep blue sports car that Thomas recognized as a Karmann Ghia. *Of course. What kind of a teenager drives a Karmann Ghia?*

An asshole teenager with a rich mommy and daddy, that's who. As Michael drove off, Thomas let out a long, shuddering breath and sank back down against the bench. *That can't be* good. *I never talked to him the first time around. I must be changing things.*

Of course I am. How could I not? And now, I've drawn the attention of a serial killer and I'm in his sights. Awesome.

Thomas walked back to the Camaro to wait for Zack. *That's right. I am changing things no matter what I do. The longer I go, the less I'll be able to predict. In my first life, I never had any interaction with Seth. Carrie's world is already a little different. It's like a map with a lot of detail near the You Are Here, then less and less, until it's just blurred colors and traces of lines near the edge.*

There is no guidebook for this. They don't even give you a brochure.

Half an hour later, Zack appeared from the direction of the track. His Adidas hung over his shoulder, tied together at the laces. His hair was messy and still sweaty. He opened the driver's door and immediately filled the car with teenage boy funk: the combination of body odor, sweaty clothes, and a splash of the Brut cologne that he always kept in his track bag.

Thomas said nothing. Zack pulled the 8-Track out of the player and switched the AM radio on instead. Barry Manilow's melodious lyrics explained, in so many words, that Barry wrote lyrics. Zack shook his head, punched a button, and The Eagles' *Take It to the Limit* came on. Zack sang along under his breath, tapping time on the steering wheel.

I can't get over how it feels to see him alive, setting records, just not being gone. I wish I could tell him everything. He had my back in the lunchroom. Why does he still seem like my older brother, when he's eighteen and I'm in my fifties? It would be nice to be able to tell him the truth.

I can see it now. "Zack, I gotta tell you something. I've already lived through this once, and in a few months, I might kill you in a car wreck. I'm going to try and change that, but I don't know if it can be changed. I'm really sorry I killed you." And what's the end game of that conversation? A long, worried talk with Mom, a consultation with some doc up in Portland, and a long stay in a nice, padded room?

Nope. I'm on my own.

Zack drove slowly through their neighborhood, his need for speed quenched for the moment by his own legs. "Thanks for coming, Squirt. It was cool that you were there. Now you can tell Mom all about it."

"I'm glad I got to see it. You were awesome. It looked like you were ready to pass out when you crossed the finish line."

Zach chuckled a little. "Just a little showboating for the crowd. I was fine."

"Really?"

"No, not really, dipshit! That was all I had. I thought I was gonna puke."

"Glad to know you're human."

"Was that Michael Hollister talking to you in the stands? What the hell was that about?"

Thomas shrugged. "I really don't know. He was asking me why I was out walking in the woods the other day."

"Good question. Why were you out in the woods the other day?" Zack took his eyes off the road for a moment, glanced at Tommy.

"I know this will sound weird, but I saw Michael go out in the woods and I got a weird idea that he was up to something, so I followed him."

"And?"

"And, nothing," Thomas lied. "I never even saw him, so I turned around and walked back out. No big deal."

Zack frowned as he pulled into their driveway. "Look, you're a big kid. You can make your own decisions about things." He turned off the Camaro's engine, but made no move to open the door. "But Michael's a weirdo. I've always thought he was a harmless weirdo, but still..."

Concern for me. That's something I have so missed, so long. Thomas turned to face Zack. "No worries, big brother. No more walks in the woods for me."

Thomas and Zack got out of the car and pushed open the gate to their front yard. Thomas let Zack go in the house first, the conquering hero. Anne was still wearing her nurse's scrubs. She jumped up, opened her arms wide to Zack, and said, "Well?"

Zack smiled, nodded, and let her envelope him in a hug that ended with her holding him out at arm's length and saying, "Okay, mister. Straight to the shower with you." She turned to Thomas. "Tommy, honey, bring Amy inside."

Thomas stuck his head out the front door. "Amy! Amiable! Come here girl! Amy!"

No dog.

"Amy?" He peered around their front yard—fenced and none too big—but she was nowhere in sight.

Down the block, Thomas heard an engine start. A deep blue Karmann Ghia pulled away from the curb and moved slowly down the street, trailing a cloud of smoke.

"Amy?"

Chapter Fourteen

Temporal Relocation Assignment Department, Earth Division.

Emillion blew A gust of air up at her bangs, pushing them out of her eyes for the moment. She leaned forward, spun her column of 180°, then feathered it to a stop. She rested her chin in her palm and studied.

"Everything copacetic?" Veruna, the worker across the aisle. She and Emillion held the same rank and duties, but similarities ended there. Veruna was taller, well put together, and an efficient worker and observer. When Margenta, who had been the TRADED supervisor for the last three cycles, moved on to her next assignment, Veruna would fill her sandals. Emillion was a little less of all those things, but no less dedicated. Different as they were, she and Emillion had been friends for millennia. Veruna met Emillion's worried expression with a smile. "It will be all right, and you know it. It's always all right in the end. If it's not all right…"

"…it's not the end," Emillion finished. She tapped her left hand twice against her heart chakra. Those had been the first words in the training manual her first day on the job. "I know that's true, but I worry about them anyway. I can't help it."

"You don't want to help it, or you would." Veruna turned her attention back to her work. Her fingers flitted in and out of the images in front of her, an artisan at work.

Emillion frowned and focused on the swirl of images. *You have a point, Veruna, though you did not make the one you intended.* "Nothing ventured," she whispered to herself. She pinched an image—a car containing a teenage boy and a small dog—and pulled it toward her until it snapped loose with an almost inaudible *thwick*. Without moving her eyes, she manipulated it, tore a piece off, and dropped it into the small waste hole at her feet. She replaced the rest of the image into the swirl in front of her. She glanced over her shoulder, expecting to see Margenta's glaring eyes, but her supervisor was not there.

Emillion smiled.

Chapter Fifteen

Michael Hollister peered in his rearview mirror, idling the engine, hoping Thomas would come outside. He leaned over to roll the passenger window down just enough for the dachshund to hear Thomas. When the dog barked, Thomas would realize what lay in store for the family pet, and it would be delicious to see.

"Amy-girl, come here, girl!"

Amy looked up at Michael with an unconcerned doggy smile. Michael reached down and wrapped long, slender fingers around her neck. Since human fingers had never harmed her, and he didn't squeeze, she did not resist. "Guess I don't need to worry about you jumping out the window, do I? You're not built for jumping, are you? Now shut up." Then he flicked her nose, hard and fast. Amy gave a quick yelp of pain and surprise. No one had ever hit her, not even with a newspaper as a piddling puppy. Michael held his finger an inch from Amy's nose, ready to flick her again. Amy tried to shrink away, but he tightened his grip as he strained to hear Tommy.

"Amy?"

The dachshund whined at the faraway voice, one she associated with love rather than rough mistreatment. She struggled as if she could reach that voice, but Michael tightened his grip.

The dog whining increased in volume. Switching hands, Michael reached behind the passenger seat and pulled out the small pet carrier he always carried. It paid to be prepared for opportunities. He sprang the door of the cage open with his left hand, keeping hold of Amy with his right. "This is most definitely not your lucky day, dog." Alone in the car, Michael heard the voice that spoke to him so often; not his conscience, but an alternate part of him that had separated long ago. *Come on, Michael. This is not some woodland creature you caught in a trap, or a stray feral cat. This is a pet. She will be missed. Her owner knows where our playground is. If you kill her, you will be caught, and you will miss out on so many other delights. Patience.*

Michael nodded and lifted Amy by the neck, then shoved her into the cage. He slammed the door closed and dropped the carrier on the passenger seat floor. She yelped in shock and sudden terror at the alien treatment, then resumed the whine of protest. He jerked his head hard left then right, eliciting a sharp crack, then shifted the Karmann Ghia into first and eased into the street while keeping an eye on Thomas in his rear view mirror.

As Thomas ran toward him, calling Amy, Michael felt a deep satisfaction.

He let Thomas get within about a car length, then gave the Karmann Ghia the gas.

Chapter Sixteen

Red-faced and gasping, hands on knees, Thomas stared at the pavement for several seconds. When he looked up, the Karmann Ghia was gone. Not even Zack could catch a car. He stood, then spun around in frustration, running both hands through his shaggy hair. "Shit. Shit, shit, shit, SHIT!"

His run had ended in futility on the sidewalk in front of the Arkofski house. Mrs. Arkofski appeared at her screen door, long white apron over her gingham dress, glaring disapproval. Thomas gave her an ineffective wave, dismissing her, but Mrs. Arkofski stood her ground, eyes promising future unpleasantness. It was the look that had sent her husband to an early, merciful grave.

I ought to flip her off.

No. If I do that, it will make things worse. He turned away and trudged toward the house.

Now what? Michael's got Amy. Unwanted images flashed into his mind's eye. The small, flayed creature attached to the plywood on the floor of the cave. The skulls, picked clean. The enraged cat in the pet carrier.

Son of a bitch. Of course. His killing place. That's where he'll take her.

No! I won't let that happen to Amy.

Unless it's already happening right now.

Another image filled his mind; Amy as a wiggly, wide-eyed puppy, tongue lolling, loving and trusting every human she had ever known. He swiped tears from his eyes. *Get a grip. It won't help anything if Mom sees I'm freaking out.*

Drawing a deep breath, Thomas went back into the house.

"Where's Amy? Didn't you bring her in?"

Make up a lie, and make it up quick. "There's a little hole in the fence that she could wriggle through. She's not in heat, is she?"

Anne's expression reminded him of later days, when he would say something that proved he was drunk again. "You know she's fixed, honey. You went to the vet's office with me. Are you okay?" She stepped forward, laid a hand against his cheek, then his forehead. "Oh, you're clammy! Are you feeling okay?"

"I'm fine, Mom. I was just running around the neighborhood looking for Amy. I'm sure she'll be back in the morning, don't you think?"

Anne parted the heavy drapes, peered out into the darkness. "I hate to think of her being out this late." She tapped her fingers lightly against the glass, lost in thought for a moment. "Come on, let's drive around the neighborhood. I'm sure she'll hear our voices and come running."

If only. Thomas tried to picture where Amy might be at that moment, and he didn't like anything that came to mind. *Great. A fool's errand I can't decline.* "Sure, Mom."

Anne grabbed her keys and they went back out into the deepening evening gloom. Despite the cold, they drove around the neighborhood with the windows down. Their cries of "Amy! Amiable!" echoed through the neighborhood, but of course, they spotted no Amy. After half an hour, Anne finally admitted defeat. "I'm sure she'll be fine. Come on, let's head for home. She'll probably be curled up on the front porch when we wake up, begging for breakfast."

She won't be, of course. But I know what I have to do.

When they were back inside the house, Thomas pecked Anne on the cheek. "I know it's a little early, but I don't feel so good. I'm gonna go to bed."

"Good idea. 'Night."

Thomas tried the bathroom door, found it unlocked, and went in. Zack was still in the shower, turning the small bathroom into a sauna. Thomas relieved himself, then flushed the toilet without thinking.

"Yeeooooww! Damnit, Tommy, you retard! I'm gonna kill you!"

"Sorry, Zack." Thomas retreated to their room and got undressed, laying his clothes across the end of his bed. It was dark out, just a little after nine, but too early to put his plan into action. He pulled the Mingus record off the turntable, sleeved it, then flipped through the half dozen albums on the floor. He found Zack's copy of The Beach Boys' *Endless Summer*. *Sometimes you just need a little sunshine piped into your ears, right?* Thomas started the album spinning, dropped the needle. He clicked the light off and laid back against his pillow in the darkness, feigning sleep.

He lay like that through the album's A side, but could still hear Zack and Anne talking in the living room. He started the record again, concentrating on the music, trying to stay awake. Not until after the A side played through again did he hear Zack slip into the room and lay down with an exhausted groan. *Just a few hours ago, Zack was setting records and everything was good. Things change so fast.*

After a few minutes of tossing and turning, soft snores came from the other side of the room. *I could sneak out the window now, but I need to grab a few things before I go. C'mon, Mom, it's getting late. Don't you have to work tomorrow or something? Go to bed! Please don't let tonight be one of the nights you stay up and watch Carson.*

The minutes dragged by. At last, the muffled TV sound stopped, then the hallway light clicked off. The door to Anne's room clicked shut.

Thomas glanced at the small windup alarm clock. The numbers glowed 10:30. *I'll give her half an hour to get to sleep, then I can take off.* He sat up to fend off slumber, then leaned back against the wall.

The only noises were an occasional car rolling down the street and the quiet ticking of the clock.

Tick, tick, tick.
Tick, tick, tick.

Chapter Seventeen

Thomas's eyes flew open with a start. He had a crick in his neck. He rubbed his blurry eyes, grabbed the little clock, and held it close.

Ten minutes after midnight. Goddammit! How could I let myself fall asleep when that maniac has Amy?

Thomas slid out of bed, retrieved his clothes, dressed, and padded to the kitchen. *If there was a gun anywhere in the house, I would sure as hell take it, but...* Thomas slid open the top drawer to the left of the sink, muttered a curse, closed it, then opened the one below. Inside was a jumble of knives: paring knives, bread knives, a cleaver, steak knives, and an Old Hickory butcher knife. Thomas reached out and touched the butcher knife's smooth wooden handle before pulling it out.

A creak came from behind him. Thomas jumped and spun around, nearly dropping the butcher knife. No one was there.

Deep breath, Thomas, deep breath. We haven't even started yet.

Thomas walked to a small cupboard in the dining room. The hinge squeaked, and he paused again to listen. Inside he saw the silver cylinder of a flashlight. He grabbed it, pointed it at the floor and pushed the switch forward. A white beam of light lit a few pieces of Cap'n Crunch he had dropped on the linoleum, another lifetime ago. *Thank God. I have no idea where I'd find D batteries this time of night in 1976. I don't think there's a single 24-hour store in all of Middle Falls.*

He slipped to the hall closet and pulled on his Middle Falls High hoodie, dropped the flashlight into its pocket, then stared at the butcher knife. *A hunting knife with a sheath would be better, but Dad took all those with him. Won't do to walk down the street with this in my hand.* Thomas slipped it up his right sleeve. At the sliding glass door, he collected Amy's little red leash and slipped it into the hoodie's other pocket.

Flashlight, butcher knife, leash. Oh, yeah, I'm loaded for bear. Let's get it over with. It would be a lot easier if I could just drive to the school, but if Mom gets up for some reason, looks out and sees her car missing, I'm in big trouble. Nope. Not worth the risk.

He took a deep breath, then stepped out into the cold night air.

***

Thirty minutes later, keeping to alleys and side streets, Thomas neared the school parking lot. The moon was nearly full, so there had been no need for the flashlight. As he walked along the fringe of the parking lot, he spared a second of battery life to glance at his watch: *1:15 AM. This whole plan seemed a lot easier when I was lying in bed. Better get my ass in gear. Don't want to have to explain to Mom why I'm not home when she wakes up for work.*

He averted his eyes from the high lights above the parking lot, letting his eyes adjust. The forest loomed directly ahead. Thomas paused to listen; all quiet. His breath puffed out in a small cloud.

A few minutes later, he located the path he had followed a week earlier. Inside the forest, Thomas thought he could hear ominous sounds near the path, but when he stopped to listen, they were gone. *It's as dark as the inside of a coal digger's butt, as Dad used to say.* He turned the flashlight on again, but there was no reassuring beam of light. His heart skipped a beat. In a panic, Thomas slapped the flashlight into his palm hard enough to bruise. The batteries shifted enough to produce a connection, and the beam reappeared. Thomas let out his breath in a rush, rubbed his hand on his jeans, and set off again.

Last time I was here, the forest felt peaceful. Now I'd swear it's closing in on all sides. He slid out the butcher knife and clamped it in his right hand. The trail narrowed, then ended.

Shit. I didn't think this through very well. Which way did I go after the trail ended? Last time, I heard the cat wailing and followed it to the cave. He stopped still, listening, but heard only the ambient night sounds of the forest.

Okay. When I heard the cat wail, I had given up on the whole thing and was heading back towards school. Then I heard the cat from my right. So it must be this way, right?

Thomas focused the flashlight ahead and began picking his way through the trees and underbrush. He found it an order of magnitude harder by flashlight. Every few steps he nearly tripped over a root, got slapped in the face by a low-hanging tree branch, or twisted his ankle on a buried rock. He worked up a sweat despite the cold.

I can't shake the feeling that I'm going the wrong way. He stopped. *Dammit. Dammit, dammit, dammit. Have I gone too far? I must have gone off at the wrong angle and now I could be—*

Thomas's mind went blank and his stomach dropped. His left foot landed on air. He tried to find his balance, lost the battle to inertia, and pitched forward. Without thinking, he threw the flashlight one direction and the knife the other. For a fleeting moment—too fast for a fully realized thought—Thomas believed he had walked off the cliff he had encountered on his previous visit, and prepared to feel broken bones. Before he could contemplate the full outcome of breaking his leg or spine this close to Michael Hollister's playground, he bounced a bit down a gully in the cliff side and rolled into a sapling.

Everything he felt told of a bruise collection to come, especially on his forearms, and he'd banged his head on a rock. The impact had knocked the wind out of him. He laid there for several seconds, trying to get air back into his lungs.

Christ. Smooth move, Weaver. He lifted his head, felt nauseous, and lay back down against the dirt and wet vegetation. *Oh, boy. Haven't felt this bad since 2016.*

Wait. Will feel. Whatever. Shit. I am never gonna get the hang of this time travel stuff.

Okay. Okay, okay, okay. Laying here feeling sorry for myself isn't going to save Amy.

I was lucky. If I'd gone straight over one of the sheer spots, I might be dead now, or worse than dead—paralyzed, waiting to be found by the freak.

He sat up, weaved a bit, directed a grateful look at the sapling. *Thanks, little tree. You done good.* He heaved himself up, stretching, testing bones and joints and tendons, expecting the lightning bolt of pain. None came. His ribs ached horribly, his face and arms had taken a beating, and he had a headache, but he could still walk.

He looked around and saw the flashlight beam in the grass at the bottom of the cliff. As his eyes adjusted, Thomas saw his path downward. It would take some daring, but he could edge down the rest of the way. He slipped several times and even fell once more, but not as dramatically. When he reached level ground, he picked up the flashlight.

It's a friggin' miracle it still works. He cast the flashlight's beam around in concentric circles, looking for the glint of the knife blade. The light fell on tangles of small trees and underbrush. *Never going to find it out here tonight. Guess I'll get Mom a new knife set for Mother's Day.* He chuckled, bringing a fresh stab of pain to his ribs. *Okay. Let's take inventory. I am weaponless, unless the flashlight morphs into a lightsaber. I hurt myself so I can't quite stand up straight or take a deep breath, but...* He fished into the pocket. *I still have Amy's leash, so I should be just fine.*

At least I've found the clearing with the freak's Kill Cave. That'll be fun to find in the dark. He shook his head in disgust and limped across the clearing, leaving the flashlight on. When he got to the cliff on the other side, he started feeling his way along it to the left.

About twenty feet later, his hands touched the ivy he remembered hanging down in front of the mouth of the cave. His stomach lurched a bit at the thought of what he might find inside. His throat tightened. He grabbed a handful of ivy, pulled it aside, tried to get it to stay, failed, wound it around some other ivy, and repeated for a minute or two. It hurt, but felt good to rip away the curtain of secrecy. When he had the entrance laid bare, it held only pitch darkness split by the flashlight's beam.

He heard a rough scrabbling, then a muffled whine.

"Amy! Amy girl, are you in there?" *Goddamn this high-pitched teenage voice!*

Use your head, Weaver. What are the chances he's in there right now, waiting? I have no idea, but I couldn't have done a better job of letting him know I'm coming. Shit.

Thomas turned sideways and squeezed into the short passage, shining the light ahead. He gathered his courage and ran the last two steps into the cave.

It had been stripped nearly empty, cleaned like a hotel room after a weeklong stay. The beam revealed no threats. He heard the scrabbling sound again, and pointed the flashlight to the far corner on his right.

The same green pet carrier from his cat discovery sat on the cave floor, turned to face the wall. The scrabbling sound came from it, and the carrier rocked from side to side a bit, but he couldn't see what was inside.

His hand crept up to his mouth, covering it. *Oh, goddammit. If Amy is in there and okay, she would be barking her head off.*

Shit. Poor choice of words. Either way, I don't want to see what's in there. I just don't want to know.

Thomas took three hesitant steps forward and nudged the carrier. The scrabbling stopped, though not the whine.

"Amy?"

Gathering himself, he reached for the handle and pulled the carrier toward him.

It's heavy. Something bigger than a cat is in there. He turned it the rest of the way, shining the flashlight directly inside, ready for the worst.

Amy's brown eyes stared back at him, full of life.

"Amy girl! You're alive! Why didn't you bark?"

Amy gave another muffled whine. Thomas kneeled and shone the flashlight at an angle into the carrier. He fidgeted with the metal catch, but his hands were shaking. Finally, he remembered to pinch the latch and slide the mechanism. The door popped open. Twenty-five pounds of squirming, twisting, terrified dachshund pushed through and clambered up into Thomas's lap.

He turned the flashlight on Amy. A rubber band was wrapped around and around her snout, and brutally so. It had cut through the fur and skin, leaving hints of blood around the band. Thomas winced, reached out and touched it gently. Amy whined again, but didn't pull away.

"Oh, poor girl. Poor Amiable. I'm so sorry he did this to you."

This is going to take delicate care. Where the band is thickest, that's where a less tight spot will be.

Thomas located a promising strand of the rubber band, stretched it only as far as he had to, and worked it over Amy's nose. The dog didn't flinch. Once he got the first loop off, the rest came away easily. When she was free of the sadistic muzzling, Amy opened her mouth wide, stuck her tongue out and barked. It wasn't the small bark you might expect from a dog so low to the ground, but an oversized sound that started deep inside her chest and made deliverymen think a much bigger dog lived in the Weaver household. The sound echoed loudly inside the cave.

Go ahead, girl. Bark away. You must've been holding it back for hours. Thomas hugged and petted Amy, who was still quivering. He looked for other wounds, but aside from the circular ooze of blood around her nose, she was unharmed. Relief gave way to a sudden burst of murderous rage.

Michael Hollister, if you were here right this minute, you would not be the one to walk out of here alive.

You freak. You goddamned freak. I can't let you get away with this.

Okay. First, I've got to get Amiable home, safe and sound, then I'll deal with you, Hollister. Thomas retrieved the leash and clipped it on her little black collar.

He scanned the cave with the flashlight. Most evidence of Michael's hobby was gone. The small, staked forest creature, the macabre line of skulls, the toolbox, were nowhere in sight. Finally, in one corner of the cave, Thomas spotted something.

He took four steps forward with the light. The small piece of plywood rested against one wall. The glove Thomas had found in the tool box was nailed to the board, turned inside out. The beam picked out the bloodstain on the palm where the cat had bitten him.

Three of the fingers and the thumb were nailed in the down position. The middle finger was nailed up.

Chapter Eighteen

When Thomas reached the mouth of the cave, the flashlight began to dim. He set Amy down, whereupon she hunkered and urinated for a very long time.

"You're a good girl, Amiable. Even in there, you wouldn't pee inside, would you?" He gave her ears a rub. "C'mon, girl, we've got a few miles to go before we sleep."

By the time he was at the edge of the clearing, the beam was too weak to matter. *No big deal when I'm on a road, but kind of a problem walking through the forest, with trip hazards every few feet.* Before the light faded completely, he shined it at his Timex. 3:45. *Okay. I can either sit here for a few hours and wait for dawn, or I can just be a man and git 'er done.* Thomas almost laughed. *Wonder where Larry the Cable Guy is in 1976?*

He's probably Larry the Ham Radio Teenage Nerd.

He clicked the flashlight off and shoved it back into his pocket.

The walk out of the forest should have been easier. At some point, the canyon would have to give way to civilization. It was slow going; his side hurt like hell, an ankle had begun to ache, it was hard to steer Amy so that the leash didn't get hung up all the time, and home and hearth seemed far distant. He stumbled over so many obstacles that he wondered if he had fallen into a *Groundhog's Day* time loop, damned to spending the same awful fifteen minutes tripping over the same things.

In time, a break in the trees allowed him to see the glow of the lights of town, so he knew which way to head. The trees and underbrush thinned out. He heard the sound of cars, then saw headlights.

Holy shit, I am completely turned around. I came out on the highway. My internal compass is broken.

Thomas took a moment to get his bearings, then set off down the road. The easy going came as such relief that the aches and pains didn't much bug him. Here, he had but to put one foot in front of the other. Amy walked on ahead, happily sniffing at every cigarette butt and french fry wrapper discarded on the shoulder. *Just a midnight-stroll-after-being-captured-and-nearly-killed-by-your-friendly-neighborhood-psychopath, huh, Amy? Wish I bounced back as fast as you.*

But let's take stock. A few weeks ago, I was a depressed fifty-four-year-old unemployed alcoholic, ending a miserable life. Now, I'm a teenager, living in 1976 and trying to stop a serial killer.

God. I tried to kill myself and woke up inside a Dean Koontz novel.

The Barnes Road cutoff was another two miles ahead. Thomas could get off the highway there, leaving only another mile or so on the side streets to get home. *Still might make it home before Mom gets up for work.*

A car traveling his direction slowed as it approached Thomas and pulled onto the shoulder. It paced him for a few yards, but Thomas was too lost in his thoughts and pain to notice it. Finally, the car pulled back onto the road and alongside him. The passenger window rolled down. The driver wore the navy blue of the Middle Falls Police. "Evening," he said, as if nothing were unusual about a boy walking his dachshund on the highway at that hour.

Thomas jumped. *Oh my freaking God. Is everyone a ninja, or am I just oblivious?* "Evening, officer." The police prowler rolled gently to a stop. Thomas bent at the waist and peered inside.

The officer leaned across the passenger seat. *Big guy,* thought Thomas. *About my age. The age I really am, just not the age I look. Looks like he used to be an athlete, but too many shifts behind the wheel of his patrol car instead of walking a beat has taken care of that. Good face, though.*

"Son, you look like you've been shot at and missed, then shit at and hit. Do you know what time it is?"

"Umm, no sir, I can't say I do." Thomas lifted his left wrist to show his watch. "It's too dark to see my watch."

The cop stared for a long moment at Thomas, then at the leash. "Well, it's 4:45 a.m., and from the looks of you, I don't think you're up early to report for your job at the mill."

Thomas nodded. "Right."

"I'm sure it's a fascinating story as to why you are limping down the highway, walking your weenie dog in the dead of night." Thomas opened his mouth to tell that story, but the cop held up a large hand. "However, my shift ends in another two hours, and I have a feeling I would still be sitting here listening. So let's start with this: do you live here in town?"

"Yessir. I go to Middle Falls High. I live on Periwinkle Lane."

"Periwinkle, huh? Do you know old Mrs. Arkofski?"

Without thinking, Thomas made a face of distaste. "Say no more," the cop chuckled. "If you're smart enough to be afraid of that lady, you're okay with me. Listen, son, you are out five hours past curfew. I can't just let you wander the streets at this time of night." He reached down to his left and pushed a button. The back door lock popped up. "You and your weenie dog…what's her name?"

"Amy, sir."

"You and Amy climb on in the back seat and I'll give you a lift home."

Thomas's throat grew so thick it hurt him. For a moment, he had the sickening certainty he was going to cry, and he was afraid he might not be able to stop. He swallowed hard. "That would be great. Y'see, Amy got lost tonight, and I've been out looking for her…"

The cop held up his hand again. "You can tell me your story while we're driving. What's your address?"

"145 Periwinkle Lane."

"Good enough. Hop in."

Settled inside the warm car, basking in dashboard's comforting glow, Thomas felt no need to tell an edited story of his evening. The officer didn't ask.

Jesus. If this was 2016, this would have gone down completely differently. Teenage boy, middle of the night, walking along a quiet road in a dark hoodie? It's hard to believe a cop would have pulled over with no lights, no siren, then offer a ride. I don't think they are nervous yet, not like they will be. Like they will have reason to be. Thomas had a sudden vision of himself as a 1970s gangster in Middle Falls, wearing a high school hoodie, having misplaced his only weapon, and leading an affectionate dachshund as his badass attack dog. He kept from laughing only with difficulty. *Lamest gangster ever.*

Ten minutes of driving accomplished what would have taken Thomas close to two hours on foot. When they turned down Periwinkle Lane, Thomas craned his neck to see the lay of the land. *Thank God. All quiet on the western front. I'd have a hell of a time explaining what I was doing getting a ride from a cop at five o'clock in the morning.*

The patrol car pulled up quietly in front of his house. "Thanks, officer. Thanks for the ride…and not arresting me and stuff." *There. That sounds like a teenager, right?*

"You're welcome, son. I don't want to see you out after curfew any more, understood?"

"Yes sir. Understood."

"Good." He pushed a button, the door unlocked, and Thomas and Amy disembarked into the chilly night air. The squad car idled at the curb in front of Thomas's house. As Thomas opened the front door, he waved to the officer, who waved back and pulled away from the curb.

Thomas closed the door behind him, feeling all the night's exertion and injury at last. He unleashed Amy, who trotted over to her water bowl and lapped at it for quite some time before stepping back and looking expectantly at him.

"Seriously?" Thomas whispered. "How can you think of food after all this?" Amy waited patiently. Thomas picked up her food bowl, dished up a bowlful of Gravy Train, then added water. *The gravy taste dogs can't wait to finish.* He set it down next to her water bowl. Amy tucked into it like she had been lost in the wilderness for weeks.

He put the flashlight away, then snuck into the bathroom. His first glimpse in the mirror made him wince. There were scratches across his forehead, his cheek, and one down the side of his neck. There wasn't much blood, and what there was had dried. *Damn. I look like Rocky Balboa at the end of the Apollo Creed fight.* Thomas took the washcloth Zack had left on the bottom of the shower and ran it under warm water, then dabbed at his face. With the dried blood washed away, he looked more human, less horror movie refugee.

His t-shirt was ripped. As Thomas pulled it over his head, he felt a jab of pain in his ribs. He lifted his left arm and looked in the mirror. A harsh red bruise, like an inverted map of Australia, was already forming.

Once in his bedroom, he wadded his t-shirt up and kicked it under his bed, shucked off his filthy jeans and eased into bed. He had just laid his head on his pillow when he heard Anne's door open and the hall light click on. Thomas turned to face the wall and was out.

Chapter Nineteen

Thomas woke to sunshine pouring in the window. A few weeks into this new life, there were still days he awoke disoriented. This was one of those. He looked down at the orange bedspread, the red, white, and blue walls, the empty twin bed to his left. He coughed, bringing a sharp spike of pain from his left side that helped him focus on where and when he was. The small clock read 11:15.

It's a Saturday morning. Mom's at work. Zack's off doing Zack stuff.

He laid back down and closed his eyes.

***

When he came to again, the disorientation and fatigue were gone. He glanced at the clock. *1:38. Crap. I feel like I've got a hangover. I've gotta get my shit together.* He pulled a clean pair of jeans and t-shirt out of his drawer and limped to the bathroom.

He turned the shower on hot, then located a green bottle of Bayer aspirin. *Damn. Did we already have childproof caps in 1976? I guess we did.* He puzzled out the cap, dropped three tablets into his palm, and began to dry-chew them. After two crunches, he leaned over the sink and spat them out. *Holy shit! How did I stand to dry-chew those things?*

Fifteen minutes later, he emerged from the shower feeling rejuvenated. *Yes! This is what it means to be a teenager. No matter how shitty you feel, feeling good is always just around the corner. If I'd fallen down that cliff as a fifty-four year old man, I'd be in the hospital. Instead, I feel like I could go shoot some hoops. Maybe.*

He toweled himself dry, lightly patting his most injured areas, then wiped the fog off the mirror. As he gazed again upon the multicolored Australia on his left side, he teased a sore tooth with his tongue. It hurt, but not sharply. *Think I dodged a bullet, there.* He drew in a deep breath, held it, then let it out; no reason to believe a rib was cracked. What to do about his face? *Lemme see. I can say I got up early and was hanging out with Billy. Maybe he and I were climbing trees and I fell off?*

She won't buy that. I'll think of something. Man. I am starving!

He jumped into his clean jeans and t-shirt and hurried to the kitchen. He put a can of bean with bacon soup on to heat and cut thick slabs of two-day-old meatloaf, which he smooshed between slices of Wonder bread slathered in mustard, then sat down to eat.

As he did, he heard Anne's car pulling in.

A minute later, she set down her purse and took in the scene: Thomas, barefooted and wet-headed, scarfing down a meal in mid-afternoon. She took a step forward, then stopped. "Tommy! What happened to your face?"

Thomas's hand jumped to his face. He reddened, then half-turned and stared down into his soup. She had torpedoed his cover story amidships.

"Nothing, Mom."

Anne sat down, reached across the table, turned his chin right, then left, a practiced gesture of maternal triage. "Cut the crap, Tommy. This didn't happen falling out of bed."

"It's nothing, Mom. I couldn't sleep last night, so I went back out looking for Amy. I fell down while I was looking, but hey, I found her!" He beamed, pointing at the napping dachshund in the living room. "Isn't that all that matters?"

The cover story, its watertight compartments crumpling, listed to port.

"You know perfectly well it's not. How in the world did you manage to fall down and get scraped up looking for Amy?"

"I..." Before he could fully engage the lie forming in his brain, he could see it wasn't going to fly.

Anne's eyes narrowed. "Where exactly did you find Amy?" A second fish exploded into the foundering hulk that might have been a successful cover story. It was about time to abandon ship.

Thomas scrunched up his face. "In the woods behind the school."

"What? No. Wait a minute. The woods at the school? That's miles away. None of this makes any sense." Thomas looked out the window in silence. "One, what would Amy be doing clear over there? Two, even if she was, how would you know she was there?"

Would you believe I had a GPS tracker installed in her collar? No? Haven't heard of GPS yet, have you, Mom? I wish I could tell you, but I just can't see how that would end well for any of us.

"Thomas, I'm waiting."

Guess she's serious. She didn't start calling me Thomas until my late twenties.

Her voice shifted from challenge to sympathy. "It's obvious something's going on. Thomas, are you in some sort of trouble? You know you can talk to me about it. Whatever it is, I can help."

Sure. Okay. I'm really twenty years older than you, even though I look like a kid. I was so depressed, I tried to kill myself and woke up back here. And other than the fact Zack is alive again—and you don't even know he was dead—everything kind of sucks. I ran into this future serial killer and now I'm all messed up with him, and I'm not sure what I'm going to do about it, but I'm going to do something.

Can you help me with all that, Mom? Really?

He continued to stare out the window.

"Fine," she snapped. Thomas saw tears glittering in her eyes. "You don't want to talk to me? Go to your room. You can come out when you're ready to tell me what you've gotten yourself mixed up in."

Thomas pushed away his lunch and stood up. "Sorry, Mom." He walked out of the kitchen.

"No. No you're not," Anne said in an injured tone. "If you were sorry, you'd sit back down and talk to me."

Thomas continued on to his room, shutting the door behind him.

Should have thought this whole thing through better. She's not stupid. Now what in the hell am I going to tell her?

He walked to the little bookcase and looked through what was there. *Wish I had my Xbox. That would make being a grounded middle-aged man a lot more palatable.* His fingers glanced across titles by Heinlein, Asimov, Clarke, and Farmer, then settled upon *A Sound of Thunder and Other Stories* by Ray Bradbury. *Okay, sure, why not. I've got time to kill.*

He flopped down on the bed, adjusted the pillow, and began to read.

A few hours later, Anne brought in a plate of dinner. "Ready to talk yet?" All Thomas could manage was a helpless stare. His mother set the plate down on his dresser.

"Billy called. He wanted to know if you could come over and play something called B & B. What's that?"

"I think it was probably D & D. Dungeons and Dragons. It's just a game."

Anne nodded. "I told him you were grounded."

"Yeah, I didn't figure you were going to let me out of house arrest to go have a sleepover at Billy's."

"Being smart with me won't help anything." On her way out, she shut the door with a little extra oomph. He returned to Ray Bradbury.

Around bedtime, Zack appeared. He took off his t-shirt. "You're in the shit now, squirt. Why don't you tell me what's going on and I'll help you figure out how to talk to Mom about it."

"Nothing to talk about. Amy got out, I went and found her and brought her home. That's it."

"Sure. Amy got out, travelled the four miles to school on her little three-inch legs, managed to get herself lost in the woods, and you happened to know exactly where to look for her? This is bullshit. Do you think we're stupid?"

"Well, it sounds like bullshit when you say it like that."

Zack leaned forward. "That's because it is bullshit, shit-for-brains. In the car last night, you said 'no more walks in the woods.' That promise didn't last very long."

"Zack, if I knew what's going on, I would tell you."

"That's another load of crap. You know something is going on, and you won't tell me. But, whatever. It's your funeral." Zack stripped down to his boxers, got into bed and clicked off the light.

They didn't listen to any music that night.

Chapter Twenty

The next morning, Anne made breakfast, but there was no happy meeting around the breakfast table. She brought Thomas a plate of eggs and pancakes in silence.

By mid-morning, Thomas finally reached the title story in *A Sound of Thunder*. It was about a company that used time travel to send big game hunters far back into the past, where they were allowed to kill dinosaurs that had been about to die anyway. The hunter loses his nerve, blunders off the pre-selected path, and returns only when the guides have killed the T-Rex. When the group returns to their own time, they find everything is changed. The hunter looks at the bottom of his boot and sees that when he fled, he had stepped on a butterfly. Over millions of years, this had somehow changed the course of history.

Thomas laid the book on his chest, tucked his hands behind his head, and stared up at the ceiling. *Of course. When I came back, unless I did everything exactly the same as I did the first time, it would change everything. And doing it all the exact same would be impossible. I've done a hell of a lot more than step on a butterfly, so what does that mean? I have to at least consider that I don't know crap about what's going to happen from now on. I've probably changed every-*

thing, now. So, that would mean Zack is safe, right? At least, safe from me killing him, right?

Thomas rolled over and put the Beach Boys on the turntable.

But if the future is wide open, that means I can make things better, right? First, I've got to figure out how to get out of this situation with Mom, but I think I've got an idea how to handle that. Then I've got to find a way to stop Michael from killing people. That's a good start, but what else can I do?

His mind replayed the image of Seth Berman pushing him backward and calling him a "homo" while Ben Jenkins looked on. *Maybe I can help Ben feel a little better, too. It's gotta suck, having to hide who you are all the time. I'd like him to know things will get better.*

Sure. And, while I'm at it, I'll stop Mark David Chapman from shooting John Lennon, the space shuttle from exploding, and 9/11 from happening. Why not?

Thomas finished the book, but was too swept up by ennui to start another. He spent half an hour watching raindrops race each other down his bedroom window. He went to the bathroom, just to get out of his room, then returned. He pulled his school notebook down and made a list:

1. Don't Kill Zack
2. Stop Michael from killing people
3. Figure out what's wrong with Carrie Copeland and help her if I can
4. Help Ben be who he really is.

Ha! How much will it creep Zack out if he finds a piece of notebook paper with my writing on it that says, "Don't kill Zack?" He'll start sleeping with one eye open.

After dinner, Anne came in again and sat down on the end of Thomas's bed, looking serious.

Uh-oh.

"Okay," Anne said, "this isn't working. I could keep you locked away in here until you're an old man…"

Too late.

"...and it's obvious you're still not going to talk to me. When I went by the hospital today, I talked to Dr. Rasmussen, and he gave me this." She laid a powder blue pamphlet on the bed, entitled *Ten Signs Your Teenager Is On Drugs*. Below the title was a caricature of a heavy-lidded, long-haired teen.

I have no business laughing, nor even looking like I might laugh. This is hard. With an effort of pure will, Thomas neutralized the urge to crack up.

"You've been acting so differently these past few weeks, I hardly recognize you. You speak differently, you even walk differently. Everything about you just feels a little off these days. That's one of the ten warning signs."

Guess I haven't been doing as good a job of fooling everyone as I thought.

"Zack told me you've been drinking my leftover coffee in the morning and wandering off to the woods after school, too."

Seriously, Zack? And you called me a narc? Still, I can't blame him. The first time around, I didn't realize how much like a second parent he had been. I didn't have any perspective.

"Sneaking out in the middle of the night is on the list, too. Tommy, I need you to level with me. No matter what, I'm your mom, and I can help you, but I need to know. Are you on drugs? Did you sneak out on Friday to see your pusher?"

Thomas had to bite his lip. *Mom, I think you've been watching too many episodes of* The Streets of San Francisco. *Okay, Weaver, get it together.* He took a deep breath. "No, Mom, I'm not on drugs. I've never even smoked a cigarette or snuck a beer." *However, if you'll be patient...* "I'm not doing drugs. I promise. If I'm acting different, it's probably because I've been pretty worried about something."

Anne scooted closer, sensing a breakthrough. "What? What's bothering you so much?"

"I don't want to tell you, because I know you'll overreact. I want to try and figure this out on my own without you just fixing it." *I really do hate to be so manipulative with her, but I can't see another way.*

Anne was quiet for a moment. Then, "Okay. I'll make you a deal. You tell me what's going on, and if I can, I'll let you figure it out on your own."

There we go. That's the opening I was looking for.

"Okay. Well…" She waited out his long pause. "I've been having trouble with this kid Michael Hollister at school. He's bigger than me—he's in Zack's grade."

"Is he hitting you?"

"No, not exactly. He's just—he scares me. I think I said something to him that made him mad at me, and now he's doing everything he can to make me miserable." Thomas looked down at the bedspread, picked off a little piece of fabric and rolled it between his fingers. "I…I figured he took Amy on Friday, and I knew where he took her. I just didn't want to tell you."

"So, when we were driving around the neighborhood calling for her, you knew where she was? And you just didn't tell me?"

"Well, I wasn't *sure* where she was. That's why I didn't say anything."

"What made you think he took Amy there?"

Thomas paused. *Should have anticipated that. Damn it.*

Were all my lies and half-truths, all my life, as crappy and transparent as this one?

"He's got like a little clubhouse out in the woods behind the school." *Yeah, sure. Clubhouse of the damned.* "No big deal, but I just knew that was where he would take her."

"And this Michael boy, he took Amy, as, like, a prank?"

"Yeah, I guess. Like a prank."

"That's not okay. I'm going to call his mother right now. He's got to know you can't play pranks like that."

Sure, Mom. Call Mother Serial Killer and complain about her demonic spawn. I'm sure that will work just fine.

"C'mon, Mom, do you have to? You said you'd let me try to figure this out on my own. What if I was in real trouble? You'd want me to be able to come and talk to you about it, wouldn't you?"

Anne narrowed her eyes. "Okay, then. How are you going to deal with this, exactly?"

"I'm going to talk to him at school tomorrow and tell him I'm sorry for smarting off to him, but it's not okay for him to do something like take Amy away."

"I think you're telling me what I want to hear in order that I'll stay out of it."

Thomas shook his head back and forth. "Nope. That's what I'm going to do."

She obviously still doesn't believe me, but that look says she'll take what she can get for now. "Hmmm. All right, we'll leave it there for now, but I'm going to check up on this. If you're having problems with kids at school, you should talk to Zack. He can talk to them."

"I know, and Zack's great about that." For a moment, he almost slipped and told her about the one-punch fight he had gotten into in the lunch room, and how Zack had rescued him. "But, sometimes I just want to do things on my own. I don't want to be Zack Weaver's little brother forever."

"I understand. But, that doesn't change the fact you snuck out of the house on Friday, no matter how good your reasons were. So, you're grounded for a week. Straight to school, then straight home. And no more sneaking out. Are we clear?"

"Clear."

"All right. Do you want to come out and watch *Colombo* with me? It's on in just a few minutes."

"I'd like to come out and watch anything."

Chapter Twenty-One

Outside Middle Falls High the next morning, Billy caught up to Zack just outside the front doors.

"So… you got in trouble?"

Thomas nodded, grinned. "Yeah, a little bit. I had the Weaver Prison Blues for the weekend."

"Holy shit," Billy said, catching a good look at Thomas's face. "Did the warden beat the crap out of you, too?"

"Long story, man. I'll tell you about it later." *Once I have another lie ready for you, too. This is getting too complicated. I've got to get to a point where I can start telling people the truth. Or, at least, most of the truth. Whatever.* "Hey, you know Ben Jenkins, don't you?"

"Yeah, I think so. Isn't he that quiet kid in homeroom with us? The one that's usually got his nose buried in a book?"

"Yep, that's him. I was thinking, maybe we should invite him over to play D & D with us this weekend. It would be cool to have another player, wouldn't it?"

Billy shrugged. "I guess. Whatever, man. Invite him if you want. I've got a cool adventure lined up for you, if you don't mind risking your precious Hooka Khan."

"You're on. Maybe Saturday night?"

"Sure, if you're not grounded again."

Inside the school, the flow of teenagers looked like Monday morning zombies, shuffling off toward the last available supply of brains.

As Thomas approached Home Room, his stomach tightened. *The last time I saw Michael Hollister, it was Friday night, and he was dognapping Amy. What's he going to be like today? Threatening? Cool as could be? I can't get a handle on this guy.*

Thomas and Billy slipped into their normal seats at the back of the class, just ahead of the bell. Carrie was in her lonely spot in the corner. Michael sat erectly in the front row, dressed like the Young Republican he was. As if he sensed Thomas's arrival, Michael turned to look at him. His expression was blank, his eyes dead.

What a freaking psycho.

Thomas tried to catch Carrie's eye, but she kept focused on a loose-leaf notebook as Mr. Burns started roll call. Mornings like this reminded Thomas why he had hated high school: a teacher droning on about something most of them would soon forget. He had begun his second chance with every intention of attentive listening.

And Mr. Burns said: "Challenge accepted."

When the bell rang at last, Thomas got up to head for French class. Billy headed for Shop. As Thomas wandered through the milling hallway throng, he noticed four blondes talking with Jimmy Halverson. Jimmy was tall, predictably played basketball, and looked in no hurry to be anywhere. In another ten years, the girls might have been referred to as Heathers. A decade later, Mean Girls. In 1976, Tommy had just thought of them as the Cool Kids.

Carrie Copeland happened by, and the main flow of traffic crowded her between the cool clique and the lockers. As she passed Jimmy, he took a casual half step backward, bumping into her hard enough to send her books and notebooks sprawling.

"What an asshole," Thomas mumbled to himself. Carrie said nothing, but kneeled to gather up her materials. The four girls smirked. "Careful, Jimmy," the blondest of the four said, "you might catch something."

Carrie's long hair fell around her face, covering it, but Thomas could imagine the embarrassment rising on her cheeks. Feigning fear, Jimmy took a theatrical step away from Carrie.

Thomas took three quick strides toward them. "Hey, Halverson."

Jimmy's face looked down from on high in disdain. "What do *you* want?"

"I've just got to know. What do you get out of making someone else feel bad? Is that really the only way you can momentarily inflate your own sense of self-worth? Or is it maybe because you know, as pathetic as high school is, this is going to be it for you? This is the pinnacle?"

Thomas saw Jimmy's eyes narrow for a brief moment. *Got 'im.* "I'm gonna pretend like I didn't understand what you just said. Move along, and you have one chance not to get your ass kicked."

"One chance? That's great." Thomas scrolled through his Facebook memories. Stories came into focus. "What was your one chance, Jimmy? A basketball scholarship? Sure. You're dreaming of an NBA career, aren't you? That was probably not gonna happen anyway, but what you don't know is that you'll blow out your knee at the beginning of your senior year. You'll never get that speed back, and the best you're ever going to do is to barely make the team at the local community college."

Jimmy gaped, too stunned to bluster. Thomas turned to the leader of the blonde pack. "And how about you, Barb? Things seem pretty sweet for you right now, don't they? Jimmy's not a bad boyfriend as far as jocks go. Here's a little secret for you. He's going to ask you to marry him next year."

Barb looked at Jimmy, eyes slightly aglow.

"You two will get married the summer after you graduate. That day won't be as happy for you as it might be, though, because Jimmy is going to sleep with Lisa on your wedding day."

Lisa blushed and took a step away.

"Your parents won't be real happy about that, Barb, because they took a second mortgage out on their house to pay for your wedding, and you'll file for an annulment before the ink has a chance to dry on your wedding license. Don't worry, though. They'll still let you live with them, which you'll do until they are old and grey."

Barb opened her mouth to chastise him, but Thomas had already turned to the future adulteress. "And you. Lisa, Lisa, Lisa. In addition to screwing the groom on your best friend's wedding day, you've got quite a life ahead of you. Ten years from now, you'll be a hundred and fifty pounds overweight, living off whatever child support you can get for your three kids you have from three different men. Don't worry, though—you'll only marry two of them. The other one will be a slam, bam, thank you, ma'am, Friday night special that you won't ever see again."

Thomas turned to the smallest of the girls, who flinched away a bit. He remembered her stints in rehab, smiled, then paused. *Shit, I'm almost as bad as they are.* He turned, spread his arms, and said, "Do you deserve all that?" He shrugged. "I dunno. We all tend to get what we deserve, in the end. For sure, though, it's at least a little karma for acting the way you do toward people like Carrie."

Thomas turned and looked at Carrie. She had straightened out of her normal slouch and was staring straight at him, making brazen eye contact. He felt a jolt of electricity at the sudden familiarity. As he went on his way toward French, she caught his arm.

The look in her eyes bored into his soul. "So. How many lives is this for you?"

Chapter Twenty-Two

Temporal Relocation Assignment Department, Earth Division

Emillion spun her cylinder, humming off-key as she worked. Lights, forms, and varying shapes that would be indecipherable to human eyes danced and moved. Two thin ribbons of blue light moved together, spun around each other in an intricate dance. In combination, they transformed first into indigo, then to a deep violet. She smiled.

"You seem much happier today," Veruna said.

"Life is good," Emillion replied to her coworker.

Veruna returned her gaze to her own work. "Life is. That is all."

Emillion's smile didn't falter. "Of course. At this moment, though, it is also good." She spun the cylinder clockwise, let it spin a few rotations, then feathered it to a stop. The violet ribbons separated, became blue again. One rose to the milky white at the top of the cylinder, disappeared. The other darkened.

"Oh. Oh no."Emillion's smile disappeared.

Chapter Twenty-Three

Thomas Weaver stood in the hallway of Middle Falls High School, reeling.

I would swear she just said, "How many lives is this for you?" What the hell do I do now? Deny? Admit it?

Since he had made the transition from middle-aged suicide to second-time teenager, Thomas had carried the weight of a secret he thought he could never share. Now Carrie Copeland was calling him on it, right to his face. "Don't bullshit me, Thomas. How many lives is this for you?"

She seems pretty freaking sure of herself. Thomas remained silent.

Carrie looked at him with what might have been tolerant pity–or perhaps insulted intelligence. "There's no way you pulled that whole Nostradamus trick without believing you really do know their future. You were too sure of yourself."

It would be great to have someone I could confide in about all this stuff. Thomas looked deep into her eyes. They were a cool green, very pretty, when she wasn't shielding them from the world. They also conveyed knowledge belying her sixteen years. When she stood up straight and pushed her hair back off her face, she was striking.

She knows. Am I not the only one? Of course. Why hadn't I considered that?

"Ummm...two?" *My God. I just admitted to someone that I am a time traveler, or spirit walk-in, or whatever the hell I am.*

"Oh," she said, eyes filling with understanding. "You're new. I guess that explains it."

"It does? Like what? What do you mean, 'new?' How many lives have you lived?"

"Me? This is lucky number thirteen for me. That's why you don't see me doing beginner stunts, like spouting off like a gypsy fortune teller at the state fair."

"Holy shit. Thirteen? No. Come on." *Thirteen times through the same life? How do you stay sane?*

Or do you?

"Oh, I'm bursting your bubble." Her look was less sympathetic than her tone. "I guess I need to remember what it was like my second time through. You're probably thinking you were just being given a second chance, maybe to fix something that went wrong in your life?"

Thomas nodded.

The bell rang. Thomas looked up to see that they were alone in the hallway. They were officially late to second period.

Carrie glanced down the empty hall. "I don't want to get in trouble. I'm trying to fly under the radar, and I'm not going to mess it up. I'll meet you in the lunchroom after third period. There are some advantages of being a social pariah. Everyone will leave us alone to talk."

"No, wait..."

Too late. Carrie turned away, cast her eyes down and let her shoulders slump, turned the corner and was gone.

She wears that attitude like a costume. Or maybe it's armor.

Trying to catch up to all the thoughts circling in his brain, Thomas broke into a run and managed to slip into the back of his French class while Miss Thompson was still taking roll. *One of the advantages of being named 'Weaver,' I suppose.*
"Mademoiselle Tolliver?" called Miss Thompson.

"Ici," said a slightly built brunette in front.

What the hell does this mean?
"Monsieur Van Den Boer?" asked Miss Thompson.
Maybe that she's got this all figured out more than I do?
"Uh-see," muttered a slouching, straight-haired male in a Blazers t-shirt.
Not hard. I don't have it figured out at all.
"Monsieur Weaver?"
"Ici," said Thomas, after an instant's hesitation.

He daydreamed his way through French, letting Carrie's revelation wash over him. *That's a game-changer. When I died and woke up here, I assumed this was it—a special one-time offer. But, Carrie said she was on, what, her thirteenth go-round? There's no way I can do that.*

But maybe, what choice do you have? Nowhere to run, nowhere to hide. Kill yourself and wake up in the same place again? Or is it different every time? If you just keep living the same lifespan over and over again, what's the point? Is there a way to win the game? Solve a certain problem and go on, or there is no end game?

If there are two of us, there's probably a lot more. Is everyone here on their second, or fourth, or twentieth life? Thomas cast a sideways glance at Wayne Farmer, one seat over. Wayne's head was cradled in his right hand, eyes unfocused, a slight thread of drool in the corner of his mouth. *If so, Wayne doesn't appear to be making the best of his opportunity. If he's on a second life, at least a portion of us are bored out of our skulls with this Land of Do-Overs.*

Wayne Farmer snored just a bit. Miss Thompson called out a question to Monsieur Farmer, who awoke with a start and asked her to repeat the question. A titter ran through the class as he wiped off the drool and gave a butchered, incorrect answer.

I don't think it's all of us, though. If it was, a lot more people would have done something like I just did and revealed themselves. It would be at least an Urban Legend, but I've never heard of anyone else claiming they were on their second or third life.

So. There's more than one, but somewhere less than everyone. Good deduction, Weaver.

Maybe I should just wait and talk to Carrie at lunch. She seems to have a better handle on what's going on. Wonder how many she's met.

Thomas spent the rest of the class thinking about Carrie's eyes, and how warm he felt when she finally let her guard down. *She's not just 'not-ugly,' she's beautiful. Who knew?*

Thomas caught up with Billy in the hall on the way to P.E., which had been a low point during his first high school days—a chance for the jocks to be jockish—but it hadn't been so bad this time around. They had played a week of badminton, at which a second life did not improve Thomas's skills. Still, aside from getting waxed 21-2 or worse in each game, at least no one was pushing him around.

After that, they had spent two weeks enjoying co-ed P.E. and square dancing. Thomas was unsure how square dancing counted as P.E. *If Ronald Reagan can make ketchup a vegetable, I guess this works too.*

If Reagan gets elected, anyway.

Thomas and Billy dressed down in the locker room, putting on minimal red shorts that would have been embarrassing in 2016 but went unnoticed in 1976, along with tight "Middle Falls High" t-shirts. They strolled out onto the gym floor, then froze.

Square dancing, which included at least brief contact with pretty girls, was over. A dozen small, mean-looking white balls rested on the half-court line.

Dodge Ball.

In junior high, they had played dodge ball with red rubber playground balls. If someone really wound up and threw, it might leave a red mark, but nothing very painful. In high school, the stakes went up. These were the size of softballs, though not as hard. They were tightly packed with feathers, and the kids called them Whistle Balls, because if you got enough zip on one, it whistled just before it smacked you. A normal kid couldn't do any damage with them, but an athlete could. In a baseball pitcher's hands, Whistle Balls became weapons.

"Shit," said Billy with an eye roll.

Thomas nodded grimly. Dodge Ball gave you no place to hide. *When you hit a kid, he goes behind you. If you miss the ball, it gets through to the back, and you're caught in a crossfire with people on both sides of you trying to make you suffer.*

Coach Raymer emerged from the locker room. Pushing past Thomas and Billy with a quick "Excuse me, ladies," he blew three sharp blasts on his whistle. "Hustle up! Front and center. I think we've learned about as much as we can learn from do-si-do-ing and allemande-left-ing. Today, we'll get the blood pumping. You all know how to play. Let's pick teams. Monroe, Halverson, you're captains. Schoolyard pick. Let's go!"

Few things in life are more predictable than a schoolyard pick. In the end, Monroe–a quarterback– picked his fellow footballers first, while Halverson went with his fellow basketball players. When the jocks were gone, the captains picked everyone in order of least to most klutzy. Thomas and Billy were chosen near the low end of that group, on the same team. Shortly after Billy, the last two draft picks remaining were Michael Hollister and Clyde Billings.

Clyde had worn braces on both legs until sixth grade. He was out of them now, but had all the grace and speed of a newborn turtle clambering for the sea. Stan Monroe looked them over, then decided that Clyde had more to offer than Michael. Jimmy Halverson ended up with Michael Hollister, who showed no reaction to anything.

"At least we get to march to our death together, right?" Billy said.

"Very comforting. Any strategy tips for surviving this?"

"Sure. Protect the gonads at all times. One of those balls whistles into your franks and beans and you can kiss ever having kids goodbye."

"Great. Important safety tip, Egon." *Shit. Ghostbusters won't exist for another decade.*

It didn't matter, as Billy had resolutely marched into the center of the floor, leaning forward as if eager to rush for the supply of balls. Thomas joined him, then noticed that Michael Hollister looked even more uncomfortable on the other side. The tight t-shirt and skimpy red shorts accentuated his tall, thin frame. He was scanning the field in front of him, looking like a fox with a foot caught in a trap.

Coach Raymer blew one shrill blast. All the athletes charged forward into the center-court chaos. Thomas and Billy took one fake-out step toward the balls, then retreated to safety at the back. That safety did not last long, for the initial volleys wiped out nearly half of both teams. Thomas tried to do a crab walk, keeping one eye on both groups of players. *Never mind glory. I want to survive this.*

One of the football players threw a low fastball at Billy. It skipped under his sneakers, but he cried, "Damn it! Nicked me!" and trotted down to the other end of the gym with a wink at Thomas.

Thomas glared at him. *Good strategy. Bastard.* Out of the corner of his eye, he saw a big, sweaty player running toward him, winding up. Thomas turned away by reflex, but not quickly enough. The ball caught him right in the throat. A howl of "Nice shot, Muller!" went up from the back line as Thomas went down, half-stunned.

Feels like he knocked my Adam's apple through the back of my throat. But it's a good excuse to take a rest, he thought, as he sort of scuttled off to the side to recover. Had he not done so, of course, he would have remained a legitimate target of opportunity. Meanwhile, the mayhem on the court continued.

As Thomas reached the bottom bleachers outside the court sideline, he kept an eye on the action, lest some sadist target him even in the bleachers. Just then, he saw Stan Monroe pick a target and fire. Thomas remembered Stan as the JV quarterback and starting centerfielder that year, with an arm like a rifle.

Stan unleashed a whistler directly to Michael's groin, bringing a brief wince from Thomas before he remembered who had just taken the hit. Michael folded over so fast he fell face first to the ground, then assumed the position—legs drawn up, fists tight to his groin, feet moving feebly while gasping for air. Every boy in the gym knew exactly what he was feeling.

Even the relaxed standards of Middle Falls High School P.E. sportsmanship dictated that such a shot entitled the victim to a few moments of safe writhing before heading to the back line, a rule Thomas had always been glad to milk. This was Michael Hollister, though. His family's position in the community had long kept at bay the bullying his odd behavior might have otherwise brought on, but it didn't change how anyone felt.

The players on Michael's side backed away, leaving him curled in the fetal position near midcourt. Stan silently mouthed, "One, two, three." On three, every player holding a ball threw with every bit of mustard he could put on it. Half a dozen balls hit Michael simultaneously, bouncing off his head, his arms, his back.

Michael whimpered a moment, but drew himself up to his knees, gathered himself, then stood; first tentatively, then straighter. His face was an absolute mask. He walked toward three of the biggest opposing players, looking right through them. They stood aside. Limping a bit, he walked past them, past the bleachers, and into the locker room.

Why do I think some poor cat or forest creature is going to die tonight?

Chapter Twenty-Four

After P.E. was over, in which he suffered no further devastating whistlers, Thomas dressed out in his jeans and t-shirt and headed to the lunchroom to meet Carrie. All the lunchroom buzz was about Michael's nut shot. Wherever Thomas looked around the room, he saw people miming the action. *By the end of the lunch hour, everyone in school will be claiming to have seen it.* He punched his ticket, collected his plate of hamburger gravy poured over toast with a side of cholesterol, and let the thoughts wander back to his father's term for this dish: "S.O.S.," which stood for "shit on a shingle." Like nearly all young able-bodied adult males of his day, his father had once been drafted into the Army, and Thomas had never heard him say a good word about the experience.

The end of the line was in sight when Carrie finally came in, carrying a small brown-bag lunch. Moving apparently by radar, she joined Thomas at his table. "Mind blown yet?" There was actually a twinkle in her eyes.

She's enjoying this. "Consider it blown."

"What's everyone talking about?"

"Michael Hollister got hit in the cajones in gym class, then given a code red by the rest of the team."

"Code red?"

Shit. What's wrong with me today? A Few Good Men *is a long time away.* "Sorry. That's from a movie that hasn't come out yet. I keep doing that today. Not sure what's wrong with me. We were playing dodge ball in gym class and Michael got hit in the nuts, fell down, then everyone let him have it."

"Oh. Sounds horrible. You don't seem too bothered by it. Are you glad for some reason?"

Shit! That revelation can wait. Shift gears. "Well, I got it in the neck just before that, but nothing like he got."

She looked at his neck with brief concern, then took a bite of her sandwich and swallowed. "So, what do you want to know?"

"So much. You said you are on your thirteenth life. Do you always wake up at the same time and place? Do the circumstances ever change? Have you figured out how much you can change the future?"

Carrie rolled her eyes a bit. "Teenage boys. I swear, always in such a hurry about things. Slow down. I'll answer as many questions as I can, but there's still a lot I don't know. First, yes, I wake up in the exact same place and time. For me, it's waking up on the couch in my parents' house with a stiff neck on a warm afternoon, the summer that I turned twelve, just a few weeks before I started junior high. Nothing particularly noteworthy about that day, it's just where I start."

Thomas nodded. *Like a "save point" in a video game.*

"Is it rude for me to ask how old you really are?"

"Of course it's rude. That's not the kind of question you ever ask a woman."

Thomas thought she was serious until he saw the ghost of a smile cross her lips.

"It gets harder and harder to keep track of these things." She paused, looked up and to her right, thinking. "I suppose I've lived about sixty-five years, altogether. Does that creep you out, knowing that I'm really an old lady?"

"Well, I was fifty-four years old a few weeks ago, so, no."

Carrie's eyes widened. "Oh. You made it that far? All the way to when?"

"2016."

"So, like *Jetsons* stuff, then? Flying cars, teleportation, that sort of thing?"

"No, not exactly. Wait. What's the farthest you've made it?"

She cast her eyes down. "I've never made it to 1980."

Thomas felt a tingle at the back of his neck. *Thirteen lives, but she's never made it out of her teens? What the hell is going on with her?*

"What—how...?" *Is there a tactful way to ask this?*

"How come I keep dying?" He nodded. Her shoulders shrugged in futility. "When I started over the first time, I didn't handle it very well. I was nineteen, but woke up in a twelve-year-old body. I messed things up pretty good. It seemed like every change I made turned out for the worse. First, my dog got run over when she was just a puppy. Then my grandma died. Then, my mom got sick and died, too. But none of them had died in my first life, so I figured it was all my fault and I gave up."

"Gave up? You mean you killed yourself?"

"Yep. Before you ask, pills."

"I get that. That's how I started over too–pills with liquor."

"Right. My third life, same story. Mom got sick and died again. I killed myself again. That time, I was pretty sure I was going to get another shot at setting things right. Problem was, I didn't know what I was doing that was causing Mom to get sick. So, I started experimenting, doing things differently each time. In life #4, I tried being the perfect child. That was better for a while. Mom didn't get sick, but right after I graduated from high school, Dad was killed in a car accident. I killed myself so often, I called it the suicide express. Don't like how your life is going? Swallow a bunch of pills and start over."

Thomas put his fork down and gave that some thought.

"I can't recommend it, actually," Carrie continued. "I've been thinking about what I was doing to my parents in those other lives, each time they found me dead. I won't do that again. I'm trying to live as long as I can this time. I'm tired of living the same years over and over. I want to see what's on the horizon after 1980."

Hmmm. The Iranian hostage crisis, MTV, a Flock of Seagulls, The Brat Pack, Members Only jackets, Miami Vice, The Challenger explosion, the fall of the Berlin Wall. Like any decade, some good, some awful—most of it mediocrity, soon assigned to oblivion.

"That's good. I'm glad." *I would like to reach out and hold your hand, Carrie Copeland, but I don't have the guts.* "So, this time... your mom and dad?"

"Mom died last year," she whispered. "But I've finally realized everyone has their own fate. Most of my lives, she's died. Is that my fault, or is it just what's destined to happen with her?"

Good question. I could ask the same about Zack and the car crash. Is it just his destiny to die young? If I don't go to that kegger, will something else get him instead?

"I've finally decided I can't control everything," Carrie went on. "Instead, I'm just lying low, trying to make as few ripples as I possibly can."

"Is that why you act so—" Thomas realized he had started a sentence that had no good ending.

"What, weird? Sad? Repressed? What?"

"Yeah, I guess. I didn't mean it like that, though. In the hallway this morning, you seemed like a different person when you were talking to me."

"I was just caught off guard. Thirteen lives, however many years it's been, and the whole time, I thought I was the only one. When I heard you bitching out the bitches, I just knew—*he's not making that up. Somehow, he knows the future.* After all this time, it was like I recognized one of my own."

"That was the first you suspected?"

"Not quite. I knew something was up that day you talked to me in class, though I wasn't sure exactly what. In all my lives, I hadn't talked to you before. If I'd stayed calm and thought about it, I would have let you just go on thinking you were the only time traveler in the world." She shrugged. "But I didn't."

"I'm glad you didn't. It's been killing me not to be able to talk about it with anyone. I don't know how you've handled it."

Carrie shrugged. "I talked to Mom about it once. I think that was life number five."

"And how did that go?"

"Not so great. I ended up having to see a shrink for a while. Eventually, I told them I was having trouble sleeping, they wrote me a prescription, and I rode the express again. I won't do that again, either."

"Ah. Yeah, that's something I was afraid of. I keep messing things up with Mom, and Zack, and I can just imagine what they would think if I told them the truth." Thomas forked some of the chipped beef into his mouth, then wrinkled his nose. "Oh, my God. That's awful." He took a drink of milk to wash the taste away.

"Why do you think I bring my lunch every day?"

"I thought it was just one more piece of your overall disguise. Didn't know it was self-defense. So. Where do we go from here? It feels like we are members of a pretty exclusive club."

Carrie looked over his head, a faraway expression on her face. "There have been times I've wondered about other people—whether or not they might be going through what I am. There's got to be others, but I never had the nerve to ask them about it."

"Now that you did, are we going to go back to pretending like we don't know each other?"

"That's probably best, don't you think? You're already ruining your reputation by hanging out with Cootie Carrie."

"I just realized something. This is your thirteenth life, but you've never been older than nineteen. You've spent, what, like 30 years in junior high and high school? That's got to qualify as an inner circle of Hell, doesn't it?"

"Yes, it does. If I have to go through Oregon State History or Algebra II one more time, I think I might go insane."

"Good, then you can help me. It's been almost thirty years for me, and I think I'm flunking Algebra."

A smile flickered in her eyes. "Maybe. What have you got to trade?"

"Seriously? I've got thirty-five years of future history you don't know, at least from the world I was living in. We're not going to have flying cars in 2016, but we made computers that carry the entire world's information and are so small they fit in the pockets of our jeans. Of course, we mostly use those computers to look at videos of cats, but no one said humanity was smart. We didn't make it back to the moon, but satellites and global positioning systems made sure you didn't get lost. We elected a black president in 2008, and the Supreme Court made gay marriage legal in 2014. We made a lot of progress."

"Are all of those things progress?"

" Maybe it doesn't feel that way in 1976, but it did at the time. It feels weird to talk about things in the past tense that are decades in the future."

Carrie shook her head. "Thanks for that, but I don't think I want to know. After spending so many years mostly knowing what's going to happen next, I'd like to be surprised for a while. I'll help you with your algebra, but please don't tell me what's supposed to happen. It probably won't happen again here in this life anyway."

"What do you mean? Do things change that much?"

Carrie nodded and took a bite out of her apple before saying, "Gerald Ford is President, right?"

"Yes, of course."

"No, it's not 'of course,' like it's written in stone. Ford has been the president, and Carter gets elected in November in most of my lives, but sometimes things change. Agnew was president once, Ford won reelection once, and another time, Ted Kennedy won."

"Wow. Okay." *President Agnew. Holy crap.* "But, why do we assume that we are the only ones who could be impacting this new world? Isn't it possible that a thousand different people woke up at the same time you did, or years before?"

"Of course it's possible. That's why I said I don't have all the answers. There is one thing I do know, though. There are certain watershed moments, large and small, that happen every time."

"Like what?"

"It's weird things. Like, Elvis Presley always dies on August 16, 1977. My dad drops and breaks his favorite coffee cup on March 27, 1977. I only remember that one because that's my sixteenth birthday. Weird things like that repeat."

Is Zack dying a repeater moment like that? How about Michael Hollister killing all those people? Speaking of which…

"There's one more thing I've got to tell you about the future, then I promise I won't tell you any more. Do you know anything about Michael Hollister?"

Chewing a bite of her bologna sandwich, Carrie said, "I didn't before today, except that his family is rich. Now I know he got hit in the groin and everyone's laughing about it. Seems pretty cruel to me, and I'm kind of surprised that you saw any comedy in it. Doesn't seem like the person you've decided to be this time."

"There's a reason for that. In my first life, he grew up into a serial killer."

"Like Ted Bundy?"

"Wait. You know who Ted Bundy is? Oh wait, right, you would have seen him on the news. Anyway, yes, like Ted Bundy. He was called the 'Necktie Killer,' and he strangled twenty-seven people."

Carrie shuddered. "You are honest-to-god serious."

"Yes," Thomas said, simply. *Maybe all the details of his animal butcher shop can wait, but one can't.* "I'm already on his radar. Last weekend, he kidnapped Amy, my dog. I thought he had killed her, but he didn't, though he hurt her. He is a dangerous person. In my last life, he didn't start killing for a few years after high school. I wonder if maybe he just didn't start the life of a full-blown serial killer until later, but still was playing his sick games all the way back in high school."

"Oh, God, I knew he was weird, but I didn't think he was kill-people-and-bury-them-in-the-woods weird."

"I thought maybe that was one of the reasons I woke up back here–to stop Michael from killing all those people."

Carrie paused, gentled her voice. "And to stop yourself from driving drunk with Zack?"

Thomas's mouth dropped slightly ajar. *Goddamn it. Of course. She would know about that. Everybody in school knew about it.*

"Yes," Thomas said firmly. "I wasn't drunk that night. I'd only had half a beer, but, yes. To stop myself from killing Zack." Now it was Thomas's turn to pause. "In all your lives—"

Carrie interrupted, "—did you have a wreck and Zack was killed? Yes. Every time."

Thomas said nothing. It took all his energy to avoid tearing up.

"I'm sorry. I just thought it was—"

"—one of those, what did you call it? Watershed moments? Like Elvis dying on the crapper or your dad always breaking his coffee cup?"

She nodded, silent now. The room clattered and bustled with students were picking up their trays, scraping their leftovers into garbage cans, and exiting the cafeteria.

"I'm sorry, Tommy. I really am. This time you'll know what's coming, so maybe you can change it. I've got to go. I'm the student aide at the office, and that's the one place you don't want to be tardy."

"Can I call you tonight?"

"No, not tonight. Let's give ourselves a rest to think all this over. We're not in a hurry, right?"

"I guess, but, man, it's been so cool talking to you. Don't shut me out, okay?"

Carrie looked at him for a long moment before reaching out and touching his hand. "I won't." She stood up, assumed the pose of the bullied, and left for the library.

Thomas sat where he was for a full minute, staring at the hand she had touched. It tingled.

Chapter Twenty-Five

Carrie was as good as her word. Over the next few days, they didn't have any more in-depth conversations, but she made eye contact as they passed in the hallways. She even smiled at him a few times.

When she's not pretending to be a pariah, she's a sweet, intelligent, saucy girl, he thought, after one such stolen smile between class periods. *That's just one of my surprises. In my middle age, I was so set in my ways. Now I'm learning to roll with changes that would have knocked me off the rails in my previous life. One day, I thought I was a solitary time traveler. The next, I found the unlikeliest possible companion on this path.*

Either way, the sun rose and set, and the school bells rang, demanding at least some sort of attention. Even with that distraction, Michael Hollister often came to Thomas's mind. He had a dream that repeated several times a week, in which Michael's victims stood in a ring, looking at Thomas, silently beseeching him to change their fate.

Amiable Amy's nose had scabbed over where the rubber bands had cut into her skin, but every time Thomas saw her, he thought of Michael Hollister and how close he had been to losing her. That was one thing, but the thought of the people who would lose parents, daughters and sons, brothers and sisters–that tore at him even more.

Upon finding Amy in the cave that night, he had vowed to do something. Now, with time marching on, he had no idea what that might be. *Get Billy and a few other friends to grab him and duct tape him to the goalposts? Even better, strip him naked, then duct tape him to the goalposts.*

Probably too much. Do I want to get into an arms race with a sociopath that is just as willing to kill you as look at you?

Probably not wise, but it feels like I've got to do something, first for what he did to Amy, for all the people who will be killed if I don't.

Now if I can figure out what.

Chapter Twenty-Six

That Saturday, the Track and Field District Finals were scheduled in Salem. Zack's primary competition in the 880, Ray Wilson from Pendleton with the UO track scholarship, was in a different district and wouldn't face Zack until the State Finals in Eugene two weeks later. Without that primary competition, Zack again sailed through both the 440 and 880. Thomas and Anne were in the stands, their shouts of encouragement lost in McCulloch Stadium.

While Zack didn't top his fastest time of the year, both Thomas and Anne noticed him easing off the throttle a bit in the last quarter lap, when he saw that he was several seconds ahead of the field. As Zack crossed the line, he glanced left at Coach Manfred, who gave him a satisfied nod. It had all been according to plan.

Zack rode back to Middle Falls on the team bus, so Anne and Thomas had plenty of time to talk. Anne cracked the window and blew her smoke in that general direction as she drove home.

When did they discover that secondhand smoke was harmful, anyway? I would have thought she would know about that by now. Maybe she's just an addict, too, and does know, but can't do a damn thing about it.

Happily for Thomas, Anne didn't bring up her previous suspicions about his possible drug use. "Don't know about you, but I'm getting hungry," she said, as they passed through a town. "I guess McDonalds is okay, but I miss the old Tastee Freeze that your dad and I went to when we were dating. Best ice cream I've ever had."

"Not there anymore?"

"No, I think the chains ran them out of business."

"Speaking of chains, is that a Herfy's sign I see up ahead? They may not have the world's best ice cream, but they've got a build-your-own-burger bar. That's got to be a close second, right?"

Anne smiled. "You got it."

Thomas made it through their late lunch and the entire car ride home with no obvious verbal missteps that might put Anne back on high alert. He counted it a triumph.

A little before 8:00 that night, Thomas bicycled over to Billy Steadman's house and walked up to the front door, dodging Billy's little sister's tricycle. His middle-aged eyes noticed the lawn needed mowing. The '62 Dodge Dart that Billy had bought a few months earlier was up on blocks. He had dreams of glory of rolling into the school parking lot in it someday, but he hadn't gotten it started yet. The house's three-tab roof was curling at the edges. The blue paint—*what we called low-income blue at the dealership*—had seen better days. *Mid-century poor, but I didn't notice it. We all were, so it didn't matter.*

Thomas knocked and waited. Through the front window, he saw Mr. Steadman reading *The Oregonian*, conspicuously ignoring the knock on the door. A moment later, Helen Steadman answered the door, a dish towel in one hand and a smile on her face. "Hello, Tommy. Seems like it's been forever since you've been over."

You think it's been a long time for you? And, hey, when I was a kid, Mrs. Steadman was just another mom. She's a looker, though. I don't remember that. Perspective, perspective. Thomas smiled down at his feet. "Hi, Mrs. Steadman. Billy here?"

"Of course. They're waiting for you downstairs. I just took a pizza out of the freezer. I'll bring it down to you boys in a little while."

Thomas looked left and right, forgetting which way to turn to get to the basement. To cover his confusion, he said, "Hi, Mr. Steadman."

Jim Steadman waved the top of the newspaper, but didn't lower it. He grunted what might have been "hello." Thomas gambled by turning down the hall and opening the first door to the right, which revealed a coat closet. Mrs. Steadman hurried toward him, saying, "Oh, would you like to hang up your coat, Tommy? Of course. Here, let me take it."

"That's okay. I'll just take it downstairs with me." He pulled opened the first door on the left. *Eureka.*

Thomas descended the narrow, curving stairs into the unmistakable smell of a poorly sealed basement, nearly banging his head on a crossbeam at the bottom. To his right was a card table where sat Billy Steadman, Ben Jenkins, and Simon Lawler. A fourth metal folding chair awaited Thomas, but the boys did not greet Thomas. Simon's gesture-rich storytelling had all their attention:

"...so, I let all my breath out and was floating a couple of inches underwater. A little kid started yelling, 'Help! Help! He's drowning!' Next thing I knew, Sandy Miller dove in and pulled me out. I acted like I was maybe dead and she gave me mouth to mouth. She figured it out pretty fast when I couldn't stop smiling, but I still ended up with her piece of Sugarless Trident." Simon mimed drowning and kissing Sandy Miller. "Spearmint. Sandy Miller chews Spearmint gum."

Billy and Ben laughed, mostly at Simon's acting ability. "I think I'm the first kid to get to second base with Sandy. She's a very good girl. And, I mean to say, she appears to be good at everything."

Coming from anyone else at Middle Falls High, no one would have believed such a story. Simon Lawler was one of those people at whom no one could be angry. He stood four feet eight inches tall, and hadn't grown since sixth grade. The jocks called him Louie, as in Louie De Palma, Danny DeVito's character from Taxi, but they were assholes. It didn't matter, since nothing bothered Simon, which made him no fun to tease. He wore dark-framed glasses with the requisite tape holding them together at the bridge of the nose. His dad insisted that Simon keep his hair cut short in a military buzz cut, so he didn't really fit in with the rest of the school in any way. It didn't matter.

Simon waved. "Thomasino. Welcome to the Land of Gorp, or whatever our esteemed Dungeon Master has named this world."

Thomas absorbed the scene: a low-ceilinged basement smelling of dryer sheets mixed with mildew, a card table that could topple over at any moment, and three losers ready to play the geekiest game ever invented. *I'm home. Feels good.*

Billy sat with his back against the wall, partially hidden behind a red book with a garish picture of an armored fighter trying to slay a dragon. "Well? Are you bringing out the big guns tonight? Will Hooka Khan be fighting, or do you want to start a new character?"

Oh, God. Hooka Khan. Totally forgot about him. My badass alter ego. Everything I wanted to be, but wasn't.

Thomas bowed slightly and said, "The mighty Hooka Khan will join the adventure, slaying evil creatures and rescuing fair maidens near and far." Thomas picked up Hooka's miniature, a pewter figurine only an inch tall, painted in loving detail: cloaked in a long green robe, belted around the middle with a rope, holding a staff that ended in a rough cross. *Can't remember where the door to the basement is, but I remember what Hooka Khan looks like. Memory is a funny thing.*

Billy smiled, making a note behind his book. "I thought you might bring him out. Here's his sheet from where we left off." Billy slid a piece of graph paper across the table. On it, in pencil with evidence of many erasures, were a number of statistics describing all Hooka's attributes, then a list of his equipment. At the top, Tommy had printed, "Hooka Khan, Level Eleven Cleric."

Thomas sat down. "Hey, Ben, glad you could come." Ben smiled back, but it was a bit tentative, hinting at *How the hell do I find myself here, exactly?* "I know it seems a little different at first. No board, no obvious winners or losers, but you'll catch on quick. Have you rolled for your character yet?"

"Of course he did, during the several hours we waited for the great Hooka Khan to join us."

Thomas looked at his Timex. "I'm right on time, doofus. What level did you start him at?"

"Seven. A little lower than you, but I figure that his natural intelligence will outweigh whatever advantage you might have in sheer abilities."

"Not sure how you'd be any kind of judge of intellect. So Ben is going to be a human fighter named—uh, named…"

"Thickuz Abrick," Ben said helpfully.

A laugh escaped Thomas. "Thick as a brick?"

"No," Ben corrected. "Thickuz Abrick. Thick for short."

"He rolled a four for intelligence," Billy explained. "I let him roll again. He got a six. He's never going to solve quadratic equations, so Ben thought it was an appropriate name."

"Rolled a seventeen for strength, though," Ben added.

"Can't argue with that," Thomas said. "So, Hooka, Thick, and…"

Simon looked wounded. "Flanger the Flummoxed, of course." He proudly held up a figurine representing a half-orc wizard. "Now, are we gonna sit around comparing notes, or are we going on an adventure?"

Billy sat up straight, stared off into space above their heads, and intoned, "The three of you are walking across a meadow ringed by trees when you come upon a small hut with smoke curling up from the fireplace. What do you want to do?"

"I would like to knock on the door and ask if they have any Venezuelan Beaver Cheese," Simon said.

"Really?" Ben said. "You like Monty Python?"

"Doesn't everyone?" asked Simon.

Ben lit up a little. "Fine, then. I fart in your general direction."

"Your mother is a hamster and your father smells of elderberries," retorted Simon, on cue.

Billy cracked up, though Thomas remained a little uncertain of what had just occurred. His

mind flashed back to the "To Do" list he had created a week earlier. *I still have no idea whether I can stop Zack from dying or not, but that's still a few months away, so that's on the back burner.*

I want to help Ben feel more comfortable with who he is, but what can I effectively do in 1976? Be his friend, I guess. But, what else? Short of telling him that the world is going to change, there's not much I can do. Maybe this helps. And Carrie? Am I helping Carrie now, or is she helping me?

Forty minutes later, Helen Steadman came downstairs bearing pizza, Doritos, and a six-pack of Coke. She spread the food and drink out on top of the nearby washing machine. Billy looked up from behind his Dungeon Master's Guide. "Mom, have I told you lately that I love you?"

"Only when I'm bringing you food. Have fun, boys."

Bolstered by pizza and caffeine, the adventure continued until 11:30, when Simon said: "You know what? *Saturday Night Live* is coming on. Do you think we could sneak upstairs and watch it?"

"Well, we might need to," Billy said, "if we weren't living in a time of technological miracles. Hang on a minute." He disappeared up the stairs, returning shortly with a portable television with a 7" screen in the front and a cord dangling from the back. He set it on the washer, plugged it in, turned it on, then extended and wiggled the rabbit ears this way and that. When the picture came into focus, Billy beamed: "Come on, move your chairs over here and we can watch it without worrying about Dad yelling at us."

The KGW logo appeared, followed by an image of John Belushi, Laraine Newman, Garrett Morris, and Chevy Chase, all sitting on folding chairs, holding musical instruments.

They did not move as Don Pardo announced the "The Dead String Quartet," nor for a time after, until they began to fall over. Chevy of course took the biggest pratfall. Then Gerald Ford appeared and said: "Live, from New York, it's Saturday night!"

"Holy Jumpin' Jeremiah," Simon said. "Was that the president? On Saturday Night Live? Is this a great time to be alive, or what?"

Chapter Twenty-Seven

That Monday evening, Thomas and Zack were in the living room, eating boxed store-brand macaroni and cheese while watching *The Muppet Show*. Anne had pulled the late shift at the hospital, and they had run out of casseroles. After watching Kermit's opening, Thomas eyed Zack. "Who's your favorite Muppet?"

"They're just pieces of cloth with somebody's hand up their butt. You know that, right?"

"Wow, that's cold, man."

"Just kidding. I like Animal."

"Figures. You're kind of an—"

The jangling ring of the telephone cut Thomas off in mid-insult. Zack jumped up and ran to the kitchen, then picked up the heavy receiver. "Hello, Zack's Mortuary. You stab 'em, we slab 'em." Zack was quiet for a moment, cradling the phone on his shoulder. "Thomas? You mean Tommy? Sure. Hang on." He raised his voice. "Hey, Squirt. It's for you." He widened his eyes, covered the mouthpiece and mock-whispered, "It's a girl."

Thomas cleared his throat, did his best to pitch his voice low, and said, "Hello?"

"Hi. It's Carrie. If you're still up for it, I'd like to hang out with you."

"Yeah!" *Too fast, stupid!*

Carrie laughed. "You're not much of the playing-hard-to-get type, are you?"

Thomas glanced over his shoulder and saw that Zack had retreated back to the living room. "No. So, when?"

"How about tonight?"

He glanced up at the kitchen clock. 7:45. "Uh, it's a school night."

"What are you? Fifteen?"

"As you know, that's a complicated question with no easy answer. Okay. When?"

"My dad just ran to the store. He leaves for work at five a.m. though, so he's always in bed by nine. How about ten? Can you sneak out?"

The thought made Thomas's stomach drop a little. "I think so. Where?" *Please don't say the woods behind the school. I've had enough of that place for at least thirteen lifetimes.*

"I've got a place in mind. You don't have a car, do you?"

"No. I don't even have a learner's permit."

"I'll come pick you up. Where do you live?"

"On Periwinkle Lane."

"That's a very manly street." She repeated it as though tasting it on her tongue. "Periwinkle. What's your house number?"

"141."

"Okay. I'll be by a little after ten. Sound good?"

"Yes. Sure. Okay. See ya."

Thomas set the phone down in the cradle and returned to the living room. The half-eaten bowl of macaroni and cheese did not beckon him, but he slid in behind the TV tray anyway.

"New girlfriend?" Zack asked. "No, wait. Back up. Rephrase that. Holy shit, have you got a girlfriend?"

"No. She's just a friend who is also a girl."

Zack's smile widened. "I remember saying that very thing to Mom, just before I lost my virginity with Cathy Spirelli. She was also a friend who was also a girl. Who is it?"

Thomas braced himself. "Carrie Copeland."

"Cootie Carrie? Interesting choice."

And there it is. Thomas clenched both fists, and something flashed in his eyes. *Who the hell is he to make judgements about me, anyway? Every single thing he's ever wanted, he's got. Everything he's ever wanted to do, he's done.*

Zack saw. "Settle down, little brother. Can't you take a joke? I'm glad to see you're in the game. I don't care who you're playing it with."

Thomas relaxed a little. "Can you do me a favor? She wants to hang out tonight."

"Sure, no problem, as long as you're home and safely tucked into bed, oh, in about the next thirty minutes. It's a school night, you know."

"Seriously?"

Zack sighed and shook his head. "God, you're ridiculous. No, not seriously. Just make sure you're home before Mom gets home from work. She gets off at midnight. If she does a bed check and you're not there, there's nothing I can do to save you."

At ten minutes to ten, Thomas was standing in his hooded sweatshirt, peeking from behind the heavy curtains of the sliding glass door, staring out at the endless rain. A few minutes later, a Ford Pinto rolled up the street, slowly enough for the driver to check the house numbers.

"I'm gone," Thomas turned to say.

"Wait!" Zack jumped up and fished his wallet out of his back pocket. It was zippered, with a logo that said, "Keep on truckin'."

He's not gonna give me a few bucks, is he?

Zack unzipped the wallet, then fished out a Trojan condom. "Better safe than sorry, little brother. I'm too young to be an uncle."

Thomas opened his mouth to argue, but glanced out and saw the Pinto waiting. "Thanks," he said, sliding the condom into his back pocket. He opened the slider and bounced down the stairs and through the puddles. Carrie leaned over and pushed open the passenger door. He jumped in and slid into the bucket seat, reached for the seatbelt, then hesitated. *Wait a minute. Pinto. Pintos go boom, and I'm not sure when seatbelts became mandatory, but they weren't in 1976. Don't think I'll strap myself inside this rolling incendiary device. But, am I willing to ride in it to spend a few minutes alone with Carrie Copeland? You bet your ass.*

Carrie had changed out of her usual shapeless sweater and long skirt. She wore a gray Middle Falls High sweatshirt, a denim jacket several sizes too big for her, and a pair of Levi's. Her hair was pulled back, and she wasn't wearing any makeup.

Beautiful.

"I'm in your hands. Where are we going?"

"You'll see. I'm taking you to one of my favorite places. I usually go there alone when I sneak out, but…"

"I'm glad you called. I had started to think I wasn't going to hear from you."

"I wanted some time to think things over. I've been on my own for so long, I wasn't sure what to make of this. Of you."

She slipped the Pinto into Drive and pulled out into the night. After just a few blocks, she turned down Patterson Road and then into the parking lot of a small white church. She drove through the normal parking spots and pulled around the side, hidden from the street.

"Do you think I need church?" Thomas asked.

"You probably do, but that's not why we're here. My dad mows the lawn for the church and I clean the inside, so I know where they keep a key." She turned the ignition off, but the engine continued to rattle, as though it was thinking of going on without her.

She saw the look on Thomas's face and said, "Hey, thirteen lives in, and this car has never left me stranded. How many people can say that?"

Thomas looked at the church. There were no lights on, inside or out. They got out of the car and sprinted through the rain to the church's small front porch. "Wait here," ordered Carrie, who ran around to the back of the church. She returned a minute later, partly soaked, holding a key. "I doubt you'll ever want to, but if you come here without me, there's a little lean-to at the back of the church. Inside is a coffee can. The key is inside it." She turned it in the lock.

A *thunk* echoed through the church. A small chill ran up Thomas's back.

Carrie looked at the hoodie Thomas was wearing. "Glad you brought something warm. I don't turn the heat on when I'm here. That would waste the church's money."

"I don't think the shiver was from the cold. It's a little creepy in here. How about some lights?" Thomas peered ahead, but couldn't see anything beyond rows of shadows.

Carrie shook her head. "I'm not really supposed to be in here, so I don't turn the lights on either. If a parishioner drove by and saw the lights on, the jig would be up. Come on." She reached down, took his hand, and led him forward into the darkness.

As his eyes began to adjust, he saw that they were walking between a dozen or so rows of pews. About halfway to the altar, Carrie let go of his hand and sat on the floor.

"Here. I always bring a candle. Usually, I just come here to think, but sometimes I bring a book and read. Sit down here, with me."

Thomas sat. Carrie pulled a votive candle out of her purse, set it between them, and lit it.

She smiled at him. "This way, even if someone that cares does happen to come by, they won't be able to see any light. This has been my getaway spot for half a dozen lives or so now."

She spoke quietly, but her voice carried. "Nice acoustics in here," he said.

She nodded, then began to sing in a soft voice. "Amazing grace, how sweet the sound, that saved a wretch like me. I once was lost, but now am found. Was blind, but now I see." Her voice was a warm alto, pitch perfect.

"I had no idea you could sing!" said Thomas, muffling his tone.

"That's what about thirty years of high school choir will do for you."

"This is so surreal, sitting here with you in a church, in the candlelight. I feel like I want to take a picture, so I'll always have it."

"You can. Look around. Look at me. Close your eyes. Hold it there."

Thomas did. The light of the flickering candle caused small shadows to creep up the pews and walls. The stained glass windows let in a tiny amount of ambient light. Carrie sat cross-legged across from him, her damp hair thrown over her shoulder.

"There. Now you'll have it forever."

Thomas nodded. He knew it was true. "After everything that's happened to you, do you still believe in all this?" He made a sweeping gesture.

"Well, that depends. I think you mean church. Religion. The Bible. The who begat who and thou shall nots? No, not really. But, God? Yes, of course I believe in God. Don't you?"

"I never have, really. When I was a kid, I just kind of floated along. My family didn't go to church. If I thought about it at all, I guess I thought that was something I would figure out later. Then, after the accident with Zack, I didn't want to think about it. Eventually, that hardened into a shell. Nothing has ever cracked it."

"I think that's okay. God doesn't need you to believe in Him in order to be real. He knows you're real. I think that's all that matters."

Thomas thought for a minute, smiled. "Will you sing me something else?"

"Sure." She sang *Let it Be*, by the Beatles.

Pop music, not a hymn, but it sounds like it belongs here. And her voice! I could listen to her forever. No hesitation, either. She has the feel of a comfortable performer.

Then, *Morning Has Broken*, another pop song delivered so as to suit their surroundings. Finally, *Amazing Grace* again, all the verses this time, and slowly, like the spiritual it had once been. When she softly sang the final verse—"When we've been there, ten thousand years, bright shining as the sun, we've no less days to sing God's praise, than when we've first begun,"—Thomas felt a lump in his throat. Tears slid down his cheeks. He looked away and wiped them with the back of his hand.

Carrie reached out and took his hand in both of hers. "Don't. That's how that song is supposed to make you feel. It's how it makes me feel, too."

She leaned forward and kissed Thomas, sweetly, then moved back.

"And here I thought I was just going to stay home and watch the Muppets tonight."

"This is better?"

"This is better."

"I…I probably shouldn't have kissed you. I don't want to give you the wrong idea. I just felt very close to you. I haven't been able to really feel close to someone for so long. I always knew, on a basic level, that they wouldn't understand who I am, what I'm going through."

"Please don't be sorry for that. I haven't been kissed in a very long time. It feels like lifetimes."

"But you were an adult. Were you married?"

"No. I mean, I was once, but it didn't go very well. I was so, I don't know…sad all my life. I can't imagine what it was like, being married to me. I drank a lot, too. In 2016, they called that 'self-medicating.' I thought I was just a drunk.

Hey, not to change the subject, but I've got a question for you."

"Okay."

" You remember what I told you about Michael Hollister? What he is going to become, and what he did to Amy?"

"Yes."

"Well, when I found Amy, I promised myself that I would do something to get him back for what he did to her."

"What did he do? You said you got her back."

"I did, but he tied her mouth shut with rubber bands so tight, they cut into her skin. If I hadn't found her when I did, it would have killed her. Anyway, I've been trying to think of something to do to him, but I hadn't been able to think of anything, until..."

"Until?"

"Until I was thinking that you said you worked as a student volunteer in the office. Do they ever leave you alone in the office?"

Carrie shrugged. "Not often, but sometimes."

"Is there a master list of lockers and combinations? Who they're assigned to?"

She looked up, thinking. "Yeah, I've seen one in there."

"How often does someone need it?"

"At the beginning of the year, every day. Now? Pretty much never. Why?"

"Could you give it to me? I would just need it for a few minutes, then I would give it back to you."

Her eyes narrowed a bit. "Again, Thomas, why?"

"Because I want to get into Michael's locker. I owe him."

"Does that seem like a good idea to you?"

"My life is a series of bad decisions."

"As mottos go, that one kind of sucks."

Thomas looked at her expectantly.

A sigh. "Boys. I don't care how many lives I have, I will never understand you. Okay, I'll see if I can get it without getting in trouble. Still think it's a bad idea, though."

"Noted." Thomas looked down at his watch. He could barely make it out in the flickering light of the dying candle. "Oh, crap! It's ten to midnight!"

"Is that a problem, Cinderella?"

"Yes. Come on, I've got to get home. Zack's covering for me, but my mom gets off her shift at the hospital in ten minutes. If I'm not home when she gets there, I'll be grounded for so long, you might never see me again."

Carrie blew the candle out. They stood and felt their way to the back of the church. At the double doors, Carrie reached for Thomas's hand, pulled him toward her, and kissed him again.

"Still not getting the wrong idea," Thomas said.

"Good," Carrie said, then laughed.

My God, that's the first time I've heard her laugh. I need to hear that again.

They made it to 141 Periwinkle Lane at two minutes after midnight. Thomas breathed a sigh of relief when he saw his mom's car was not in the driveway.

"Call me whenever you want. I like your hideaway."

"I'll call you again soon."

Thomas was out of the car, in the house, undressed, and pretending to be asleep before Anne pulled in. His dreams that night were happy ones.

Chapter Twenty-Eight

At school the next day, Carrie stopped Thomas in the hall. "I think you're bad luck."

"Me? Why?"

"When I got home last night, Dad was standing in the kitchen with a glass of milk, waiting for me."

"Oh, shit."

"Yeah. It wasn't great. If he had known I was sneaking off to meet a boy, it would have been a lot worse."

"What did you tell him?"

"Mostly the truth. That I'd had a hard time sleeping since Mom died, and that I had often gone to the church in the middle of the night, because I feel close to her there."

"And he bought that?"

Carrie scowled. "Yes, he 'bought it.' It's true. At least, it had been true until last night."

"...when you snuck out and met a boy."

"I already feel bad enough, lying to Dad. He hasn't done anything to deserve that."

"So what happened?"

Carrie shrugged. "He grounded me for two weeks. Thirteen lives, zero groundings. One day hanging out with you, and look what happens."

Thomas held up his hands, protesting his innocence.

"Anyway, I think I better stay in for the next few weeks, let things cool off with Dad."

"I understand."

Over the next few weeks, Thomas regretted not having more nights with Carrie, but fell completely into the 1976 groove. The longer he was there, the more 2016 seemed like a dream. Cell phones, Google, and huge flat-screen televisions that got hundreds of channels seemed unreal. School obligations, trying to stay out of hot water with his mom, and getting to know Carrie were things his senses told him were real.

They hadn't snuck out since Carrie had been caught and grounded, but one Wednesday afternoon over lunch, they were sitting in the lunch room, when she mentioned that she thought she could risk it again soon.

Just then, Jimmy Halverson's little brother Randy approached them with three friends. Randy was tall and gangly like his brother, with dirty blond hair and a flare-up of acne across his forehead. He wore a serious expression, as though whatever he had to tell Thomas was important. "So, Tommy. Is this like a science experiment? Find the skankiest girl in school and try to find out what grows in her petri dish? Cuz I think I can save you the time. I don't know from firsthand experience, of course, but I've heard it's naaasty."

Thomas slumped in his seat, then started to push away from the table. *That's enough. Time to do something.*

Carrie reached out and touched his hand, looked deep into his eyes, shook her head. "Please. Don't," she whispered.

Thomas took a deep breath, bottling the desire to smash Randy's bad complexion into the tile floor over and over. He forced himself to smile at Randy. "Randy, you're even more pathetic than your brother. You want to know something? Your life isn't going to turn out so hot either. That acne farm you've got going there is just getting started."

Randy's hand flew to his forehead, then he forced it down to his side.

"You're going to have three kids before you're twenty-two. Wait until you see who you father them with. You'll remember this day, and reflect on your bad taste. You'll be divorced before twenty-five. Paying child support on those three kids will keep you in the poorhouse most of your life. Have a good life." Thomas slowly turned back to Carrie, tensing ever so slightly, as if Randy might hit him.

Color drained from Randy's face, accenting his complexion woes. "Whatever. You're such a loser," Randy said to Thomas's back. The words were tough, but any steam was gone from them. He turned and hurried from the lunchroom, entourage in tow.

"You've really got to stop doing that," Carrie said. "It's just not a good idea in any way."

Thomas nodded. "You're right. I've never been very good at keeping my mouth shut when I should. But on to other business. You know we missed Prom, right?"

"Nice change of subject, but I'll play along. Does us missing Prom bum you out? Don't tell me that when you woke up again in 1976, your first thought was, *I'm going to Prom!*"

"Well, no."

"Good. It's not high on my priority list. My turn to change the subject. " Carrie opened a notebook and took out several sheets of paper, holding row after row of numbers and names. "I shouldn't reward you for telling people's misfortunes, but here you go."

"Yes! Thank you. I haven't wanted to bug you about it, but I'm really glad you got it."

"I think the information you're looking for is about halfway down the second page."

Thomas flipped to the second page, ran his finger down the column of names until he saw: *Hollister, Michael. Locker #726. 04-22-16.*

"Perfect. I'll copy this down next period and get it back to you. Now, one more favor."

"Sorry, that's my limit for the day."

"Can we meet Friday night?" Thomas asked.

"It's harder for me to get away on weekends. Dad doesn't work on Saturday, so he doesn't conk out right at nine, like he does the rest of the week. Plus, we just got caught. If he catches me again, I'll be grounded for the rest of this life."

"Can't you tell him you're going to go spend the night with a friend?"

"Sure, that could work, except I don't have any friends. Except for you, that is. And I don't want to lie to my Dad."

I should probably let that pass. Then he didn't. "So, sneaking out is okay, but lying, not so much? Got it." He saw her eyes flicker, softened his tone. "Okay, how about if we wait until eleven? Will he be asleep by then?"

"Yes, I'm sure he will be. He almost never stays up that late. Why is it important to get together Friday?"

"It just is. I miss you. Is that a crime? Whaddya say?"

"Ohhh...all right, all right."

The smile in her eyes went right to his soul.

Chapter Twenty-Nine

Thomas put his plan into action the next day. During first period, where he could see Michael sitting in his accustomed front row seat, Thomas raised his hand. "Mr. Burns? I'm not feeling so hot. Can I go to the bathroom?"

Mr. Burns stared at him, annoyed. The students around him twittered. "Not feeling so hot," and "go the bathroom," meant only one thing. Diarrhea is funny to almost every teenager. "Fine, Mr. Weaver." He jotted a quick note on a pad. "Here's your hall pass. Don't dawdle."

Thomas walked very deliberately to the front of the room, grabbed the note, and hustled for the door. Once outside, he speed-walked to the stairs, took them two at a time, then hurried to his own locker. He dialed his combination, but his locker wouldn't open. *Slow down, Weaver.* He took a deep breath, re-entered the combination, and it opened. He reached in and removed a small brown bag, tucking it inside his jacket, then walked to locker 726. Another deep breath. He entered the combination he had memorized and felt the door pop open.

Neat as the first day of school, the inside of Michael Hollister's locker smelled strongly of cologne. The small top shelf held a zippered lunch box—the kind a busy salesman might take out in the field—and a small white bottle with a red top. Thomas reached out and turned the bottle so he could read the label. *Old Spice? If I didn't know better, I'd think he was the middle-aged man stuck in a teenager's body, not me. What kind of a kid wears Old Spice? A freak, that's who.* Below the shelf, a white windbreaker hung on one hook. A stack of books sat at the bottom of the locker, spines up.

Thomas reached for the lunchbox and smiled.

Three minutes later, he walked back into his classroom.

Anthony Massey sniggered, "Hope everything came out all right."

Two hours later, Thomas walked into the cafeteria, grabbed a tray, and went through the food line. He didn't bother to look at the menu. It didn't matter. He was there for the floor show.

He took his tray to the back corner, where Carrie awaited. Thomas sat down across from her, a broad smile on his face.

"Thomas, I have never seen you smile like that. It's a little frightening."

He raised his eyebrows, but the smile remained. "So, what's up?"

"What's up, yourself? What have you done?"

Thomas reached inside his jacket and pulled out the folded piece of paper with the locker combinations. "Here you go. Thank you very much."

Carrie's look rebuked him, but she said nothing. She got out her bologna sandwich and apple.

If I opened the refrigerator in her house, wonder if it would just be stacked with bologna sandwich makings and apples.

Michael Hollister came in through the double doors and headed to a vacant seat in the middle of the lunch room, newspaper tucked under one arm. It didn't matter where he sat. Like Carrie, Michael had always eaten alone.

He unfolded the newspaper and opened it to the business section, then unzipped the lunch box. He removed a sandwich baggie, a bag of Fritos, and a Reese's Peanut Butter

Cups candy bar. He opened the Fritos and ate a few, then slipped the sandwich out of the baggie and took one big bite.

Thomas leaned right, making sure of his field of vision.

A look of horror spread across Michael's face. He spit the half-chewed bite out onto the table, then pulled the bread apart. When he saw what was inside, his hand flew to his mouth.

It was a futile gesture.

Michael projectile-vomited across the table, directly into Freddy Jimson's lap. Marti Taylor, sitting adjacent, sustained some collateral damage. As Michael's head drooped, Freddy and Marti leaped out of their chairs.

Michael raised his head and vomited again. Freddy and Marti were fortunate they had taken such decisive action, because this time Michael christened both their vacant seats.

Every eye in the room was on Michael. The sound of conversation, silverware scraping plates, everything, faded to dead silence. The only sound was the soft swoosh of the industrial dishwashers in the back, cleaning trays.

Michael wiped his mouth with the back of his hand. Even from some distance, Thomas could see the one word that he mouthed.

Weaver.

Michael stood shakily and scanned the room until he found Thomas. Michael fixed him with eyes that held a thing Thomas had heard and read about, but never seen in the flesh.

That is the face of murder. The real deal, as in first degree premeditated.

"What have you done?" whispered Carrie.

Chapter Thirty

At 11:00 Friday night, Thomas stood at the corner of Periwinkle and Hyacinth, staring up at the street signs.

She's right, isn't she? Who named these streets, anyway? An interior designer?

Just then, the headlights of Carrie's Pinto turned the corner. Thomas picked up his bag and waved.

Carrie turned to him as soon as he closed the passenger door. "What in the heck did you do to Michael Hollister?"

Thomas squirmed. "Aren't we going?"

"Not until you answer my question. What did you do?"

"Well, I told you what he did to Amy, right? This morning, I let Amy out in the front yard to do her business before school. When I let her in, though, I picked up one of the presents she left behind, put it in a bag, and took it to school. In first period, I went to his locker and spread the turd around on his sandwich."

"You didn't!"

"You saw his reaction, right? What else do you think would cause that."

Carrie couldn't stifle a giggle. "But, my God, Thomas. Did you see the look he gave you?"

Thomas shrugged. "Yeah. I admit, I was immediately a little sorry I had done it. Just for a moment. Now, I remember he's got a lot more than that coming."

"He's going to do something to you. He's going to get even."

"I don't let Amy outside any more without watching her. What's he going to do? I don't think he's going to kill me."

Carrie put the Pinto in gear and pulled slowly back onto the street.

A few seconds after she turned the corner, a blue Karmann Ghia turned its lights on and followed, far enough behind that it wouldn't be noticed.

Chapter Thirty-One

Once they were inside the church, Carrie said, "Come on, Thomas, I hate surprises. What's in the bag?"

I love that she calls me Thomas, instead of Tommy. In so many ways, she is the only person that really knows me.

"We may be too old to be hanging out with a bunch of teenagers at Prom, but that doesn't mean we can't have a little party of our own."

Thomas set the bag down on one of the pews. He pulled out a small, battery-powered cassette player, turned it on, then hit Play. Bread's *Make it With You* started to play.

He reached back in the bag, pulled out half a dozen small candles and a pack of matches. He sat the candles around them, one on each of the pews, and lit them. Dim light glowed from them, casting shadows like ghosts dancing in a cemetery.

Next, he pulled out a small comforter that Anne normally kept draped over the back of the couch. He laid it out flat on the floor. Finally, he pulled two cans of coke out with a ceremonial flourish, opened them both, and offered Carrie one.

"I know it's not much, but this was the best I could do with—"

Carrie reached her hand out and touched Thomas's lips. "Hush." She kissed him. The world kept turning, but for the two of them, it stopped for several long moments.

When the kiss finally broke, Thomas said, "Whoa. You've never kissed me like that before."

"I've never felt like this before."

When they finally left, an hour before the sun came up, they were not followed.

Chapter Thirty-Two

Late Sunday morning, Thomas stood in the front yard, watching Amy as she wandered around, re-investigating the smells she had already sampled a thousand times. He looked up and down the quiet street.

Feels like we pushed our luck a little bit last night, staying out so late, but it was oh, so worth it. Feels like I can still feel her lips, though.

In homeroom Monday morning, Michael Hollister was again not in his normal seat.

Carrie caught Thomas's eye, glanced at the empty seat, then back at Thomas. His attempt at a devil-may-care smile came out a sheepish grin.

Michael Hollister was absent from school for the rest of the week. Rumors spread throughout the school: he had contracted one or more terrible diseases and was in the hospital dying, or that he had been so humiliated that he had moved out of state, or that the whole thing had been filmed for an episode of *Candid Camera*. That one was a favorite of the kids, all hoping to be on TV except for Freddy Jimson and Marti Taylor, who hoped to God there was nothing to the *Candid Camera* rumor. By the end of the week, the story was stale. The whole thing had begun to settle into Middle Falls High lore.

At the end of lunch on Friday, as Carrie stood to leave, she finally said the words Thomas had been waiting to hear. "Ten o'clock?"

I think Mom's working the late shift tonight. Easy. Thomas nodded, the grin spreading into a smile on his face. He watched her walk away into the mass of students.

Is she slumping less? I think she is. She's either happy and having a harder time being miserable, or her self-control is slipping. Either way, I like it.

As it turned out, Anne was not working the late shift, but awaited Thomas and Zack at home. Dinner was already on the table. As they sat down, Anne slipped a thick slab of meatloaf onto his plate. "I've got a surprise for you boys."

Thomas and Zack looked at each other. Parental surprises were so seldom a good thing.

"Don't look so petrified! I just want to take my two handsome men on a little date. When I was driving home from work this afternoon, I saw that *Logan's Run* was playing at The Pickwick. Remember? We saw the commercials for it, and you both said you wanted to see it? This is your lucky night. My treat, including popcorn."

"Umm...what time is it playing?" Thomas asked.

"Why? Got a hot date? Other than your old mom, that is?" *Yes, Mom, as a matter of fact.* "The marquee said that the movie starts at eight, so we should probably get there about 7:45. It's supposed to be pretty popular, and we don't want to end up sitting all the way up front."

So two hours, starting at eight. Won't be over until ten. I'm going to be late to my date with Carrie. We did think it through, and we have a plan if I can't make it, but I'd rather make it than go out with Mom and Zack.

Anne's face fell. "I thought you would be excited to see it."

Thomas forced a smile. "Oh, I am, Mom. Just thinking of some homework I have to do this weekend. Can't wait to see the movie."

Anne narrowed her eyes. "Okay, then. Let's eat up and do the dishes, then we can go. If we hurry, we can drive through the A&W and get us all root beer floats."

Mmmm. Meatloaf and root beer floats. I wonder what fine wine would pair with that?

I feel like a shitty son, though. She's trying so hard, being a much better parent than I ever was an adult on any level, and I bet Zack doesn't want it any more than I do. I don't need to be a jerk. "Sounds great, Mom."

"This is cool, Mom," echoed Zack. "We'll have fun."

Anne glanced at each son. Neither flinched. "Good. It's settled. Pass the ketchup."

Thanks to the previews, cartoon, and Anne's insistence on watching the credits, the lobby clock glowed 10:15 as they walked into the cool spring air. By the time they had driven home and Thomas could make an excuse to go to bed, it was nearly eleven, and his stomach was in knots. For the last half hour of the movie, all Thomas could think about was that Carrie was probably waiting at the meeting spot. The plan was that if he didn't show up, she should leave after a few minutes and go to the church. It was close enough that Thomas could easily bicycle over.

Just as he was getting ready to crawl out the window, Thomas heard footsteps. He froze, a perfectly guilty tableau, one foot up on a stool and the window half open.

"In a hurry?"

Thomas exhaled. *Zack. Just Zack.*

"When mom asked you if you had a hot date tonight at dinner, I about choked. Who would have ever guessed the day would come that you had a date on a Friday night and I didn't? You know that if Mom comes back for any reason, we're both busted. You for sneaking out, and me for not telling her."

Thomas didn't say anything. Just looked at Zack, waiting.

"Aw, what the hell. Get out of here. If we get caught, we get caught. I'll put on one of your stupid records and she'll think we're both back here."

Would it embarrass him if I jumped down and gave him a hug? Probably.

"Thanks, Zack. You're the best."

"Truer words have never been spoken, weirdo."

Chapter Thirty-Three

Carrie waited in the church, humming *How Great Thou Art*. She hadn't bothered to bring a book, so she walked slowly up the aisle, thinking of Thomas, tracing her hand from one pew to the next.

When she heard the door open, she turned with a smile.

Standing in the door was Michael Hollister.

"Hello, Carrie. No Tommy tonight?"

Chapter Thirty-Four

Temporal Relocation Assignment Department, Earth Division

Margenta walked the aisle between the endless desks, pausing at each, tapping a finger. After a look at the worker's spinning column, she passed to the next. She came to an empty desk with an opaque column that was turning almost imperceptibly.

Her eyes locked on Veruna, sitting across the aisle. "Emillion took a personal day," she said.

Margenta's look expressed her opinion of personal days. "She's due for one, I suppose. Off to Arcadiam for the day, perhaps?" Margenta's eyes, normally hard as marbles, softened. "Few things are more pleasurable than getting a moon tan on the night beaches of Arcadiam.

"Don't think so." Veruna returned her eyes to her work.

Margenta's eyes narrowed. "Wait a moment. She didn't go to Earth, did she?"

Veruna gave a reluctant nod.

Margenta adjusted her half-rim glasses, then passed a hand over the column in front of her. It spun faster. The opacity sharpened into clarity. She stopped the spin, then sent it moving counterclockwise. She moved it forward, then back, forward then back.

She removed her glasses, rubbed the bridge of her nose. "This is too much. She's gone too far this time. It will take a lot of effort to get this straightened out. I'll bring her up before Council."

Chapter Thirty-Five

Thomas Weaver braked his bike to a gravel-spraying stop in the church parking lot, then listened. After a few moments, the chorus of crickets and frogs resumed.

He swung off the bike, laid it down, and walked around the church. Carrie's car was hidden in the shadows. Thomas smiled, flew up the stairs, and pushed open the door.

"Carrie? Sorry I'm late. When I got home..."

No one was there. Thomas paused, listening. There was no candle, just moonlight filtering through the stained glass windows. No sign of life.

"Carrie?" No answer.

Thomas walked down the aisle, peering into each row of pews. When he reached the altar, he turned around. *I am not going in those back rooms. I think that's where they keep religious stuff. I have no business there.* He sat down in a pew to think.

Carrie's car is outside. The door was open. No Carrie. What the hell?

He heard a sound coming from outside, walked back to the front and stepped into the cool night air. "Carrie?"

An orange Ford Courier turned into the parking lot, aiming its high beams at Thomas, halting a few feet from the steps. Thomas shielded his eyes from the glare. After a moment, the lights clicked off and the engine cut. A tall, lean, clean-shaven man emerged, dressed in a Levi's jacket and trucker's hat. He did not look happy.

"Who are *you*?" the man asked.

I'm someone trespassing in a church after hours, of course. And who the hell are you? Whoever you are, none of this can be good. "I'm Tommy. Tommy Weaver."

The man nodded and shut the pickup door. "Tommy Weaver," he repeated, as if the name were a bite of stale toast. "Okay, Tommy Weaver, what are you doing here? This is private property. What were you doing inside our church?" He nodded at the open door.

Who the hell is this guy? I think I've got a right to know why the hell he wants to know.

Sure, 'Tommy,' do that. Teenage kids in the 1970s always knew all their legal rights. They always smarted off to angry truck-driving men.

The sword of the 1970s cuts both ways. If I lip off to this guy, he might just kick my ass and bundle me in for a citizen's arrest for trespassing. Like I need more people asking me tough questions.

Back on your game, 'Tommy.' "I was supposed to meet a friend here."

Hard eyes narrowed. "A friend? This 'friend' wouldn't be my daughter, by any chance?"

Holy shit. It's Carrie's dad. Thomas took a deep breath, then nodded. "Probably." The man's eyes hardened. *Shit. He thinks I'm being a smartass.* "Are you Mr. Copeland?"

"Yeah, I'm Gerald Copeland. Carrie told me she was coming here because it made her feel close to her mother. Looks like she was feeling close to a boy, instead."

He does not sound happy about that. Can't blame him. Thomas shook his head. "No, she's always come here. It's only been–"

"Don't bullshit me, boy. You're in deep enough already. My daughter's not home, and she's evidently not here either. I think I'm about ready for some truth, starting with you."

He's right, I guess. This isn't the time for BS. But, the truth is always so complicated.

"Mr. Copeland, I'm not sure what's going on. I was going to meet Carrie here tonight, but I was late. When I got here, her car was here, the church was open, but she's nowhere in sight."

Copeland's head jerked back. "Her car's here? Where?"

Thomas pointed to the side of the church. "She parks over there. In case someone drove by, they wouldn't see her car."

"Someone? Like me?"

"Yeah, but not just you. Anyone who went to church here. We weren't doing anything wrong. We were just talking."

Copeland scowled. "Pretty sure I already told you not to bullshit me, boy. I know damn well why teenagers sneak off to dark places in the middle of the night."

Sure. But how many middle-aged teenagers do you know?

One of these days, if I'm not careful, I'm going to blurt something like that out.

Copeland walked over to Carrie's Pinto and laid a hand on the hood. "It's cold. What time was she supposed to meet you here? To not do anything wrong?"

"Ten o'clock."

Copeland looked at his watch. "11:25." He returned to the spot where Thomas could not escape the scene without getting past him. "You're here, her car is here, but she's not. I'm thinking you would know something about why that is."

"Honest, Mr. Copeland, I have no idea. I was late because my mom took me to a movie and we were late getting home. I came here, the church door was open, and she wasn't here. If she didn't get home, I'm worried about her."

"Boy, I'll just bet you are. I think there's something you're not telling me. I don't know if it has to do with drugs, or fooling around, or drinkin', or all of the above, but I'm sure as hell gonna find out. You best get home. If I find Carrie tonight, I'm going to be having a talk with your folks. If I don't, the police will do that. Is your family in the phone book?"

Thomas nodded. "My mom is. Anne Weaver."

Copeland walked up the steps, pulled the door shut, then turned to Thomas. "Where's the key?"

"I don't know, sir. It was unlocked when I got here."

Carrie's father fixed Thomas with another disbelieving glare. His voice dropped into menace. "Get the hell out of here. Obviously, I'm not going to get anything out of you tonight. You'll be hearing from me, one way or the other."

Thomas climbed on his bike and pointed it toward home.

This is as lost as I've ever felt. In either life.

Chapter Thirty-Six

Thomas pedaled along the shoulder, keeping an eye out for lights approaching from either direction. *Shit. "Get the hell out of here." And do what, exactly?*

No way.

At the next corner, Thomas turned back toward the church.

No idea where to look for her. Why would she leave the church? If she did leave, why wouldn't she take her car? None of this makes any sense. I'll circle back toward the church and ride the streets around it.

After less than an hour of pedaling, covering every possible piece of pavement within a mile of the church with no sign of Carrie, Thomas stopped the bike in front of a darkened Veltex gas station.

Useless. Completely useless.

Shoulders slumped, he turned and pedaled toward home. It wasn't far.

Thomas leaned the bike against the house and walked around to the window to his room. Years before, Zack had stacked flat paving stones under the window years to facilitate sneaking back in. After a moment's effort, Thomas was inside. He undressed and got into bed without waking Zack up.

Pretty sure I'm not going to sleep tonight.

He let one thought chase another around his brain. Soon, he was out.

Chapter Thirty-Seven

Thomas woke with a start. It was light outside, a beautiful Saturday morning in evergreen western Oregon.

Spent the whole damn night dreaming I was still on the bike looking for Carrie. Or Amy. Which was it?

He rubbed his eyes, turned to look at Zack. Still out.

Everything is still good in his life, but mine has gone from great to absolute shit. What's first on the agenda today? Telling Mom I've been sneaking out at night? Meeting with the cops? Having bamboo shoved under my fingernails?

He stood. Amy was curled up at the foot of his bed, head resting on her paws. She raised her head and blinked. "Sorry, Amiable," he whispered.

He took two steps toward the bathroom, when a name jumped into his head in that way that makes everything seem to click into place.

Michael Hollister.

Wait. Michael wouldn't have anything to do with this. Would he?

An image followed the name. Michael, vomit pooled in front of him, hatred in his eyes, and one word on his lips: "Weaver."

No way. He's sick, he's a freak, and maybe he's going to be a killer someday, but not yet. He wouldn't risk killing someone right here in his hometown, when he's still a teenager. He wouldn't kill Carrie to get back at me, right?

Who am I trying to convince?

Thomas hurried on to the bathroom.

Hollister, if you've done anything to Carrie... Something about that line of thought seemed too dark to confront. *I can't believe he would actually do anything to her, but I've got to know.*

I've got to go back to the goddamn cave. It's the last place on Earth I want to go, but what if she's there right now? What if she needs me?

He opened the door to get dressed, to make one last trip to Michael's kill cave. In his hurry, he bumped into his mom.

"Tommy! What are you doing up so early?"

"Mom. Oh, crap, everything is all messed up. I've been trying to make everything better, but instead I've made everything worse." Thomas felt tears, but held them back.

"Tommy, what in the world? Everything was fine last night. What's happened?"

"Let's go sit down." He averted his eyes. "Might as well get it over with."

As they sat on the couch, Thomas looked up at Anne's worried eyes. *How much can I tell her? What can I not tell her? I wish I could tell her everything, but I know how that will turn out.*

"Okay," Anne said. "What's going on?"

"You're not gonna be happy."

"It's six o'clock on a Saturday morning. I've got to be at the hospital in an hour to work a twelve-hour shift. I'm already not happy. Tell me what's going on."

"After we got home from the movie last night, I snuck out." Anne opened her mouth, then closed it as Thomas hurried on. "I've been seeing this girl named Carrie. I was supposed to meet her last night, but I was late getting there because we went to the movie. When I got to where we were supposed to meet, her car was there, but she wasn't."

"Let's slow down. What time did you sneak out?"

Thomas hesitated. "Right after I went to bed."

"So, Zack knew." Thomas shook his head, but Anne cut him off. "Don't start. If you snuck out that soon, Zack was obviously awake. I'm going to have to talk to him too."

Thomas nodded miserably. "It gets worse. Carrie wasn't there, but her dad was. He thinks something bad might have happened to her. I think so, too. He said he was going to talk to the police this morning and that they would want to talk to me, too."

Anne was quiet for a moment. "I don't know this Carrie. What do you think has happened to her?"

"Like maybe somebody kidnapped her, or took her somewhere."

Anne gave a patient sigh. "Don't be ridiculous, Tommy. This is Middle Falls, Oregon, not Los Angeles. Young girls don't get abducted off the streets here. Why would anyone do that?"

"Well, I think Michael Hollister might have done something to her."

"Who? Michael? The boy that took Amy? Why in God's name would he do something to this girl?"

Thomas's shoulders sagged. *I shouldn't have started this. Too many blind alleys I don't want to walk down.* "Mom, I think he might have done it to get back at me."

"For what? Rescuing Amy? If anyone needs getting back at, it's him, and I don't care how rich his parents are, the law is still the law. After this, I'm calling them, and that's final. But first I'm going to have the rest of the story."

Thomas exhaled a deep sigh. "Mom, I haven't been telling you the truth about everything."

"I'm beginning to realize that. Now's a good time to start telling me not just the truth, but all of it. I don't care how embarrassing it is. You're talking about an abducted girl, and this is adult business, and you no longer get to keep any secrets. Do you understand me, Thomas?"

"Okay." *At least as much as I think I can. But in the end, Mom, you're wrong. Some secrets, I have to keep.* "I told you that

Michael had like a clubhouse behind the school, and that's where he took Amy, right?"

"Yes. Did you lie to me?" The sad, resigned defeat in her eyes almost made him break down.

"More like I left out a lot of the truth, Mom. He had this weird little cave where he took animals and tortured them to death. I followed him out there one day–that's how I found his torture stuff, and I released a cat that he was probably going to add to his skull collection–but he knew I'd been there. He took Amy to scare me into not telling anyone about it."

Anne opened her mouth again, but Thomas held up his hand. "Please, Mom. This is hard, and you asked for the truth, and I'm telling you. Let me get through it." She nodded, made a *keep-going* gesture. "I was really pissed at him for taking Amy like that, so a few days ago, I snuck into his locker at school and put one of Amy's poops into his sandwich."

Anne's hand went to her mouth, eyes wide. "He didn't."

Thomas could not repress a smile. "He did. He ate it, then puked all over the lunchroom."

She half closed her eyes, shook her head. "That's the most disgusting thing I've ever heard of in my whole life, and I'm a nurse. Seriously, Tommy?"

He nodded. "Now, I think he might have done something to Carrie to get even with me for that."

Anne sat in stunned silence for about ten seconds, then pointed at him. "You, just sit here. Don't move." She walked into the kitchen and dialed five numbers into the rotary phone. "Evelyn? It's Anne. I'm scheduled to be on at eight, but I've got an emergency at home. I'm not going to make it in." Thomas could hear surprise, irritation, even frustration in the disembodied voice. "Yes, I know. I'm sorry. I'll be in tomorrow." Without waiting for a response, Anne set down the receiver, then started a pot of coffee and lit a Viceroy. She sat back down on the couch.

God. She looks closer to the age when I committed suicide. It's like she just aged a decade.

Anne exhaled a cloud of bluish smoke. "I'm having trouble with all this, but I really don't understand why you put...feces in his sandwich. Why did you do that?"

"Didn't you hear what I said? He was torturing animals to death. He had a cat locked up in a cage that would have been next, if I hadn't let it go. He's a sick freak, and I wanted to get back at him for taking Amy. Now, I wish I hadn't. I wish I could go back and undo it."

And maybe I can. Carrie rode the suicide express a dozen times. I could start over too. Thomas looked at the worry and uncertainty etched in every line on her face. *If I did start over, what do I leave behind here?*

A grieving mom and brother, wondering why I did it.

Shit. There are no good answers.

Anne said, in suffering-mother mode, "Someday, Tommy, you will have to learn that you can't just undo everything and start over. But I notice we're now talking all about Michael's feces sandwich, instead of a missing girl." Thomas made as if to speak, but Anne bore in. "Now look at me. The truth, the whole truth, and nothing but, if you love me at all."

Shit. She has never said that to me before, that way. Ever.

"Tommy, did you have anything to do with this girl's disappearance? Are you helping her run away?"

"I wish I was, Mom. I would feel a lot better right now."

"And why would you feel better?"

"Because I'd know where she was, and that she was safe. I like her a lot, and I don't know where she's at or if anything happened to her, and it scares the crap out of me. And I think Michael may have done something to her. He's evil, Mom, really evil, not just a bad kid." *Damn it! What if she gets nosey about that?*

"I should think that's obvious, if he tortures cats and kidnaps...*dognaps* dogs. Okay, we're going to tackle this head on. Go take a shower so you'll look more presentable. I'm going to get dressed and have some coffee. Then we're going down to the police station and see if we can get to the bottom of this."

Thomas suppressed a sigh of relief that would have been unexplainable. He got up and went to their bedroom, passing boxer-shorted Zack in the hallway. "What's all the excitement?" Zack asked.

"Tommy, go on," Anne said. She shot Zack a look. "Come sit down, Zackary, we need to talk."

Thomas looked up at Zack's expression, which needed no words to convey: *I don't know what you did, you little freak, but you drug me into it, and I am going to beat your ass.*

Chapter Thirty-Eight

Fifteen minutes later, Thomas came back into the living room looking as respectable as he got. Zack was alone on the couch, watching out the front window. Anne emerged from her bedroom at the back of the house, purse over one arm. "Ready?"

Zack craned his neck and stood up. "I don't think you're going to have to go see the cops. I think they're making a house call. I'll get dressed." He went back to the bedroom. Thomas pulled the drapes aside and watched as Middle Falls' one unmarked police car slowly rolled to a stop. A dark-haired man in his mid-thirties stepped out, wearing slacks and a short-sleeved white shirt. He reached in the car, grabbed a sportcoat, slipped it on, and walked up to knock on the slider. Anne stepped forward and opened it.

"Morning, ma'am. I'm George Madison, a detective with the Middle Falls police force." He produced a badge. "Were you expecting me?"

"We were getting ready to drive down to the station, Detective. I'm Anne Weaver, and this is my son Tommy. My other son is getting dressed. Please come in. Would you like to sit down?"

Detective Madison looked around the small living room. "Is that coffee I smell?"

"Yes. Would you like some?"

"If I'm not taking your last cup, yes, Mrs. Weaver, thank you."

"Please call me Anne, Detective."

Is my mother sort of flirting with this cop? thought Thomas. *She's certainly trying to be charming. I wonder if she realizes how obvious she is.*

"Fine, then, Anne, thank you." The detective pulled out a small blue notebook and opened it. "Would it be okay if we sat at the kitchen table?"

"Absolutely. I'll bring the coffee."

Madison settled into the chair at the end of the table and looked Thomas over, glancing at his notebook. "So, Tommy, am I safe in saying that you've met Mr. Gerald Copeland?"

"Yes," answered Thomas.

"Mr. Copeland came into the station bright and early this morning. He says someone kidnapped his daughter. That she's not the stay-out-all-night type of girl, although he did admit she had been sneaking out to see you."

Thomas sat in silence. *You're pretty good, Detective Madison, but there wasn't a question in there anywhere, was there?* He stared back, willing himself not to break eye contact. *I've got to remember I am a teenage boy and act like one, or this guy will be able to tell something's up. I'm not sure what he'll do if he catches a weird vibe, but it probably won't be helpful.*

Anne set a cup in front of the detective. "Cream or sugar?"

"Thank you, no," said Madison, picking up the cup. "Black is fine." He turned his attention back to Thomas. "Well? Is Carrie Copeland the stay-out-all-night type of girl? Maybe her dad has the wrong impression. Dads often do."

"Absolutely not. Carrie's gone through a lot—"

"Right. Mr. Copeland said her mother passed away this last year."

"—and she went to the church to think. She felt close to her mom there. When we wanted a place to go and talk, that's where we went."

Madison blew on his coffee, took a sip, and smiled. "Good coffee, ma'am. Thank you. Is that where you two were last night? At the church?"

"I was going to meet her there, but Mom took us to the movies."

"What did you see?"

"*Logan's Run.*"

Detective Madison scribbled a note. "Then what?"

"Well, I was going to meet Carrie at ten o'clock. I couldn't tell Mom I was leaving, though, so I didn't get to the church until around eleven."

"And how did you get out of the house?"

Thomas squirmed. "Through the window in my bedroom."

Madison looked at Anne. "What's your other son's name?"

"Zackary. Zack."

"Do they share a bedroom?"

Anne nodded.

The detective raised his voice. "Zack? Can you come join us for a moment?" Zack appeared as if he had been just around the corner. Detective Madison stood up, introduced himself, shook Zack's hand. "Could you have a seat with us at the kitchen table, please, Zack? Just need you to help clarify a few things for me."

"All right, officer." Zack sat down.

"What time did you go to bed last night?"

Zack cleared his throat, found his voice. "Around eleven."

"So, you were in the room when Tommy here snuck out?"

Zack flushed, glanced at Anne. "Yes."

"Okay, then what happened, Tommy?"

"I knew Carrie had already gone to the church, so I rode my bike over there."

"You knew she had gone there? Did you call her?"

"No. I guess I should say we planned to meet there, and she's pretty reliable, so I assumed she'd be there waiting for me."

The detective wrote something down. "What is it, about a mile from here to there?"

"I guess. Never measured it."

"So. If you snuck out a few minutes after eleven, you probably got to the church about a quarter after." He flipped a few pages back in his notebook. "Mr. Copeland said he found you at the church before 11:30." The detective chewed on the end of his pen. "Doesn't leave a lot of time for nefarious deeds, does it?"

"That would explain, I guess, why Tommy wasn't as excited about the evening as I'd expected he might be. He had plans, and his old mom was cramping his style," said Anne, slowly, enunciating as she went. To hear the hurt in her voice, one would have had to be a member of her immediate family. Both Thomas and Zack winced, and Zack gave his younger brother a look of disgust.

Detective Madison looked at Anne. "Is everything I'm hearing true to the best of your knowledge? Going to the movies, what time you got home, what time the boys went to bed?"

"Yes. There's been more going on here than I knew about, but that was all true."

"Well, don't be too hard on yourself. I think that's true of most houses with teenagers in them." He flipped the notebook shut, then slipped it back in his jacket pocket. He sipped his coffee, looked at Thomas, then nodded once. "I might have a few questions for you later, but for now, I think that's everything I need. Thanks again for the coffee, ma'am."

"Please do call me Anne. And you're welcome. Let us know if there's anything else we can do to help."

The detective took one step away from the table, then paused to lock eyes with Thomas. "Anything else I need to know, Tommy?"

Whoa. This guy's good. If I was fifteen, I would have spilled whatever I knew. I would have implicated Michael Hollister, and that would have opened more lines of questioning than I would have answers for.

"No, sir."

Madison's eyes bored into Thomas's for a few seconds. He smiled. "Okay, then. If I have any more questions, I'll drop back around."

Anne, Thomas, and Zack stood in the kitchen watching the detective get in his car and drive away. Anne just turned to look at Thomas, visibly thinking something over.

"Mom? I know you're probably mad at me—"

"I am. I'm damned mad. I'm also disappointed, hurt that you've lied to me, feeling very alone that Zack was in cahoots with you about all this sneaking out, and wondering why you didn't tell the detective about Michael Hollister."

And there's the live electric wire again. Grab it and get fried. "Well, Mom, I think it's probably illegal to put a dog turd in someone's sandwich. I didn't want to confess to that."

Zack burst out laughing. "Is that what it was? All I heard is that he puked up his lunch. I didn't hear why. You put sh...dog turds in his lunch? I didn't know you had it in you."

The look on Anne's face stifled all the mirth from Zack. "This is when I need you to help me, Zackary, and be a big brother," she said, as if every word aged her a month. "You're almost an adult. This is a real problem and nothing about a missing girl is funny."

"I understand," Thomas continued. "I'm probably grounded for the rest of my life. But before I serve my sentence, I need to go do something."

Anne's eyes said otherwise. "Tommy, you don't get to decide what you need to do any more. But I'll listen to you explain."

"It's really important. I want Zack to go with me to the cave behind the school."

"Is that really necessary?" Anne glanced at Zack, whose face revealed nothing. She lit another cigarette, sighed out a cloud of smoke. "I suppose if there's any chance at all you know where she might be, we should check on it. Why didn't you mention it to Detective Madison when he was here? Besides not wanting to tell him about what you did to Michael's food?"

Thomas squirmed. "I didn't think he'd believe me. I promise, after we check that place out, I'll be grounded for life."

"Okay. Be back here in less than two hours, and no other stops, understood?"

Zack grabbed his keys off the dishwasher and walked toward the Camaro. Thomas hurried into the dining room, pulled the flashlight out of the cupboard, and hurried after Zack. As soon as he climbed in, Zack's fist rammed knuckles deep into the fleshy part of Thomas's bicep, giving him a Charlie horse.

"Ow!"

"That's for dragging me into your mess with you, dumbass. I should give you a lot more than that. Just when I think you can't be a bigger idiot than you already are, you prove me wrong."

"Sorry, Zack. Didn't mean to get you in trouble too."

"Apparently I slept through most of the story this morning. What the hell happened?"

"When I got to the church last night, Carrie was gone, but the door was open and her car was there. Her dad showed up and thinks I have something to do with it."

"You are such a dipshit. Who the hell goes to make out in a church? You are the weirdest little shit I know." Thomas did not answer. Then Zack came unglued in several minutes of sustained laughter, so wracking that he could barely drive. When he finished, he asked: "So why'd you put dog shit in Michael's lunch? Because of his kidnapping Amy? I would have just kicked his ass for that myself."

"Yeah, that was it. The guy abuses animals. That's why I think Carrie might be in his animal torture cave."

They pulled into the school parking lot. "What's the deal with this cave, anyway?"

Shit. Am I going to have to confess to every lie I've ever told today?

"That day I was in the woods after school? I followed Michael Hollister to a weird-ass cave. He'd been torturing little animals there and had a cat caged up. I let the cat go, and that's why I was so freaked out by the time I got back to the car."

"You little shit. I knew you were lying to me. Why the hell was Michael killing things out there?"

Training.

"He's a weirdo. He gets off on hurting things. Killing them."

"And what makes you think he gets off on it? I do a lot of things that don't get me off, but I still do them."

How about because we know a lot more about serial killers and their behaviors in another thirty years?

"You don't do anything like this, and you know it."

Zack shook his head in angry frustration. "And this is the guy you're all mixed up with, huh? Okay, show me where this cave is."

The third trip to the cave, in full daylight, was quicker and easier. Thomas remembered the right place to turn off the path, and managed to find the edge of the cliff without tumbling off. "Here," Thomas said, "there's a little trail down to the clearing."

The vines and ivy had begun to hang back down over the mouth of the cave, but it wasn't fully covered. It looked innocuous in the daylight. "This is it?" Zack asked, doubtfully.

"Yeah, this is it." Thomas turned the flashlight on and led the way into the pitch darkness, turning sideways. He hesitated, but Zack shoved him in.

Thomas flashed the light along the floor, hoping not to see anything, but his mind's eye already saw Carrie, crumpled on the floor.

Nothing.

"Looks like an empty, stinky little cave to me. Are you sure this is the one?"

Thomas scanned the entire cave with the light: floor, corners, walls, ceiling. Nothing. "Yeah." His voice wavered.

"You didn't really think she was in here, did you?"

"Yeah, I really did. I was hoping she wasn't but was afraid she was. Let's get out of here."

As they began to make their way back, Thomas swore inwardly. *Of course he came back and finished cleaning everything out. He's not an idiot. Still, I had to check, or I wouldn't have been able to live with myself.*

They made it back to the house well before their deadline. Anne was waiting at the door.

"Mr. Copeland called while you were gone."

"What'd he say?" Thomas asked.

"No sign of Carrie yet, unfortunately. He asked if you would wrack your brain and see if you can come up with any reasonable explanation."

"Jesus Christ! Does he think I haven't already been doing that? I don't think he wants to hear what I've come up with."

Thomas spun and headed to his bedroom. He sat on the edge of the bed and took the Creedence Clearwater Revival record off the turntable. He slipped on a Charles Mingus album, set it to repeat, and lay down. He spent the rest of the day tossing and turning, picking up a book and throwing it down, unread.

He was still there, the same record still playing, when Zack came to bed many hours later.

Chapter Thirty-Nine

Sunday brought nothing more than Thomas laying on his bed staring at the ceiling. He ran the same scenarios over and over in his mind, looking for any explanation for Carrie's absence. There was nothing he could do, no reason to want to do anything that was in his power, and nothing to look forward to.

On Monday morning, he was awake before the sun came up, early enough to see his mom leave for the early shift at the hospital. By the time Zack got out of the shower, Thomas was ready and waiting to leave for school. *I know it. She will be sitting in homeroom, with some story to explain this whole weekend.*

Just inside the school's front door, Billy, Ben, and Simon were waiting for him. Not talking, cutting up, or laughing; just waiting. Thomas spotted them, nodded without stopping or speaking, and headed for his homeroom. They caught up to him, flanking him.

"What's up, bro?" Billy asked.

"Nothing."

"Really? That's not what everyone else is saying," Simon said.

Thomas stopped dead. "What do you mean?"

"You are topic number one in the hallways of greater Middle Falls High this morning." Kids parted around them in the hall, staring as they passed. "We half-expected to see you come in with handcuffs or a ball and chain attached."

"What the hell? Seriously? What have you heard?"

Ben glanced at the other two, hesitated. "We're hearing a lot of stuff. We knew it wasn't true."

Billy added, "We heard you and Carrie ran away to get married, or you had kidnapped her and the police had already arrested you, or she had run away to California to become a singer, but she was framing you for...something. The details didn't make a lot of sense."

"That's because it's all bullshit. You guys know that, right?"

"Yeah," said Ben, "of course we do. So what's really up? What can we do to help?"

"I don't know," Thomas said. "I was supposed to meet Carrie on Friday night. I was late. When I got there, her car was there, but she wasn't. Then her dad showed up and got really pissed off, since he didn't know she was sneaking out to see me. He thought I had something to do with her being gone. The cops did come and talk with me Saturday, but they just asked me some questions. I didn't do anything. I was with Mom, going to the movies on Friday. That's why I was late to meet Carrie. Are you guys sure she's not here?"

Simon shrugged, said, "I don't think so." A girl with short blonde hair and an equally short skirt eyed Thomas in passing. "If she was here, I think everyone in school would know it."

"You're probably right, but I still want to get to first period and see for myself."

"Okay, that's cool," Billy said. "See you guys at lunch, maybe."

Billy and Thomas took the stairs two at a time and hurried to a dark, deserted room 222. Thomas flipped the lights on, and both took their usual seats.

Two minutes later, kids started to stream in, saw Thomas, and stared until they caught themselves. Those who were alone just looked. Where there was a group, the whispers came.

Mr. Burns arrived right before the first period bell rang. Right behind him, Michael Hollister walked in and took his seat at the front. He didn't look at Thomas.

A dull, preoccupied morning of classes gave way to lunch, where Thomas stood in line and got his food without even looking at what was being served.

I have never felt less hungry.

Out of force of habit, he made his way to the back corner where he had sat so often with Carrie. He looked around the room for Michael Hollister, but didn't expect to see him. Since the Sandwich Incident, Michael had taken to eating elsewhere. *In his car, probably, since we aren't supposed to leave campus during school hours.* Once again, all eyes and whispered babble seemed to center on Thomas. When Ben, Billy, and Simon emerged from the end of the line, they took seats next to and across from him, semi-shielding him from prying eyes.

"Thanks, you guys, but they don't bother me. Heard anything new?"

They exchanged glances.

"C'mon, whatever it is, it can't be that bad. Wait. You didn't hear anything about Carrie, did you?"

"No. Some of the jocks in English were saying..." Billy shook his head.

"What? Saying what?"

"They were saying you had killed her and buried her in your back yard. They're a bunch of assholes, though."

"Amen, brother," Simon chipped in. "Assholes. Holders of the coveted Asshole's Medal with Crossed Plungers."

Thomas laughed along in spite of himself. "I appreciate you guys hanging with me. It's good to know who your friends are."

"What was it d'Artagnan said?" asked Simon. "All for one, and all of you to protect me when I walk through the valley of the shadow of death, right?"

Chapter Forty

At track practice that afternoon, Zack and Coach Manfred planned Zack's next few days of training. "Let's get your distance work in today and tomorrow, your intermediates Wednesday and Thursday," said the coach.

"Sounds good, Coach. Stretch only on Friday?"

Coach Manfred nodded. "We'll have you ready to go."

"I feel good. No..." Zack's eyes wandered over to a group of boys standing in the middle of the field, huddled together, gesturing toward him.

"Weaver, you with me? Now is not the time to lose your focus."

"No, I know. I've got it, Coach. I'll be ready."

"Okay, get warmed up, we'll start with some timed 880s. Take it easy, though."

"Sure, Coach. You got it."

Zack started his warmup routine, stretching, taking a few high steps, then stretching again. He noticed one of the boys gesturing at him again. He jogged over to them. "What's going on?"

Thirty seconds later, Zack tore for the parking lot full tilt. Five minutes later, he brought the Camaro into the driveway at home hard enough to sling gravel into the small yard.

    Anne met him at the door, ready to give vent to outrage. Then she saw her son's face.

Chapter Forty-One

A few hours later, Thomas was in his room staring at the ceiling. Anne knocked on the bedroom door, then stuck her head in. "Honey?"

"Yeah?" Thomas rolled onto his side. "What? Did you hear something from Mr. Copeland?"

She and Zack both stepped into the room.

Thomas looked from one to the other, swallowed hard, and closed his eyes for two long beats. "Okay. Whatever it is, just tell me."

Anne's composure cracked, with tears rolling down her cheeks. She and Zack had delayed this conversation for hours. She had made phone calls, talked to the police, tried to get the details right. Most of all, she and Zack had tried to come up with a better way to tell Thomas the truth, and there was none.

"Oh, goddammit, what, Mom? What?"

Anne took a few tentative steps, sat on the edge of the twin bed. Zack hung back, out of place in his own bedroom. "Tommy, honey. I wish I didn't have to tell you this." She reached out and held his hand.

Thomas froze inside. His voice went flat. "Whatever it is, Mom, just say it."

Anne reached up, wiped away the tears, and drew a deep breath. "Carrie's gone. The police found...they found her body."

For a moment, all Thomas could do was blink. Then, the pain, the loss, the finality of—*they found her body*—exploded in his heart. He closed his eyes tight, looked for a place inside him where there wasn't pain. It didn't exist.

I knew it. What else makes sense?

"Oh, Tommy. I'm so sorry." Anne reached her arms out and hugged Thomas. He was stiff as a statue.

Thomas leaned back from her and cleared his throat. "Where did they find her?"

"Tommy, do you really need to know?"

"I do."

"In the rest area just north of Roseburg."

Thomas nodded, completely calm. "Rest area? Yeah. Figures."

"Figures? Why? What do you mean?"

Thomas shook his head, stared at the wall. "Doesn't matter." *Nothing will ever be okay again, will it? I'll never catch up to her. I have no idea how this works. Does this world keep resetting, or are there a million different worlds with a million different Carries in them? If I find Carrie again, would she even know who I am? The Carrie who truly knows me, is gone to God only knows where—her starting point, a new life altogether, who knows? She killed herself and started over a dozen times. What happens when someone murders you instead? Do you get to go on to something new?*

The thought broke him inside. He laid down, pulled his knees up a bit, and turned his back to Anne. "I just want to lay here." *For the rest of my life, or until I figure out how to kill Michael Hollister.*

"There's something else I need to tell you."

Oh, for fuck's sake. You haven't told me enough? Thomas rolled over and looked at her.

"There's someone here who wants to talk to you."

"The cops here already? I'll come out right now and they can take me away, if they want."

"No, not the police. Someone who wants to talk to you."

"Goddamnit, Mom! I don't want to see anyone. Just tell me what is going on!"

Anne paused, bit her lip, then shook her head. "Come out as soon as you can," she said, leaving the room. Zack remained behind, leaning against the wall. He started to say something, but couldn't. As tears filled his eyes, he shook his head and followed Anne out of the room.

Thomas looked out the window. It was still light out, but overcast. The clock read 7:45.

Thomas turned, swung his feet over the bed.

So here it is. Carrie's gone. Michael killed her, but she would still be alive if not for me. I loved her, now she's dead, and it's all because of me.

Why do I keep killing the people I love most?

Thomas pulled the record off the player and smashed it against the edge of the table. It broke into half a dozen pieces. He flung the biggest piece against the wall, where it shattered into smaller pieces.

That's Thomas Weaver's #1, all-time classic hit, "Destroying Whatever He Loves!"

He put his head in his hands, drew a deep, shuddering breath, and walked to the mirror over the dresser. He stared at his reflection. In most ways, he looked as he had upon his arrival back in 1976, just a few months earlier. His eyes, though, looked familiar in a different way. *And I know it well. Those are the eyes of a middle-aged alcoholic at the end of a long bender.*

Thomas glared into his reflection for a full minute. Then he heard subdued voices coming from the living room.

What in God's name does Mom have up her sleeve now?

Chapter Forty-Two

Thomas took two steps into the small living room and stopped dead. Standing in front of him was someone Thomas hadn't seen in more than forty years.

James Weaver looked almost exactly as Thomas remembered him. He was still tall, if not quite as lean as the day he'd walked out on them. A full head of hair, with wisps of grey, framed a tanned and angular face with an expression that rankled Thomas at first sight.

Who the hell has a tan this time of year in Oregon? You, asshole. Riding in on your white horse in a time of family crisis. Well, you can go fuck yourself. Last life, I never saw you again. Not even at your funeral. I liked that just fine.

When Tommy stopped, his father took a tentative step toward him, arms out. Tommy stepped back. "No. No way. You don't get to abandon us, leave us to fend for ourselves, for how many years? Five? Then come riding back in on your white horse?" Thomas's voice, high-pitched anyway, climbed a dangerous octave. *Hold it together, Weaver.* Thomas looked out to the driveway. Parked beside Zack's Camaro and Anne's old station wagon was a glinting new Cadillac. Then he glanced at Zack, sitting in the recliner, looking out the window, his face inscrutable.

"Son. Tommy. Don't be like that. There's a reason for everything. Someday you'll understand." His voice was the deep, masculine, smooth tone of the successful salesman.

Bullshit, Dad. You're what, pushing forty? I lived a decade past where you are and never understood. I guess you liked that family better. At least you stayed with them until you died.

"I will, huh? That's crap, *James*. I'll never understand why you left us. You and Mom didn't want to be married anymore? Fine. You wanted to run away and play house with a new wife and kids? Who gives a shit?"

"Tommy!" exclaimed Anne, but Thomas continued.

"But what about us? Do you know how good Zack does in school? Do you know what a great athlete he is? How much everyone likes him? He is just like you, except he's not an asshole."

Color drained from James's face. "That's enough!" Control asserted itself. "Look, son. I'm sorry. It's obvious things aren't going well here." He cast a glance toward Anne. "It stinks to high heaven of cigarette smoke in here. For God's sake, Anne, you're a nurse, you should know better." He turned back to Thomas. "A dead teenage girl and visits from the police to interrogate my sons shows me things have gotten completely off track. Believe me, I'll be around more."

"You know what, *James*? I don't ever want to see you again. If it weren't for all this, you wouldn't even be here. I'll tell you one last thing, though. You might want to get a checkup. You're already carrying the stuff around inside you that's gonna kill you. I won't go to your funeral this time, either."

"Tommy! Please don't be this way!" Anne's voice was almost a wail.

"Tell *James* that, Mom," snarled Thomas. He pushed past his father, threw open the sliding glass door, and slammed it behind him hard enough to make it bounce back a few inches. He heard Anne say, "This was a mistake. I shouldn't have called you." Her words faded away as Thomas leapt off the porch. He glanced into the Cadillac to see if the keys were inside, but they were not. He ran around the side of the house, got on his bike and pedaled away, wanting only to be away from his home.

Finally, half a mile from the house, Thomas let the bike come to a stop. Tears of anger streamed down his face: at his father, Michael Hollister, himself.

He rode through Middle Falls for hours, keeping to the side streets. On an impulse, Thomas rode out to the falls that gave the town its name.

If these are the middle falls, where are the beginning and ending falls?

He listened to the water's gentle cascade, twenty-five feet onto the rocks below. Oregon had far more impressive waterfalls than this: Multnomah, Bridal Veil, Toketee, Latourell were but a few. Tourists didn't trek from Northern California or even Eugene to see Middle Falls, but in the darkness closing around Thomas, they were some small comfort.

I've done it again. Ruined everything. I don't care how many lives the universe gives me, I'm going to find a way to fuck it up.

He stood over the falls for a long time. *Suppose I climbed over this railing and stepped off the edge.*

Would that kill me, though, or just break my neck, and make me a quadriplegic? Another problem for Mom to have to take care of. I might wake up in the hospital instead of back in my bedroom again.

He stood there a long time, contemplating.

I've got to stop taking the easy way out at some point. Gotta quit running away from the pain.

Then there's Mom. In the other life, I quit on her. I just ripped my father a new one for quitting on us. Now I'm looking at quitting on her again.

This has to end. I am done running.

Thomas swung a leg over his bike, put his weight on a pedal, and rode back toward town. Just over halfway home, he realized that he wasn't far from the small church, and he steered toward it. Its front door was slightly ajar. Golden light poured out into the darkness.

Church services on a Monday night? Since when? This is around the usual time Carrie and I went there, and no one was ever there but us.

He started to turn the bike away when he noticed that the parking lot was empty.

Weird. Church open, lights on, no cars in the parking lot? He coasted up to the church, listened to the crickets for a few moments.

Images flashed unbidden through Thomas's mind—Michael attacking Carrie, knocking her down, straddling her, and choking her until she stopped moving.

Carrie. A small sob escaped his lips.

He laid his bike on its side and went to the front door. He peeked in, saw nothing but the neat rows of pews. The familiar smell of the place raised a lump in his throat.

Carrie? Are you here, somehow? He took a few soft steps inside. A woman emerged from the room at the side of the altar, smiled, and said "Hello."

She looked sixtyish, none too tall, a little on the plump side, silvery-white hair mostly pulled back except for several strands hanging down her forehead.

Oh, for Christ's sake. This is the last thing I need. A well-intended grandma trying to save my soul.

"Can I help you?" She had an accent Thomas could not place.

Thomas shook his head, found his voice. "No. I was riding by and saw the lights on. Usually, this place is all locked up and dark. I was just curious." He turned to leave.

"Why don't you come in and sit down and rest for a few moments. You look tired. I know I am. I've been here waiting all day and night, and waiting wears me out like nothing else. I'm Emily Leon." She walked toward Thomas, offered her hand.

Thomas sighed. He met her, shook her hand quickly. "Thanks, but I really should be heading home."

"You're Thomas, aren't you? Thomas Weaver?"

"What?" Thomas's head jerked back. "How could you possibly know that?"

"There are more things in Heaven and Earth, Horatio, than are dreamt of in your philosophy."

"Huh? What?"

"Shakespeare," Emily said. "Hamlet." She sat down in the nearest pew, patted a spot beside her. "Come. Sit down for a moment, then you can be on your way."

Thomas's eyes narrowed, but he slid into the pew. Now she looked younger, but with eyes that harbored ancient secrets. "You still didn't tell me how you knew who I am. And, who are you, exactly?"

"As I said, I am Emily Leon. I am just a visitor here today. On a mission, I suppose you could say."

"A mission? Like, 'saving African orphans' kind of mission?"

"No. More like a 'saving Thomas Weaver' kind of mission."

What the hell? Who is this crazy woman? I don't need this shit.

"Or perhaps this shit is exactly what you need."

Thomas's mouth fell open. *So, the old lady is a mind reader. Sure, why not.*

Emily's expression grew more serious. "That's closer to true than to untrue, but let's not waste time playing games. Let's agree there are some things that cannot be explained and leave it at that." Thomas said nothing. "For instance, a middle-aged man who tires of his life, tries to end it, and wakes up young, with a chance to do it all again."

This time his jaw fell wide open. He closed his eyes, ran his hand through his hair, and looked again. *Still there. If I'm hallucinating, it's a good one. And the Amazing Kreskin couldn't have pulled that off, no way.*

"No, Thomas, Kreskin couldn't have." She reached out and touched his hand. "As you are probably realizing, I am not from around here."

Thomas nodded, shocked to silence.

"In some ways, I am very different from you. If you knew everything about me, you might call me an angel. That's what often happens when people meet one of us. In other ways, though, I am as ordinary as anyone else you will ever meet."

Don't think I've ever met anyone less ordinary than you, lady.

"Of course you have. But I have a job, and I like to think I am good at it. It is my job to watch over certain souls here on Earth. Including yours. And Carrie's."

"Then you've been doing a pretty shitty job of it."

Emily closed her eyes for two beats, three.

Holy shit, angel or not, that stung her.

She nodded. "Perhaps. Sometimes I try to help, even though I know I shouldn't. So often, things don't turn out the way I intend. It's *The Universal Law of Unintended Consequences.* As many millennia as I have seen, I should understand it by now, but I am still a work in progress. *I am but an egg.*"

"Okay, sure. If you want to make things up to me, why don't you spin us all back in time, so I can save Carrie. Wait. Even better, do you know where Carrie is? The soul I sat with in this church?" He paused. "The girl I love?"

Emily drew in a deep breath and held it for a long time, but did not answer.

"You do, don't you? But, you're not going to tell me, right? Of course. If you can't do that, I'll settle for you making Michael Hollister drive his car into a tree at eighty miles an hour."

"This will be hard to understand, but I watch over Michael Hollister just as I do you or Carrie."

"If you're responsible for that batshit crazy weirdo, then there's nothing left for us to talk about."

"I am not *responsible* for him, Thomas, any more than I am responsible for you. My job is to watch, but everyone has the inalienable right of free will. There are more worlds, just like this one, than you can possibly understand. On all of them, there is or was a Thomas Weaver. I only watch over one of them." She leaned toward Thomas, laid a hand gently on his heart. "This one. This soul."

Looking into the kindness of her eyes, Thomas felt an odd feeling he remembered only in the moments after waking from a vivid dream.

"I have a simple message for you, and I've traveled very far to share it."

"What?"

"Thomas Weaver, don't lose hope. Don't give up. I empathize with you, but don't let the darkness envelop you. If you start over again, you will be recycled away from this life and I will not be able to put right what I have mistakenly put asunder. I know you were contemplating that tonight."

"Being recycled and starting completely over sounds good to me."

Emily nodded, smiled sadly. "Do you know the most powerful force in the universe?"

"No, but if you tell me the answer is in the Bible, I'm gone."

"You know; we all know, though humans spend much of your lives denying the answer. Here on Earth, you call it 'love.' It is the force that drives the entire universe. It feeds the machine of creation."

"Ha!" A bitter bark of laughter escaped Thomas. "John Lennon will be so glad to know he got it right—"All You Need is Love."

Thomas turned away for a moment. When he looked back, Emily Leon was gone.

Chapter Forty-Three

Thomas took his time pedaling homeward through the darkness. *So she is The Watcher. And she knows who I am—who I really am. She proved that. Okay, so there's a group of angels who sit and watch over all of us. Talk about shit jobs.*

Coasting down a slight hill, Thomas turned right onto Periwinkle Lane.

If I can believe I'm a middle-aged man living in a teenager's body, I guess I can believe she's an angel. What did she really tell me, though? She knew where Carrie was, but she wouldn't tell me. She said she watches over Michael just like she did Carrie and me. I don't like that. What else? Not much, other than telling me not to kill myself again.

Great. An angel shows up, tells me what not to do, doesn't tell me what to do. Clear as mud!

Thomas stopped in front of his house. He glanced at his wristwatch, but it was too dark to read. The only light in the house was a single lamp showing through the living room window. He saw his mother, wrapped in her old housecoat, obviously waiting for him. He ran inside, but before he could say anything, his mother grabbed him and held him in a fierce sobbing hug.

"Tommy, I'm sorry. I just felt so completely over my head, and out of touch, and I didn't know what to do. I shouldn't have thrown your dad into this. He's not part of our family any more, and it made everything worse. And Tommy, most of all, it breaks my heart what happened to Carrie. The only way I can imagine how you feel right now is by imagining if I lost you or Zack. Can you please forgive me?"

Thomas nodded into her shoulder and whispered, "Okay."

She held him out at arm's length and scanned his face. "Now, where have you been?" It was not in the tone that evinced the right to demand an answer.

Oh, nowhere. I rode around town, thought about throwing myself over the falls, then I met a weird old lady that was probably an angel.

"Nowhere, Mom. I know you meant well, but I couldn't stand to be in the same room with him. I rode around town, then out to the falls. On the way back, I stopped at the church where I used to meet Carrie."

Anne clucked softly and pulled him close again. "It's okay. If it helped you, and got you away from my mistake, then it's fine."

"I've got school in the morning, I guess. Life goes on, right?"

Anne forced a smile. "Yes, it does. I've got the early shift in the morning and I can't miss another one, so I'll already be gone when you wake up."

"I love you, Mom."

"I love you, Tommy. Go try and get some sleep."

Chapter Forty-Four

When Zack and Thomas pulled up to Middle Falls High the next morning, they had to maneuver around several large news trucks with huge satellite dishes and logos like KEZI *SkyLink* and KGW *Eyewitness News*.

"What the hell?" Zack said. "Haven't seen those guys since the windstorm blew the roof off the gym three years ago."

Thomas felt sick to his stomach. *I should have known this would happen. If it bleeds, it leads. Carrie, wherever you are, I'm sorry this is happening in your name.*

Ben, Simon, and Billy were waiting for Thomas at the edge of the parking lot. "We're sorry, man," said Billy. "We heard when we got to school." He laid a hand on Thomas's shoulder.

"This sucks so bad, Tommy. I don't know what to say, but I'm around if you need to talk," Ben said.

"Now the vultures are here to pick at the bones," Simon added, nodding toward the news trucks. Then he clapped his hand to his mouth, glanced at Thomas out of the corner of his eye. "Shit. Sorry. I didn't mean…"

"It's all right. I know you didn't," Thomas said.

The three friends formed a phalanx around Thomas, somewhat like an undersized and complexion-challenged band of Spartans. It didn't help. As soon as they got near the school, the pointing, nodding, and whispering began, worse than the day before.

As they passed a tanned, big-haired reporter with fake eyelashes, Thomas heard her ask Amanda Jarvis: "Were you close to the victim?" He hurried on. *Not sure I can handle Amanda telling the world she and Carrie were besties, when all she had ever done was make fun of her. Not sure I can handle any of this.*

Thomas and Billy put their heads down, perp-walk style, and went straight to homeroom. Every head turned when they walked in. Here, where everyone knew him, there were no more whispers or questions, just steady stares. Thomas ignored them and sat in his accustomed seat.

I think I've gotta get out of here. There's no way I can put up with this shit for an entire day. Zack will have track practice, but I can cut out and walk home.

Michael Hollister walked just past Thomas, then paused and pivoted toward him. A small smirk played across his lips. Their eyes met.

He knows I know. Goddamn him, he knows.

"Sorry to hear about your, umm, girlfriend, Weaver."

That was it.

Thomas covered the distance between him and Michael in a blink, ramming his shoulder into Michael's midsection. Both went sprawling over two rows of desks, a cacophony of flesh hitting metal and wood.. Thomas landed directly on top of Michael, knocking the wind out of him.

Anthony Massey whooped, "Ho, it's on!"

Michael's eyes were wide with surprise. He tried to push Thomas away, but Thomas shifted position to put both knees on Michael's biceps, drawing a scream of pain: "Ow, get off, Weaver! What the hell is wrong with you?"

Thomas said nothing, but drew back a right and hammered it into Michael's face. It connected with a meaty, satisfying sound, followed by a left. Right, left, right, losing count.

No matter how many times he hit Michael, it wouldn't bring Carrie back, but as long as he was hitting him, it almost didn't matter.

Blood streamed from Michael's nose; his left eye began to close up. Tears streamed down Thomas's reddened face. Thomas laced his fingers into Michael's hair, pulled his head up off the ground, and slammed it into the floor. Again. And again, each time with a sickening *ke-rack* like the sound of a power alley home run ball leaving a white ash baseball bat.

Thomas wouldn't remember how many head-slams it took to send Michael's eyes rolling back in his head, but that was when he wrapped both hands around Michael's neck. Every muscle in his arms was fatigued, so he straightened them and lifted his body up, putting all his weight on Michael's throat.

"Holy shit, Weaver's gonna kill him! Actually kill him! Oh, man!" Anthony Massey again, doing the play by play.

Thomas stayed on Michael's neck as the battered face went brick red, then deepened into purple. He was no longer resisting.

Behind him, Billy said, "Tommy, don't!" but Thomas was beyond hearing anyone. His lips pulled back from his teeth at the effort.

The light faded from Michael Hollister's eyes.

Chapter Forty-Five

Temporal Relocation High Council

Emillion stood facing nine floating desks. Each was occupied by a tall figure wearing long robes that seemed made out of pure light. Each was a different swirl of colors.

"Makes it awfully hard to see their faces, doesn't it?" Emillion muttered.

Margenta stood with her back to Emillion. She offered no reply.

"Margenta? Why have you called this meeting of the council?" Thus spoke the being in the very middle, her robe made up of swirls of blue and white. Her face was obscured, but her musical voice emanated from a world far away.

Margenta remained ramrod-straight. "Thank you, Blessed One. One of my Watchers, Emillion Askanzi, has repeatedly interfered in the outcomes of the lives we are charged to watch. I have counseled her repeatedly. I have paired her with Veruna, one of my very best. Despite all, she acts irresponsibly. She flouts our laws of non-interference. In this most recent case, she has interfered in the orbiting lives of a number of the souls she is charged to watch. The repercussions have been widespread, and the ripples are still spreading. I am petitioning to have her permanently removed from my division."

"Show me."

"Of course." A column rose in front of Magenta. An image appeared above her head: Emillion, at her desk, spinning her own column. Margenta moved her hands and the image inside Emillion's column came into focus. A young man in an automobile, speaking to a small dog, then snapping its neck in one swift motion. The image panned back. Emillion grabbed the image of the boy and the dog, twisted it until it snapped free, then dropped it into a receptacle at her feet. The image began to move again. The man drove on, ignoring the dog. The image went dark.

"I see. Show me the result."

"There were a number of ongoing echoes from the interference. I cannot know the extent of the damage. Here is one of them." Margenta spun the column, then slowed it. Now the same man was standing in a church, facing a young woman. They were speaking, but the image was silent. No sound was necessary. He stepped toward her. They fell together. Margenta spun the scene ahead to show the man dragging the woman out of the building.

"This was a direct result of our interference?"

"It was."

One more image appeared. Emillion herself, recognizable even in human form, sitting in the same church with another young man. A small rustle moved across the council.

"Emillion?" Blue/White Robe's voice was still soft.

Emillion cleared her throat. "Yes?"

"Is there anything else we need to know?"

"I suppose not. Wait. Yes, there is. My job is to watch, to observe, to project. I understand. But, I am given free will as well. I have a heart and soul just as surely as those I watch over. Do you want automatons watching over our charges? Surely, if you did, you could build a machine to do what I do. Is there no room for choice?"

Margenta's lips tightened. "No," replied Blue/White Robe. "No, Emillion, there is no room for that type of choice. What is your proposed solution to this?"

Emillion lifted her chin, squared her shoulders. "The young woman that you saw murdered. I want to bring her back. Her soul is in limbo. There are souls on Earth who have completed their assigned tasks. Instead of allowing them to die, she could walk into their life and finish her own."

"I see." Blue/White Robe's voice grew softer. She looked to her left, where the rest of the council nodded in answer. To her right, they did the same. "Margenta, there is no benefit to removing Emillion from your division."

"But...!"

Blue/White Robe held up a long-fingered hand. "Removing Emillion simply moves the problem from one area to another, solving nothing. She is unrepentant. Her "solution" will only wreak more havoc, cause more ripples. We cannot have it."

Margenta stood frozen, holding her breath.

"It is the decision of the Council that Emillion Askanzi must earn a new perspective. She is not fit to fulfill the rigors of her position at this time. She will be immediately reborn."

A small gasp escaped Margenta. Sudden fear in her eyes, she turned to say something to Emillion.

Emillion was gone.

Chapter Forty-Six

A healthy, lusty-lunged baby girl was born to Harvey and Louise Esterhaus at St. Nicholas Hospital in Sheboygan, Wisconsin. Since the second trimester of her pregnancy, they had planned to name her Lisa, but when Louise held her for the first time, she said: "Hello, Emily."

And Emily she was.

Chapter Forty-Seven

Thomas Weaver slumped forward in the chair opposite the principal's desk, arms dangling, knuckles sore. His head rested on the desk. His arms were too fatigued to bother pushing the hair out of his eyes.

I never realized. Strangling someone really takes it out of you.

In strode the principal of Middle Falls High School, Mr. Vincent, carrying a manila folder and taking a seat at his desk. With an effort, Thomas lifted his head and leaned back. *Mr. Vincent? Where the hell are the cops? How long does it take for them to get here after you've killed someone? Are there a lot of murders that need investigating in Middle Falls on this particular day?*

Mr. Vincent leaned forward, dropping his meaty forearms on the desktop. He was in his early sixties, heading for a dance with a widowmaker heart attack if he didn't get his weight, blood pressure, and cholesterol under control. His nearly-bald head came to a slight point. It reminded Thomas of Humpty Dumpty.

"Well, we've got a mess on our hands here, don't we? You want to tell me about it?"

Thomas managed a slight shake of his head. "Not particularly."

Mr. Vincent scowled. It was not the first time he had heard such a response, nor the hundredth. "That attitude will not do you any favors, uh..." He glanced down at the folder in front of him. "...Thomas. Look. Here's where we are. Your mother has been called. I understand that she is on her way down here."

Thomas did his best to repress a flinch. *Oh, my God. What is this going to do to Mom?*

Wait. What? Mom is on her way down here?

Where the hell are the cops?

"Mr. Vincent? I'm not sure I understand. Have the police been called?"

The principal leaned back a little, pulled out a pack of Camels, lit one. He inhaled, blew a line of smoke toward the yellow-blotched ceiling tiles. "We don't call the police over every school fight. If we did, they'd be here most days, and that wouldn't do. This is a high school, not a war zone."

Thomas took a deep breath, held it, then exhaled slowly. "School fight? Is that all this was?"

"Yes, it was." Understanding lit Vincent's face. "Wait. Just how badly do you think you hurt the Hollister boy?"

"Pretty badly, didn't I?"

"Well, you certainly got the best of it. He's at the nurse's office right now. Looks like he's going to have a shiner, probably two, his nose is broken, and the nurse is checking him for a concussion. Other than that, and the bruising around his neck, I believe he is fine. I was just talking to him, trying to get to the bottom of this. Fortunately for him and you, strangulation is more difficult than one might imagine. The assault victim, I am told, tends to pass out long before passing away."

Shit. I can't even kill somebody right.

"Were you trying to really hurt him, son?"

I sure as hell was. "No. I guess I wasn't. Things just got a little out of control."

Mr. Vincent nodded. "That's what I thought. That's usually the way these things are. One boy pushes another, neither one wants to back down, then it escalates." He pulled a piece of paper from the folder, then spent much of a minute reading. "Looks like it's a good thing Mr. Burns walked in when he did. According to him, you had both hands around the Hollister boy's neck and were vigorously applying pressure."

Not vigorously enough.

The door opened again: Miss Mullins, the office secretary. "Mr. Vincent, Mrs. Weaver is here."

"Send her in."

A moment later, Anne Weaver walked in, still dressed in her white nurse's scrubs. *She looks pissed. Go figure.* "Please, sit down, Mrs. Weaver."

Anne sat beside Thomas without looking at him. "How is the other boy?"

"Definitely worse for wear, but according to our nurse, he's going to be all right."

"Good. Thank God for small favors. What's going to happen next?"

"This is a grave situation, as I'm sure you understand, Mrs. Weaver." Mr. Vincent took a long drag on his Camel, blew smoke skyward. "This is too serious to let pass. I am going to suspend Thomas for the remainder of the school year." The judge let his sentence sink in. "It's less than two weeks. I'll arrange for his schoolwork to be delivered to him, and you'll need to bring him in one Saturday to take his final tests."

"Of course. If I'm working, I can have his brother Zack bring him to school."

"Zack? Zack Weaver? Of course. I should have made the connection!" Mr. Vincent gave Thomas another once-over. "Are you an athlete, too, Thomas?"

Thomas narrowed his eyes. *Screw you, too, dude.*

The principal looked at Anne. "Well. I don't think there's any reason I need to keep you here any longer, Mrs. Weaver. I'll have someone in the office get in touch with you about—"

There came a knock, then the office door swung open. Miss Mullins looked flustered. "Sorry to interrupt, Mr. Vincent.

Mr. and Mrs. Hollister and their lawyer are here and insisting on seeing you immediately."

He sighed. "That's fine. I'll see them in just a moment. Please ask them to wait."

They did not wait. Three people walked in: two men in nearly identical dark blue suits and a thin blonde woman dressed in a tan skirt and matching jacket. They all looked as though headed to a fundraiser for the less fortunate. The elder man, whose hair was silvering up nicely at the temples, opened the festivities. "Clayton Hollister, Vincent. I want to know why the police aren't here."

Mr. Vincent cleared his throat. "Mr. Hollister, if you'll wait outside, I'll be with you in just a moment."

"If I walk out of this room right now, it will be so my attorney, Mr. Radishaw–" he nodded at the other blue-suited man–"can file a lawsuit against your school for falling below a normal standard of care in protecting its students."

Mr. Vincent opened a desk drawer and fished around until he produced a card. He handed it to Mr. Hollister. "This is the School District's legal counsel. Please direct all legal matters to their office."

"I just saw my son. He has been beaten with an inch of his life by this young thug."

Thomas did his best to make his posture reflect the insignificance of his 5'6", 153 lb. frame.

"Bruises already showing, blood coming out of his nose, unable to focus his eyes. We think he might have permanent neurological damage."

Hey, score one for the good guys.

"Mr. Hollister, our nurse gave uh…" He glanced down at the report on his desk again, "Michael, a thorough exam. She doesn't believe it was that serious."

"Are you willing to bet your job on that?"

Mr. Vincent flushed, then looked down and spent a full thirty seconds reading the report in front of him. When he looked up, his face was calm. "Mr. Hollister. I'm sorry that this incident happened. Our students' safety is our primary concern. Unfortunately, where teenagers congregate in large numbers, this type of thing is inevitable. And while I am always concerned with the safety of every student, I do not allow anyone to come into my office and threaten me. That includes you. I'm no more receptive to such threats than I am to condoning violence on school campus."

Clayton Hollister's face paled as his lips tightened.

I'll be damned, Vincent, you're worth something after all. I think I'll help you. It's about time to take this snob down a peg. "Before you sic your attorneys on the school, Mr. Hollister, there's something you might want to be aware of."

Hollister looked amused, like a batter just realizing that the incoming knuckleball had too much spin to begin floating around. "Might I? Very well, young man, please enlighten your elders."

Before Anne could step in, Thomas plunged forward. "Hollister, your son is sick. There's a cave in the woods where he tortured animals. And it's a good thing I knew that, because he took our little dog right out of our yard and hid her there. If I hadn't known where that place was, he would have killed her, just like he killed all the other animals in there. I'm sure you're going to deny it, but before you do, you should know that I have some proof. He cleaned out most of the cave when I found it, but he left some evidence behind that I have, and I'll bet it would be pretty easy to match to him. You're going to want to get your lawyers on speed dial, because you're going to be needing them a lot to keep Michael out of jail. The best thing you could do is get him into therapy, because most people who start out tormenting animals usually escalate."

Everyone present seemed too flabbergasted to speak. *Shit. Speed Dial. There is no speed dial in 1976. Ah, screw it. That's why everybody's staring at me like I've got two heads. Whatever, I don't give a shit.*

Radishaw leaned forward, whispered into Mr. Hollister's ear. Hollister pulled away, glared at him, then to Mr. Vincent and Thomas. "You haven't heard the last of us, young man. A price will be paid."

"Don't threaten my son." Anne, her voice, flat, emotionless.

"I see where Michael gets it. All of it," added Thomas.

Clayton Hollister's outrage seemed near to boiling over at Anne, Mr. Vincent, and Thomas. He opened his mouth, then closed it, turned and strode out, leaving Margaret and Radishaw trying to catch up.

Thomas glanced at Anne, who looked as if she felt seventy years old. "Mr. Vincent," she said, "my son Zack is graduating next week. I would like Tommy to be able to come to the ceremony. Will that be allowed?"

Mr. Vincent leaned back in his desk chair. It squeaked ominously. He templed his fingers together and stared at the ceiling. Then he moved forward, scanned through a file, and made a pronouncement. "This Hollister boy will also be graduating that night. Thomas is not allowed on school grounds, but the graduation will take place downtown. There's nothing that will stop him from attending. But, Thomas." He waited until Thomas met his eyes. "Do I have your word that you will not bother Michael Hollister again?"

Thomas glanced at Anne, then met the principal's eyes. "Yes, sir."

"Very well. I think that's all, then, Mrs. Weaver. Miss Mullins will be in touch to arrange for Thomas's final homework and tests."

"Thank you for being so understanding, Mr. Vincent. I will take care of things from here."

Chapter Forty-Eight

Thomas opened the door to his mom's station wagon, which she had not parked in the shade. The resulting blast of heat made getting into the car feel like crawling into Hansel and Gretel's oven, turned on low for a nice slow baking. He wanted nothing more than to close his eyes, curl up, and drift away.

It was not to be.

Anne turned the key, cranked her window down, then turned to Thomas. "I hope you don't think you're going to be sitting around for the next few weeks watching *Split Second* and *The Price is Right*."

Thomas opened his eyes a slit. "I hadn't thought about it."

Anne pursed her lips tight. "I've just about given up on understanding what is going on with you, Tommy. I've done my best, but it doesn't seem to matter. You just keep getting into more and more trouble. This is the worst yet." She trailed off, lit a cigarette, and didn't put the car in gear. "We need to make some changes. I'll start with me, but believe me, it's going to include you and Zack as well." She stubbed the freshly-lit cigarette into the ashtray, took the pack out of her purse, and crumpled it up.

Thomas stared at her, uncertain what to say, lacking the energy to express it if he did.

"Here's how this is going to go. Every morning before I leave for work, I will leave you a list of work to do. By the time I get home, every darned thing on that list had best be done, and I mean done right. Are we clear?"

Thomas nodded, then managed to roll down his own window. Sweat stung his eyes. He remained quiet until they pulled into their driveway. "For today, can I just go to bed?"

"As soon as you clean the bathroom and do the dishes from last night, you can go to bed. In the meantime, I'll make a list for tomorrow. We will do this every day, seven days a week. If we get everything done around here, I'll see if Mrs. Arkofski needs help around her place."

"You really know how to hurt a guy."

"That's the idea, all right."

Thomas got out of the car and went inside the house. Anne backed out of the driveway, let out a long sigh, and returned to her shift.

Thomas got to work. When it was all done, he went to bed.

Chapter Forty-Nine

When Thomas opened his eyes the next morning, it was a virtual replay of the first morning of his return to 1976. Sun poured through the window, over his head, all over Zack's messy and empty bed. Thomas swung his feet onto the floor, reached up to rub his eyes. His arms ached from the previous day's fight.

Shit. Why does it feel like I can never do anything right? Even when I try to do something bad, I manage to screw that up too. Carrie's gone, Michael is still here, and I am lost.

A long, hot shower, triggering the miraculous recuperative powers of a teenage body, solved at least the physical component of the pain. Magneted to the refrigerator was a brief note from Anne:

Tommy—
Clean Gutters
Weed flower beds
Mow lawn
Wash windows inside and out
—Mom

Thomas took it down, set it on the counter. *Hell, I should be doing more around here anyway. I'm a full-grown man, and I haven't been exactly pulling my own weight.*

He pulled a bowl down, filled it with Raisin Bran and milk, and sat at the kitchen table.

Maybe doing some real work will clear my mind, help me think. Just because I'm not quite strong enough to kill Michael Hollister doesn't mean I can't take care of him one way or another. I've got to think of a way. I've read hundreds of murder mysteries and Perry Masons. The killer always gets tripped up some way. Michael is a rookie killer, so I'm sure he made mistakes. I've just got to get the police to take a closer look at him somehow.

Thomas crunched a mouthful of cereal. *If I just go to the police, especially after what happened yesterday, they won't believe me. It might even make me a suspect again.*

Thomas finished the cereal, put his bowl in the sink, and picked up the list.

Better get started. This is gonna to take me all day, which I think is the plan.

Thomas went to the small shed at the back of the house that held their lawn care tools. He pulled the wooden extension ladder down off the nails and headed for the gutter at the front of the house.

He spent the entire day working, doing the work not merely well enough to cross items off the list, but well enough to withstand any maternal scrutiny. As he worked, he turned over, examined, and rejected various methods of alerting the police to Michael Hollister.

Plant drugs on his car and then narc on him? Pretty risky. To plant drugs, one has to have some to begin with.

Plant drugs in his food and let that take care of him? Not just risky, but what if he kills someone with his car while loaded? Isn't my whole life right now about how not to get certain people killed in avoidable car accidents?

By the time Zack rolled the Camaro into the driveway, the gutters were done, the grass was mowed, and Thomas was dripping sweat into the front flower bed, trowel in hand.

Zack got out of the car, peered over the top of his sunglasses and said, "Kunta Kinte, I presume."

Thomas wiped the sweat away, said, "Don't be racially insensitive, Zack."

"Huh? What the hell are you talking about?"

"Never mind. Nothing." Thomas went back to attacking a flat sticker bush that had taken root under a rhododendron.

"I've gotta say, in a matter of months, you've gone from being totally anonymous to being a famous freshman. Good job. Next year, you should try being known for something other than trying to kill somebody."

Zack strolled by Thomas and into the house. A minute later, he reappeared, a glass of lemonade in his hand. He slid down to sit on the porch, leaned against the railing, and sighed. "Nothing better than a frosty cold beverage on a hot day, while watching my little brother sweat his ass off."

Thomas picked up a large clod of dirt, calculated the distance between he and Zack, then crumbled it up with a sigh. *Gotta grow up some time.* He settled for extending his middle finger.

Zack smiled. "That's a lot more effective when you're not wearing Mom's old lady garden gloves."

Thomas ignored him and went back to work. When he looked up again, Zack was gone and the shadows were growing longer across the front yard. Anne's station wagon pulled into her spot and she got out, still wearing her scrubs, which were spattered with a brown residue. *Maybe this will cheer her up a little. We really ought to appreciate her more. She goes to work and gets splashed with shit to feed us, clothe us, put a roof over our heads, and come to the principal's office when one of us almost chokes a rich kid to death. We should get off our lazy asses now and then to keep this place looking pleasant for her to come home to.*

Anne looked at the freshly mowed lawn, the huge pile of weeds, and her sunburned son. "Get the gutters done?"

Thomas nodded.

"You can knock off for the day, then. I'll have a new list for you tomorrow."

I hate this. She's not mad. I don't even know if she's worried any more. It's like everything has been burned out of her. I wish I could talk to her.

I wish I could talk to anyone.

Chapter Fifty

The next few days were much like that—an endless cycle of hedge trimming, porch painting, vacuuming, and polishing silver. As Thomas worked, his brain was free to work on the real problem.

The breakthrough came four days into his internal exile, the Friday after the fateful Monday when he had failed to kill Michael Hollister. By 2 PM, he judged he was far enough ahead to take a break. His mother was at work, would not be home until at least 5:30. It was Senior Skip Day, so Zack was blowing off steam with his friends at the lake. Home, a place lacking in both bikinis and beer, would be the last place he would come.

Thomas took a pair of Anne's surgical gloves from under the bathroom sink. He pulled out a new spiral notebook, opened it, and printed neatly in the upper right hand corner:
Michael Hollister
Civics
5/24/76

Then he rewrote the same thing directly over the top of the first impression, pressing hard. He turned to the second page of the notebook and ran his gloved finger over the same spot. He couldn't see anything, but there was definitely an indent there.

He took the pencil and scratched it back and forth on the back of the notebook until it was dull. He turned back to the second page, put the pencil awkwardly in his left fist, and wrote in big blockish letters:

Dear dum asses.

I am the Oregon Strangler. I killed that yung girl you found at the rest stop.

Why haven't you caught me? Because you are dum asses.

She was my first but she will not be my last.

OS

Thomas hunted through the dining room drawers for a plain white envelope and a thirteen cent stamp. He wet the stamp on a sponge and attached it to the envelope. *No sense in taking chances, even if they don't have DNA tests in 1976. They will eventually, and I don't want to confuse the issue if they test it later.* He folded the paper, stuffed it into the envelope, and looked up an address in the phone book. In the same block printing, he addressed it to "George Madison, Middle Falls Police Department, Middle Falls, Ore."

Hmm. Not the kind of thing you just drop in our mailbox for the mail lady to pick up. Too memorable. Mom told me not to leave the house, but with any luck, I can bike down to the mail box and back in ten minutes and she'll never be the wiser.

It took him fifteen minutes, but she never was the wiser.

Chapter Fifty-One

That night, Anne returned home to discover that Thomas had once again completed his daily assignments. She inspected the work with wordless disinterest, then went to the refrigerator and got a Tab. She reached into her front pocket, but it contained no Viceroys.

Four days. She's just existing. She's emotionally wrung out, she's trying to cold turkey the only addiction she's ever had, and she's exhausted from another shit-splattering twelve-hour day at the hospital. Probably not a great time to have a life-changing conversation, but I can't stand to see her go on like this. I can't take her looking at me like I'm a stranger.

Of everyone involved in this mess, she deserves the best, and has gotten the emotional equivalent of Amy's Yard Sandwich. Every time.

Enough, come what may.

"Mom?"

"What, Tommy?" She sat in what had once been his dad's chair and pulled the lever so her feet went up, then kicked off her sensible nurse's shoes.

"I know you're tired, but I'd really like to talk to you."

"Now?"

"Well, yeah. I want to tell you what's really going on with me."

"This would be, 'What's really going on with Tommy, version four, or five?' I've lost track."

"That's fair. I know this has been killing you, and I bet a part of you has blamed yourself." He thought he saw an eye flicker and harden. "It's not your fault one bit. The problem is that the truth is too weird for anyone to believe, and I don't want to get locked up in the nut wing. So I've been holding back on you, and you knew, and it hurt you. Still does. This ends now, for better or worse."

"And why tonight?"

"While I've been working this week, I've been thinking. All my life, I've let things control me. I'm not gonna do that anymore."

Anne cracked open the Tab, took a sip, then almost smiled. "'All your life?' Tommy, you're fifteen. You haven't had a life yet."

"Yeah. That's the problem in a nutshell. I'm not fifteen years old, not really."

Anne's eyes fell a bit. "So I wasn't actually there when they got the forceps and worked you out of me? If you aren't fifteen, then just how old do you claim to be?"

"You might want to have the guys from the hospital come with their butterfly nets and take me away, but I don't care. I'm going to tell you the truth."

Anne clamped her lips against a reply, then sat up a little straighter.

"This is going to be hard to hear and harder to tell. I just ask, please let me tell it straight through without stopping me. When I'm done, I'll answer any questions you have, and then you can have me hauled off to the rubber room if you want. Deal?"

Anne hesitated, then nodded. "Sure. Deal."

Great. Now how do I start? At the beginning, I guess.
What the hell is the beginning?
It's where I decide it is.

"Mom, this is the second time I've lived this day. This is the second time I've been fifteen. Next week will be the second time I watch Zack graduate."

Anne's eyes narrowed in doubt.

"I know I look like I'm fifteen, but I'm really fifty-four years old."

"Oh, Tommy," she said, shaking her head in sorrow.

"No, really. My body is fifteen. My mind, my thinking, is fifty-four." Anne's face was compassion for a lost soul. "I'm gonna give you the short version of this. Please?"

"I'm here. I'm silent. Mostly. Go on." The tone of resignation tore at his heart.

"When I lived this part of my life the first time, I was a normal kid. I didn't get in much trouble. I got okay grades. I wasn't as good as Zack was at anything, but that was kind of okay."

"I never thought I'd feel so nostalgic for that," she blurted. "Tommy, I'm sorry. I couldn't help that. I'll hush."

"Mom, it's all right. You have every right. Anyway...the summer after he graduated, before he left for OSU, Zack took me to a party at the lake. It was kind of fun, but Zack drank a lot. A big rainstorm came and broke the party up. I ran to the Camaro, but Zack had passed out on the ground. When I finally got him to the car, I knew he was too drunk to be able to drive. I didn't want us to get in trouble, though, so I put him in the passenger seat and drove home."

Anne had put her feet back on the ground, the Tab forgotten.

"I didn't really know how to drive a stick yet, but eventually I got going, and we were doing okay. Everyone else had already gone, but I found my way out from the lake and onto the highway. At first, I was driving slow, because I didn't know how to drive. But, I was a kid, so eventually I started to go a little faster."

Shame touched Thomas's cheeks. Tears filled his eyes.

"I still didn't know how to shift very well. When I tried to shift into fourth, I had to look down to do it. When I looked back up, there was a deer in the middle of the road." Thomas closed his eyes, spilling tears. "I didn't even think. I just jumped on the brakes and turned the wheel. We missed that deer, but the Camaro started rolling. When we stopped, all I could think was that I had ruined Zack's car, and that you were going to kill both of us."

Thomas paused, gathered himself, looked at Anne's expression of alarm.

"That's when I looked for Zack. He wasn't in his seat any more. He'd been thrown clear and he was laying on the road."

Anne's hand flew to her mouth. *She doesn't believe me yet, but she feels the impact. Sorry, Mom, gotta get this off my chest.*

"He was dead, Mom. I killed Zack." He was crying.

"Oh, honey." Anne shook her head, but still reached out to him. Thomas blew out a full breath, tried to get his voice under control.

"Life just wasn't ever any good after that. I went back to school, I even went to college myself for a while, but nothing turned out right." He laughed slightly. "You and I ended up living together. You were old and retired, and I was dead inside. Then I did something selfish and awful and gutless."

He could not read whatever was in her eyes, except that it involved pain. *No stopping now.*

"Finally, when I got canned from my crappy job selling cars, and couldn't take it one more day, I swallowed a bunch of your pills–which I had filched from your meds, just to show you what sort of a wonderful character I grew up to be–and killed myself. Except I didn't, I guess, because I went to sleep in 2016 and woke up back here on Easter Sunday, 1976. You know the rest, I guess."

"Do I?"

"Oh, hell, I guess not really. But if you look back, that's about when I started to say odd things, sound different, seem weird, right?"

"Maybe," Anne said, but her eyes showed a crack in the front of skeptical sadness.

"See, in 2016, I knew things. I knew how people's lives had gone. One of those things was about Michael Hollister. He became a serial killer and killed twenty-seven people, before science caught up with him and they nailed him. After I killed myself and woke up back here, the first time I saw him, I thought of his future. I thought about all those people he was going to kill. I didn't want them to die, so that's why I've been trying to stop Michael ever since I got back here. As usual, though, just like the way my first life played out, I've totally screwed it up."

"Oh, Tommy, Tommy, Tommy," she sighed. "You seem to be very sure of all this."

"That's not hard when it's true, Mom. I just wanted to make a few things right. I wanted to manage not to kill Zack. I wanted to stop Michael from killing people. I wanted to make things a little better for a few friends. So far, I haven't made any of those things happen. Now I'm getting closer to the time I killed Zack. I'm afraid it's going to happen again."

Anne's face seemed to retreat into the fortress of nursing patience. "That's…that's quite a lot for me to process."

"I know how crazy it sounds. That's why I've haven't told you. You can agree, at least, that I would be reluctant to tell a story like this, and I might think my own mother would have a hard time buying it?"

Anne laughed, just a bit. "I can go that far with you, at least. Is there more?"

Hmmm. I met an angel in a church who could read minds and disappear when she wanted to. Do you want to know about that?

"Yeah, there's some other stuff, but I think we've made enough stops on the crazy train for one night, don't you?"

"I suppose." Anne attempted a smile. "Tommy—"

"You know, you stopped calling me that not too long after the accident. I've been Thomas a lot longer than I was ever Tommy."

"Okay, *Thomas*, I'll do my best, even though you've got to understand how wrong that rings in my ears. I wish I could say I believe you. I can tell that you really believe that what you're telling me is true. And it helps me, because you were right; it hurt me deep down that you weren't trusting me. You and Zack are all I have. I've tried hard to do the best I could, and it felt like rejection. If you are really fifty-four, you'll get that, and why it hurt. So, no matter what, I'm glad that you trusted me enough to share this with me."

"I do get it. Coming back now has reminded me of everything you sacrificed, how hard you worked to give us a good start. That's partly why I told you, because by God, you deserve the truth. But you don't believe me."

Her eyes softened. "All right. We're being honest, full truth, no baloney. Tomm...Thomas, how can I, no matter how much I love you? How can anyone? You know that what you're telling me sounds impossible, goes against all science. No offense, and I'm not hinting I think this is what's up, but it sounds like an LSD trip."

"It does. A bad one, at that."

"So is there a way you can prove it to me? Predict the future, or something?"

Thomas shook his head. "I can sit here for hours and tell you what happened during my lifetime—who the Presidents were, what kind of stuff was invented, where we went to war—but none of it matters because you can't verify any of it, and you will never be able to. Maybe this time Carter beats Reagan in 1980, if they both even run after the mess Carter makes...who knows? As soon as I woke up here, I did things differently and everything has changed now. My first life, I never saw Dad again after he left. Not even at his funeral."

Anne's eyes widened. "If this is true, you know when he's going to die."

Thomas shrugged. "No. I know when he died then. That doesn't mean he'll die at the same time, or the same way this time. Lots of things stay the same, but a lot changes, too."

Anne raised her hand. "Hold on. Don't go anywhere. It was a long shift, with lots of coffee to keep me going. I've got to go to the bathroom."

Or sneak away and call for the medics to take me away. How can I ever let her see the truth?

Two minutes later, she was back. This time, she sat beside Thomas on the couch. "I don't know where we go from here."

I do. Yes!

"Mom, what if I could tell you something that there is no way for me to know?"

Anne shrugged. "I don't know. You could tell me all kinds of things that are going to happen in the future and I wouldn't know if it was true or not. You've always had a good imagination. Plus, based on what you said, maybe they wouldn't happen the same way."

"Right. True. But, what if I could tell you something from the past, something that absolutely no one else knows?"

"I can't imagine what that would be."

A small smile lit Thomas's face, then faded. "In 2009, your Uncle Ted died."

A flicker crossed Anne's face.

"You didn't go to his funeral." He paused to let that sink in. "That was so unlike you. You were the kindest, most generous person I knew, so it was really odd that you didn't go to a relative's funeral, when it was only a half hour's drive away. I also realized that I had never met Uncle Ted, which was weird, too. By then I'd met all the aunts and uncles, on down to the third cousins. But, I'd never met Ted."

Anne's eyes looked over Thomas's shoulder, focused on nothing he could see.

"I probably should have just left you alone about it, but you know me. I don't know when to stop. I want to stop now, but I think I have to see this through. Honesty."

He could see her hand clench the armrest. Her voice radiated dread. "Go on. Tell me."

"I kept pestering you about it, and you kept not telling me. Finally, I broke out my secret weapon. A bottle of Grand Marnier that I'd been saving as a birthday gift for you. You didn't drink much, but you loved that liqueur."

"I haven't had that in ten years! You don't...maybe I'd better not speak too soon. Maybe you do. I'm sorry, Thomas, this is hard."

"I am sure it is, and don't feel bad. All of this is sure to be emotional. So what happened was that I got a few glasses of that down you and...well, you didn't come clean, exactly, but I got the gist of what had happened, why you never went anywhere near Uncle Ted. Do I have to tell you what you told me that night?"

Anne shook her head vehemently. She wiped tears away, but more came. It took all she had to meet his eyes. "Thomas. How could you possibly know that?"

"Because, Mom, my mind is fifty-four, and because that happened the way I describe it. I believed you then, and I would believe you now if you confirmed it, but I won't ask you to. I hated to bring up something so painful. I never will again, but it was the only way I knew to really show you who I am. I want you to believe me. I think I might go a little crazy if I don't have someone to talk to. I had Carrie, but..."

"Hold on. You mean you told Carrie about this? And she believed you?"

"That's one of those 'other things' I wasn't going to talk to you about yet. Carrie had done the same thing. Lived the same life over and over."

"More than once?"

"Yes." *No reason to tell her about all thirteen of her lives, or that she committed suicide in all of them. This is complex enough already.*

"This is so hard for me. But I hear a maturity in your tone, your words. Sounds weird in a teen voice, but the way you think of all this sounds like anything but a teenage boy. Even so, it's still hard."

"I'd be a little worried about you if it wasn't hard for you. This is the most unbelievable thing anyone has ever told you. I understand. I don't expect you to take it all in immediately. It's just that, I'd been lying to you since I got here, and I couldn't keep that up. There was an old Facebook posting—"

"A what?"

"Crap. Sorry. Gotta remember when we still are. It doesn't matter. There was a story about a professor who asked a boy to hold a glass of water out in front of him. It was easy for the boy. It was only a glass of water. But, after fifteen minutes, the glass started to shake. Another ten minutes and the boy dropped the whole thing. It wasn't the weight of the burden, it was how long he'd had to hold it. That's how I was starting to feel—like I was already shaking and about to drop the whole thing."

Anne nodded slowly, but didn't speak.

What a friggin' rollercoaster ride. She believes me, though. She can tell when I'm telling her the truth. So what's she going to do with a time traveling son?

"I can't believe it, but I believe it. I believe you." She rediscovered the can of Tab, took a drink. "Still, I can't let this change everything. You might be older than me on the inside, but your outside still looks like the fifteen-year-old boy I've always loved. So, for all the world to know, that's who you are. Agreed?"

"Agreed. I don't know enough secrets to convince everyone else about who I really am, anyway. And Mom, if there's one person I'd want to be able to tell the whole truth to, it'd be you. I'm happy with that."

Something in Anne's eyes glowed from deep in the soul. "One question, then I want to turn my brain off for the rest of the night. Did you really try to kill Michael Hollister?"

"I did. I mean, that wasn't my intention when I woke up that morning, but when he walked by me in class, all I could think about was what he did to Carrie. I don't even know what happened after that. I really thought I'd killed him, but I guess I just choked him until he passed out, dammit."

"But, how can you be sure he killed her? Just because you remember him killing people?"

"That was part of it, but there was more. Remember, he ate Amy's turd because of me—"

"Okay, if what you say is true, you know why this has to come out." Anne faltered a bit finishing the sentence, then laughed until the tears came. "God, I know I am not supposed to laugh about that, but if he grew up to be a serial killer, then it was the least someone could do, feeding him dog poop. Okay, sorry."

"No problem, Mom. You needed that. And you heard what I told his dad about his animal abuse hobby. So, I knew he wanted to hurt me, and he thought hurting Carrie was the best way to do it. He was right. That's why I asked you where they had found Carrie. As the West Coast Strangler, Michael always put his victims at rest stops. That's why I wasn't surprised when you told me."

"Okay. That might not be enough to convince a judge and jury, but at least I see why you did what you did. Can we agree that's not a good solution, though? No more of that? And please, promise me, no more dog poop sandwiches for anyone?" He could see the stifled laughter as her Mom/nurse persona asserted control.

"Yes." *If the letter works, I won't need to. Is there even a snowball's chance that will work? Based on my track record, the Magic 8 Ball says, "Don't count on it."*

Anne polished off her Tab. "Hungry?"

"Yeah. Starving. Confession is good for the soul, but it makes you hungry, too."

"Well, that, and the full day of chores I left you."

"Good point. Can we talk about a parole from the endless labor?"

Anne ignored that, walked into the kitchen, and put a frying pan on the stove.

Thomas watched her take hamburger out and start forming it into patties. Hamburgers sounded good. He leaned back into the cushions of the couch, and for the first time in months, he relaxed.

Chapter Fifty-Two

Anne let up on the chores list, but she still left Thomas one or two things each day. He didn't mind. Their house was looking rather spiffy relative to their modest neighborhood.

It was mid-afternoon on Thursday, the day before Zack's graduation. Thomas sat at the kitchen table, Algebra II book open in front of him, scratching the back of his head.

Carrie Copeland, where are you when I need you?

The thought made him wince. *Shit.*

He refocused on trying to solve the equation in front of him when he saw Zack's Camaro slide into its customary parking spot. Zack slammed the driver's door behind him. That caught Thomas's attention.

The only time Zack ever hurries is on the track. What fresh hell is this, then?

Zack slammed through the sliding door at the front of the house and exploded into the kitchen.

"Holy shit, did you hear?"

If only I had a small object I could keep in my pocket that would tell me news from all over the world instantaneously.

Zack didn't wait for a reply. "They arrested Michael Hollister."

Thomas jumped up from his chair. "What? When? How? Why?"

Zack stopped dead. "I don't know. That's pretty much all I know. We were in the middle of rehearsal for graduation. They were trying to teach us how to walk together, as if we haven't been doing that since kindergarten. We were listening to the same crappy song over and over again and I was about to lose my mind. It was hot and we were all sweating our asses off because Ms. French was making us wear our stupid robes. Revenge for calling her 'Ms. French Kiss' all those years, I suppose."

Thomas made an impatient *come on, come on* hand gesture.

"Oh. Right. Anyway, two police officers came in and asked to speak to Michael. One of them was that guy that came here to the house. I didn't even think Michael was going to show up for Graduation. He's still looking pretty nasty from the beating you gave him, but he was there."

That almost sounded like pride in his voice. Like Zack is proud of me.

"They stood off to the side talking for a little while, then he put his hands behind his back, they cuffed him and took him away. He looked like he might be crying."

Oh. My. God.

Thomas sat back down, hard.

Was it me? Did I do it? It had to be, right? How else?

Thomas let his head drop, not wanting Zack to see the tears that were forming.

"Oh. Hey. You're not gonna lose it on me again, are you."

Thomas was silent, but shook his head.

Zack moved close to his brother and put an arm around his shoulder. "It's okay. I get it. You can lose it if you want."

Chapter Fifty-Three

By the time Zack, Anne, and Thomas arrived at Graduation the next night, everyone knew the story. The version circulating at Middle Falls High was that Michael Hollister had been enough of an idiot to send a letter taunting the cops, saying he would kill again. The details were a little fuzzy on how they had tracked this letter back to Michael, but somehow they had.

Well, that worked. But he's not convicted yet. His dad has the kind of money that can buy justice.

Thomas spotted Ben and Simon milling around inside.

"Where do you want to sit, Mom? I'm gonna talk to some friends for a minute, then I'll come sit with you."

Simon spotted Thomas and waved him over. "How is Middle Falls High's great white boxing hope? Do you prefer Thomas Ali, or Thomas Frazier? We were just bummed that we didn't get to see you pound the ever-lovin' shit out of Hollister. We would have been cheering you on, and that was before we knew he was going to get arrested."

Thomas blushed slightly. "I shouldn't have done it. You know smug he is. He said something to me about Carrie and the next thing I remember, I was sitting in the Principal's office."

If that had happened in 2016, half a dozen kids would have filmed it with their iPhones and it would have been on YouTube instantly. Another advantage of growing up in the seventies.

"I've been locked up at the house, so other than Zack telling me that he'd been arrested, I haven't heard anything. What have you guys heard?"

Ben started to speak, then hesitated. "Sure you want to know?"

"I'm sure."

"As usual, there's a million rumors, but the gist of it is that Michael was a big enough idiot to send a letter to the cops and somehow they traced it back to him. That was enough to get a search warrant for his house. Even his dad's lawyers couldn't stop that from happening. When they searched his room, they supposedly found a necklace that belonged to Carrie."

Goddamn it. That was a trophy. The sick bastard took a trophy to remember her by. I hope he rots forever in prison. It won't bring Carrie back. Nothing will. It's the best I can do. I've got to let go of the rest.

"And then they searched his car," said Simon.

"When they searched his car, the rumor is that they found some hair and..." Ben looked away, swallowed. "...and, some blood. They're going to test it to see if it's Carrie's blood type and if the hair matches hers. I have no idea how they can tell that. There's some other really crazy stuff, like they found some pretty awful Polaroids, but you know how it is."

"I do. Where are you guys going to sit?"

"No idea," Ben said. "Maybe we can catch up with you after."

"Maybe. Mom wants to take Zack out somewhere after the ceremony, but I have a hunch that's not gonna happen. See ya."

Thomas found Anne, sat down, and waited for things to get underway. All around them, people glanced at Thomas, then looked away. Anne noticed.

"Are you famous or something?" she asked.

"Famous for being the guy that beat up a killer, I guess. I can think of better things to be famous for."

To the strains of *Pomp and Circumstance*, the 279 graduates of Middle Falls High School, Class of 1976, began filtering in to take their seats on the auditorium floor. As a Weaver, Zack was among the last to enter.

Thomas leaned over and whispered to Anne, "Is Dad coming?"

"I don't think so. I haven't seen him or talked to him since he was at the house."

"Good."

The ceremony was as long and boring as any high school graduation. Chipper teacher's pets gave interminable speeches on the value of looking forward, keeping America great, and how putting your nose to the grindstone solves all of life's ills. The commencement speaker was a local pastor who reminded them of the importance God would play in the success or failure of their lives.

One final punishment of ultimate boredom before the system sends them off to the workforce.

At last the time came to hand out the diplomas. By the time Zack got to the stage to receive his, the ceremony had gone on for two and a half hours. Out of the corner of her mouth, Anne said, "I hope Zack doesn't do something stupid here."

Thomas chuckled a little. It would be entertaining to see Zack lift his robe and moon the audience, but he probably wouldn't.

When the announcer finally said, "Zackary David Weaver," Zack bounded up the stairs, turned, took a small, courtly bow to the audience, and accepted his diploma like an adult. Anne let out the breath she had been holding. *She knows it could have been much worse.*

It didn't take long after that. After the expected burst of mature maternal emotion, once outside in the cool night air, Anne grabbed Zack.

"We're going out to grab a late dinner to celebrate. Are you coming?"

Zack, so tall in his cap and gown, looked down at his mom and kissed her cheek. "Yeah... no. Places to be, people to do and all that, you know."

Anne lifted her eyebrows at Zack, a sure-fire warning. Even that wasn't enough to bring him back to earth.

"Gotta run. Love you!"

And he was gone.

"Looks like it's just the two of us, Mom."

"In more ways than one, huh? Soon, he'll be gone for good."

Hopefully only in the empty nest sense, rather than the previous life's sense.

Anne's eyes were misty. "So, where do you want to go? I'm buying."

"Anywhere. Or, we can just go home, heat up some leftovers, and see what's on TV."

Anne whispered into Thomas's ear, "Sometimes I love having a middle-aged teenage son."

Chapter Fifty-Four

The next week, Thomas got their old lawnmower out of the shed, gave it a tune-up, and put signs up around the neighborhood, offering to mow anyone's lawn for $5. He soon had a sunburnt nose, grass-stained socks, and all the work he could handle.

Maybe I can get enough to buy myself a beater car before Zack leaves. I really don't want to have to ride the bus all next year. I remember in Back to the Future, *Michael J. Fox made himself rich by betting on sporting events. Unfortunately, I didn't bring a sports almanac with me, don't remember any of it, and would have no idea how a fifteen-year-old kid could place a bet in Middle Falls, Oregon, anyway.*

Each day, he took his pay and added it to the roll he had tucked away at the back of his sock drawer. *Another fifty lawns and I might be able to swing a '62 Dodge Dart in serious need of new springs and tires.*

Zack spent the summer like a burned out businessman on a three-month holiday. The worries and responsibilities of high school were behind him, and he was not the type of person to anticipate any troubles that college might bring. Time passed, Thomas mowed, Zack partied, and every day the date of the accident drew one day nearer. The closer it got, the tighter Thomas felt.

Everything I've seen since I got back here tells me that things change. Nothing has played out the same. Still, I remember Carrie telling me that Zack had died in every single one of her lives. It's possible that Zack's death is one of those watershed moments, and there is nothing I can do about it.

Finally, the day arrived: Friday, August 13th, 1976. The day had loomed so large for so long that it felt a little disorienting to see it dawn.

Thomas woke up early, showered, and checked his mower before hitting the first of three jobs he had scheduled for the day.

Things are different already. Last time, I think I slept 'til noon and didn't do a lick of work.

He got home from the third job a little after noon and made himself a ham sandwich and soup. He was almost done when Zack wandered into the kitchen, hair askew, sleepy-eyed.

"What time is it?"

"Almost 1:00, princess. Must be nice to do nothing but sleep all day."

Zack smiled muzzily, smacked his lips, and said, "Yeah, actually, it is. Hey, by the way, there's another party tonight, out at Victoria's house. I promised you I'd take you to one of my parties before I went off to college, so we better do it tonight. I'm leaving for school pretty soon. Capiche?"

Okay. That doesn't necessarily mean anything. Same date, but it's a party, not a kegger at the lake, right?

"Ah, that's all right, Zack. You don't have to."

"You're right, I don't, but I promised you on your birthday that I would take you and introduce you. I'm getting a little partied out, so this might be the last one I go to before I leave for school."

Which is better? Change the scenario even more by not being there, or try to change things as they might happen by being there? Crap, nothing is ever easy.

"Okay. That's cool."

Zack looked Thomas up and down. "You're filling out a little bit. Maybe you'll be an athlete yet. We leave at seven, so be ready."

Thomas nodded, got up, and went back into his bedroom to add the day's pay to his bankroll. *This whole thing feels different. When I was a kid, I was excited. Couldn't wait to go. Now, I wish I could be anywhere else.*

A little before seven, Zack wandered out into the living room smelling like Brut cologne and Irish Spring. "Ready, Squirt?"

Thomas had been busy finding nothing in the paper about Michael Hollister's upcoming trial. "Ready!" He tried to sound more enthusiastic than he felt.

"Did you leave Mom a note?"

"Yeah."

But I didn't say, 'By the way, this is the same day I killed Zack last time.' No sense in worrying her more than she already is.

"Okay, let's roll." Zack jumped down the stairs, jogged to the Camaro and did a perfect Starsky and Hutch slide across the hood.

I don't like this at all.

The Camaro rumbled to life. After a short pause, the 8-track started to play. Thomas held his breath, but it wasn't *Trampled Under Foot*. It was *My Time of Dying*; not much better. Zack cranked it up so the bass caused the windows to rattle.

"Hey, Zack," Thomas shouted. "Wanna listen to something else?"

Zack fished under his seat for a minute, then brought out another 8-track. He blew the dust bunnies off of it, then held it up for Thomas to read: *The Bay City Rollers Greatest Hits*. "Sure, dorkus, let's get jacked up to party with a little Bay City Rollers! Yeah!"

Thomas laughed. "Why do you have a Bay City Rollers tape?"

"Grandma gave it to me for Christmas last year, remember? She said that the clerk at the store had told her it was what all the kids were listening to. I think he just had a few too many copies of this in the store room and he knew a sucker when he saw one."

"How about the radio?"

"How about if we listen to The Hammer of the Freakin' Gods and get in the mood to party?" Zack cranked the volume knob until Thomas felt it in his chest.

"Okay," Thomas said, but it didn't matter. His words were lost in a tornado of bass, guitar, and the wail of Robert Plant.

They drove through town and took enough turns that Thomas felt thoroughly lost. *Still not sure how everyone manages to get around without GPS.* Zack seemed confident, making turn after turn, then slowed and turned down a long driveway that twisted through a quarter mile of woods before opening into a clearing with an oversized lodge-style house. There were already half a dozen cars parked around the circular driveway when Zack pulled up behind a white Jeep and killed the engine.

Thomas opened his mouth wide, trying to pop his ears after the onslaught of the music in the car, then heard Molly Hatchet blaring from inside the house.

"Looks like they started without me. What kind of a party can it be, though, if I'm not there yet?"

Good old modest Zack. Gotta love him.

Zack and Thomas walked through the open double front doors, but the inside was mostly deserted. A set of double French doors opened onto an expansive multi-level cedar deck. Beyond that, Thomas could see a swimming pool.

"Jesus, who lives here?"

"Victoria Marsh. Her parents own the cement plant. I guess they're doing okay for themselves," Zack said. "Okay, you're here. Grab a beer if you want one, you're on your own now. Don't cramp my style."

Zack wandered past a table containing clear plastic glasses of beer, grabbed one and downed it. He looked at the immense figure behind the keg. "Tiny."

"Zack."

Zack plucked another cup of beer up and headed for the pool, where three girls in bikini tops and cutoffs were moving to catch the last rays of sunlight.

Thomas looked around the house, which was decorated as tastefully as any house was in 1976, forgiving the multiple animal heads that hung around the immense room. He thought of Dudley Moore in *Arthur*, talking to the mounted moose head: "This is a tough room. But I don't have to tell you that."

"Daddy's quite the hunter, isn't he?"

Thomas jumped. "Uh, hi."

"Sorry. Didn't mean to sneak up on you. I'm Victoria."

Victoria Marsh was a pretty blonde with a radiant smile. *Oh, she's going to have it rough in life. Beautiful, blonde, and rich.*

"Nice to meet you. I'm Tommy Weaver."

"Oh, I know. I'm glad you came. I think everyone knows who you are since, well, since…you know."

Thomas just nodded. *No doubt the first of many awkward moments.*

"Make yourself at home. Where did your brother wander off to?"

"I think he's out by the pool."

"Figures. That's where the girls are. Ta-ta."

He walked onto the back deck and nodded at Tiny, who lifted a cup of beer toward him, but Thomas held up a hand.

"No thanks. I don't drink."

"You're at a kegger, man. Everyone drinks."

Thomas smiled, "Everyone but me, but thanks."

"You sure?"

"Dead sure. Appreciate it." *Great choice of words, Weaver.*

"No problemo," shrugged Tiny. "More for me."

"There you go."

The night crawled by. Whatever interest young Tommy might have found in the various mating and drinking rituals of the mid-seventies teenager meant nothing to Thomas. He did his best to keep an eye on Zack, but that proved all but impossible. Every time Thomas saw him, he had a new cup of beer in his hand, and his arm around a different girl. For Zack, every party was a smorgasbord of bacchanalian options.

It'll be all right. If he passes out, I'll get him home. I'm not a scared fifteen-year-old kid any more.

After it started to get dark, glow lights and tiki torches lit the back yard. The music shifted from the Doobie Brothers and Lynyrd Skynyrd to the Commodores and Marvin Gaye. A lot of people had paired off and headed to a bedroom, or even behind the bushes lining the pool area.

Thomas looked to the sky, praying for a sudden thunderstorm that might once again end the party, as well as his suffering. There were clouds, but they didn't look that threatening.

He felt a brush of warm skin against his and looked into the bottle-green eyes and lavish smile of Amanda Jarvis. Thomas nodded at her.

"You're Tommy, Zack's little brother, right?"

"Right. You and I've had classes together since sixth grade, when you moved here."

Her glassy eyes didn't seem to compute that. She laughed in what she imagined was a sultry way.

This is like an off-kilter echo of the kegger at the lake. Nothing else has matched up this closely. Or maybe I just don't remember most days as clearly as I do this one.

"So. My cousin is here at the party tonight, but she's not having a very good time." Amanda stuck her lower lip out in a face she no doubt considered irresistibly persuasive. *And it's repellent.* She laid a hand on his arm. "She wants to leave, but I'm still having a good time. Would you hang out with her for a while? Kind of keep her occupied?"

"I don't mind, Amanda. Where is she?"

"Over there by the fire pit, by herself. Her name is Georgia."

"Ah," he said, feigning unfamiliarity. "Sure. I'll go talk to her." *At least that will help pass the time.*

Thomas maneuvered through the slow dancers, stepped over one prone body on the deck, checked and saw it wasn't Zack, then sat down next to Georgia and said, "Hey. I'm Tommy."

"I'm Georgia. I saw you talking to my Amanda. Did she send you over to babysit me so she can get more stoned or drunk before we leave?"

He laughed a little. "You know how girls like Amanda are. This is it, for her. High school is the pinnacle." Thomas paused, thought back to his Facebook feed, forgot himself for a moment. "Once she graduates, she'll go to work for some company as a receptionist, hook up with the boss, get pregnant, then get dumped." *Weaver, you idiot! This is not the time or place!* "I kind of feel sorry for her."

Georgia turned her full attention on Thomas. "You're unusual. Have you been to a lot of these parties?"

"Nope, this is my first one. You?"

"Unfortunately. Amanda uses me as cover with Aunt Molly. She thinks we're at the movies right now."

"Oh, great. What aren't you seeing?"

Georgia laughed a little. "Tonight, I think we aren't seeing *The Omen*. Too bad, it looked kind of good."

"Right, the one about the creepy kid with 666 tattooed on his skull."

"Oh, have you seen it?"

Thomas started to say, "A long time ago," but wised up. "Nah, just heard a lot about it."

"So, why is this your first party? Aren't you one of the cool kids?"

"Nope," Thomas said. "I'm one of the Dungeons & Dragons kids."

"Never heard of that."

"You are not alone."

Their conversation went on much longer than it had the first time around. Thomas explained about Dungeons & Dragons. Georgia wasn't all that interested, but listened anyway.

She talked about astronomy, and Thomas was interested in that, so he didn't have to fake listening.

While they talked, the night grew dark. When the fire lit Georgia's face, she looked quite fetching. *Smart, too. Probably too smart for me. But the big problem is that I am a middle-aged man, she is a teenage girl, and it doesn't matter how mature and intelligent she is. We don't do that.*

I guess in Carrie's case, the fact that we were both recycled from past suicides overcame that for me.

Thomas's reverie was interrupted by a boy laughing and shouting, "Weaver just puked in the pool!"

Georgia raised up from her chair and asked, "Does he belong to you?"

"Kind of. He's my big brother. This is his last high school party, and I think he's overdone it."

"Apparently."

"'Scuse me." Thomas stood up for a better view and saw Zack laying vertically to the pool, his head hanging over the edge. A slick of beer and bile spread out on the water in front of him.

"That's gross, Zack!" screamed a girl, backing away and scanning her front for vomit splatter. Thomas ran to Zack, kneeled, and rolled him away from the pool.

"Zack, you okay?"

"Never better," slurred Zack. "Why do you ashk?"

"Because you just spewed all over the pool."

Zack didn't answer. He was passed out.

Thomas looked around. Tiny Patterson was still manning the keg. Leaving Zack where he lay, Thomas approached Tiny. "Hey. Zack's wasted. I think I need to get him home."

"What a lightweight," Tiny said.

Thomas nodded. "Here's my problem. I can't carry him to the car. Can you give me a hand?"

Tiny replied with a massive, echoing belch. He then walked to Zack, picked him up, and tossed him over his shoulder. *Never imagined anyone could do that, but there we go.* He waved a goodbye to Georgia, then jogged ahead of Tiny to the Camaro. He opened the passenger door and stood back.

Tiny deposited Zack in the seat, although not without bonking his head into the door frame. "Oops. Sorry."

"As hungover as he'll be tomorrow, he'll have a heck of a time distinguishing one headache from another. Thanks, Tiny."

"No problem. Tell Zack I had to carry his scrawny ass to the car when he wakes up."

"Sure will."

Thomas looked in the ignition; no keys. He searched Zack's pocket until he found them. *Shit. Almost forgot.* He reached across Zack, found the seatbelt, and struggled with it until Zack was buckled in. "You are like dead weight, dude."

Thomas clambered into the driver's seat, moved it up, adjusted the rearview mirror, and turned the key. The 8-track clicked, then began to play *Trampled Underfoot*.

Oh, hell no.

Thomas ripped the tape out and threw it in the backseat. Silence. *Perfect. Okay. It's been a little while, but I've been driving all my life. I'm fine.*

Thomas flicked the headlights on, checked for the high beam indicator, slipped into reverse, gave it a little gas, and slowly let out the clutch. The Camaro backed slowly into the pickup behind him with a mild *bonk/crunch* sound. "Sorry," he said to himself, then slipped the gearshift into first and pulled out. *We will worry about auto insurance, fault percentage, and all that when I get Zack home alive.*

Rain drops, thick and warm, spattered against the windshield.

Of course. Why not? Driving home in the dark is always more fun when it rains. Thomas fidgeted until he found the wiper controls. He waited while the windshield turned muddy, then cleared.

He drove down the long driveway at five miles per hour, found the county road, and turned right.

Really should have paid better attention on the way in here. Liable to wind up in Eastern Oregon if I'm not careful.

The road was deserted. Thomas kept the Camaro just under the speed limit. After a few miles, he saw something in the road and slowed below ten miles per hour. It was a doe, eyes reflected in his headlights, standing in the middle of the road staring at him. Thomas pulled the Camaro over to a complete stop ten yards away.

No way that is the same doe. Just a coinkeedink, right? Step aside, Bambi.

Thomas beeped the horn. The deer didn't move immediately, but eventually sauntered away to his left.

Was that it? Was that the moment? Are we in the clear now?

I'm not taking any chances. I won't get a second, unless I manufacture it with tranquilizers and vodka, or a noose or something.

Thomas downshifted and headed back toward Middle Falls. The rest of the drive into town was uneventful. The rain continued to fall, the wipers slapped, and Thomas sat ramrod straight, hands at 10 and 2, watching everything.

In town, Thomas relaxed a little bit as he coasted up Umpqua Street to the red light at Main Street, the town's busiest arterial intersection. Relief and many other emotions were flooding through him. Zack sat buckled safely in the seat beside him; he hadn't even barfed again. Not that Zack was any prize, naturally, with drool running into the vomit on his Pink Floyd T-shirt. *Don't care. Glad you're still here, brother.*

A long horn blast came from behind him. *Damn. Too wound up and then unwound to notice the green light.* He gave the Camaro a little gas and started across the intersection.

As he did, a four-door sedan's driver reaped the outcome of a misjudged yellow light, screaming into the intersection. Thomas picked it up from the corner of his left eye. "Shit!" he yelled as he slammed on the brakes.

The car behind him hit the Camaro's rear bumper, adding a new bit of minor damage. The oncoming sedan was able to swerve just enough to miss the Camaro before it finished running the red light. The driver had his arm out the window, middle finger extended above.

Thomas's heart felt like the stereo's bass cranked to the maximum. He let out a deep breath, looked right. Zack slumbered on. Thomas turned the ignition off, undid his seat belt, and jumped out of the car. Behind him, a heavy middle-aged man was also getting out.

"Sorry I hit you, son. I thought you were going through. Damned good thing you didn't, though. Did you see that guy? Like a bat out of hell! If you had gone when the light turned, they'd be scraping you up off the road."

Thomas nodded. Before anyone could see his hands shaking, he stuck them in his pockets.

Fear.

Adrenaline.

Gratitude for being alive.

He cleared his throat, but couldn't clear the tremor from his voice. "Yeah. I guess I was daydreaming when the light changed. Saved our asses, though."

"Our?"

"My brother's asleep up front."

The man looked at Thomas more intently. "Are you old enough to have a license?"

"I've got my permit. My brother's got a license, though, so we're good."

Thomas looked at the back of the Camaro, using the man's headlights for illumination. A small smudge scarred the back of the Camaro's bumper.

"Since you've just got your permit, and since your brother is "sleeping" in the front, I see no need to report this. I don't want to get you kids in trouble."

"Sure. Whatever." *Asshole. Pushing a kid around so you don't have to report an accident for which you surely would be found at fault, and they would crank up your insurance premiums.*

Whatever. Just glad we are alive.

Thomas climbed into the Camaro and drove Zack safely home. When he pulled into Zack's spot, he turned the key off, looked at Zack, still passed out, and cried.

Chapter Fifty-Five

The house felt strangely empty when Zack left for Oregon State a few weeks later. Everything seemed to echo and reverberate in a way it hadn't while filled with Zack's plus-size personality.

Thomas didn't mourn too long. He spent a few of his hard-earned dollars on some posters of his own, bought paint to cover the Bicentennial-themed walls, and otherwise made the room his own. It felt a lot better than the last time the room had become his.

Billy Steadman's parents had moved to Maine a year earlier than they had in his first life, but Thomas had made sure to write down all his contact information before he left. *And I will write him actual letters and pay enormous long distance charges. I will not lose a friend like that, then get him back after thirty years when someone invents social media.*

When he rolled into school the first day of his sophomore year, Ben and Simon were waiting inside the doors, just like always. "Hey, man," Thomas greeted them.

"Hey, Tommy!" they answered. "You need a haircut," added Simon, rubbing his fresh crewcut. "All the cool kids are acting like it's 1965 all over again."

"That's all right, I'll pass, Sgt. Rock."

"Anything new?" Ben asked.

"Oh, right! I haven't seen you guys in a couple weeks. Come on, let's go outside. We've got time before assembly."

Thomas led them out to the back of the parking lot where a sky blue 1964 Plymouth Fury was parked. At least, it was sky blue where there wasn't rust or primer.

"Whaddya think?"

"I think," Simon said, "that someone at the school district forgot to pay the trash company this summer, and heaps like this are the price we have to pay."

Thomas laughed. "Okay, so it's not beautiful. It had one feature that I couldn't resist. The guy only wanted $400 for it."

"That's a pretty irresistible feature, all right," Ben said.

"I'd be sold," laughed Simon.

Thomas opened the door proudly, revealing the torn upholstery and foam peeking through.

"It's not quite in the same league as Zack's Camaro. But, it runs good, and it beats holy hell out of riding the school bus every day."

Ben and Simon both immediately stopped laughing at him.

"So," Simon said, "my very, very good compadre, what do you say to picking me up before school in the morning?"

"I say I'll pick both of you up every morning if you kick in two bucks a week for gas and oil. This thing burns through both."

They turned and walked together into their brand new school year.

Chapter Fifty-Six

Zack's first track meet of the season was an invitational at Corvallis on January 29th, 1977. Anne and Thomas drove up to root him on. Zack hadn't been home often, just once for Thanksgiving and a week at Christmas. They both missed him. Based on the bear hug he gave them both when he saw them before that first meet, the feeling was mutual.

"How goes it, big brother?"

Zack put his arm around Thomas. "It's tough out here, little brother. Beautiful coeds everywhere, parties every night. I don't think this is the life for you."

"Hopefully there's some studying going on occasionally too?" Anne asked.

Zack looked wounded, then turned back to Thomas. "That's the other thing. They expect you to actually study here. No more bullshit, look-something-up-in-the-encyclopedia-the-hour-before-class-starts kind of work. Seriously, it's cutting into my social commitments."

Thomas nodded toward the track. "You gonna kick ass and take names today?"

A serious expression crossed Zack's face. "It's different here. I'm a much smaller fish in a much larger ocean. I'm gonna give it my best, though."

Thomas and Anne found seats in the cavernous old Bell Field stadium. They had brought blankets and a thermos of hot chocolate. Zack was only scheduled to run the 880 today, which didn't run until halfway through the events. Anne and Thomas rooted loudly for all the Beavers, not just out of loyalty, but to try and keep warm.

Finally, they spotted Zack peeling off his warmups and doing his stretching exercises. He approached the starting line, scanned the stadium until he located them, then got into his stance. Ten runners took off at the gun and they were bunched in a pack when they hit the first turn. Coming out of that turn, two runners had a few steps of separation. Neither one was Zack. Thomas and Anne both yelled at the top of their lungs, but it was lost in the crowd noise.

By the end of the second lap, it was obvious that Zack wasn't just laying back waiting for an opportunity. He was giving it all he had. The field had separated by then, making it easy to see that he had come in fifth out of ten finishers. After he had showered, Zack met them back at Anne's station wagon.

"See? I told you guys. It's tough out here. Pretty much every kid on that field was the best athlete in their school."

Anne hugged him, kissed his cheek. "You did wonderfully! How was your time?"

"Actually, two-tenths faster than I ever ran last year. Good for fifth place." He shook his head.

"How about dinner out? Maybe Sizzler? I'm buying."

"I was so nervous this morning that I threw up. I'm starved and empty, so I might make you regret that offer."

Chapter Fifty-Seven

Thomas's sophomore year was much less eventful than his first year. No serial killers to track, no blossoming romance, no brothers to worry about not killing. Older boys did not pick on him to any significant degree. *Because once you go psycho one time, they never know if you might do it again.*

At OSU, Zack's track meets went along like the first. He continued to work hard and improve, but he wasn't setting the world on fire. He had once dreamed of improving enough to run in the Olympics in Los Angeles in 1980, but reality was chasing that dream away.

One Saturday evening in mid-March, Anne and Thomas were in the living room eating pork chops and mashed potatoes, watching Jessica Savitch read the news on NBC. The phone rang.

"I'll get it," Thomas said, hustling to the kitchen. "Hello?"

"Tommy?"

It was Zack, but he sounded strange. Far away. "Hey, brother! How was the meet today."

"Good and bad, I guess. Any day we beat the freakin' Ducks is a good day, but…"

Thomas waited through a five-second silence.

"Zack? Are you there? You okay?"

"Uhh...yeah. I'm here. I'm calling from the hospital. I'll say one thing for this place. They've got the good drugs."

"What the hell's going on?"

Hearing Thomas's tone, Anne jumped up and grabbed the telephone. "Zack? Zackary? Are you okay? What's going on?"

"Hi, Mom. Yeah, I'm kind of okay. I was running the 880 today. I was running against that guy I beat in the state finals last year. I knew I wasn't going to win the race, but I was sure as hell gonna beat him. I was ahead of him, too, but..."

"But, what?"

"On the second lap, I heard a pop in my left leg. Next thing I knew, I was face down, eating track gravel. They brought me into the hospital here in Eugene. The doctor just told me I completely ruptured my Achilles tendon."

Anne's hand flew to her mouth. Her voice remained calm. "We'll be there in an hour."

They made it in fifty minutes.

Chapter Fifty-Eight

Zack took the rest of the semester off. It was possible that he could have gotten around the campus in a wheelchair, then crutches, but everyone thought it was in his best interest to take a few months to recuperate and return for Fall Quarter. The best news was that his coach had told him his scholarship would be good whether or not he was able to rejoin the team. Both of them knew Zack would never run as fast as he had before.

He hobbled around the house in a full-leg cast, with the toes facing slightly downward to allow the tendon to heal. The Camaro sat unused in the driveway. Thomas offered to drive it for him, but aside from bringing it home from Corvallis, Zack was uninterested. He was a lost boy, laying on the couch, watching game shows and the afternoon movie. As smart as he was, Zack hadn't been a big reader and he didn't change that habit now.

The third week of March was Spring Break. The Sunday before it started, Thomas plopped down in the chair beside Zack, who was laid out in his semi-permanent spot on the couch.

"Hey, lazy butt."

Zack ignored him.

"Wanna go do something tomorrow?"

Zack turned. "Sure. What's up, wanna shoot some hoops? Go hiking? Run down to the Y for a swim? I'm up for anything." He turned back to the TV. "Oh, wait. I forgot, I'm crippled up and in a cast. Guess you're gonna have to do it yourself."

"Seriously. How long has it been since you've been out of the house? Three weeks? A month?"

"Look. I don't tease you about being a doofus and being socially retarded...well, wait a minute. I do, but I've been meaning to stop."

"Michael Hollister's trial starts tomorrow."

That caught Zack's attention.

"It was originally scheduled for six months ago, but his dad's lawyers keep getting it postponed. It's finally going to start tomorrow. I was thinking we could both go."

"Yeah. I'd like to see that. I'm not very portable at the moment, though."

"We can make it work. We can take my car—"

"—We can take our lives in your hands, you mean."

"—and I can fix up the backseat so you can ride back there. Whaddya say?"

A champagne bottle popped on the TV screen. Bubbles floated across it. Lawrence Welk said, "This week-a, we are celebrating our wunnerful nation. To start us off-a, here's Norma Zimmer, and God-a Bless America."

Zack hung his head. When he looked up, his eyes hinted of desperation. "Okay. I can't take any more of this. What time does it start?"

"Ten A.M. I don't know if there's going to be a crowd there or not, so I want to be there when the courthouse opens at nine."

They left the house the next morning at 8:30. Thomas hadn't anticipated that Zack might be an asset. Thanks to him, he was able to park in the handicapped spot right in front of the courthouse. They got passed through every line and slowdown without having to wait. When they got to Courtroom A, the big double doors were locked.

A guard noticed them. "You boys here for the trial?"

"Yes, sir," Thomas said.

Zack leaned on his crutches and looked winded, which was only partially an act. He hadn't walked so far since his injury.

The guard checked his watch. "You're here too early. It doesn't start for another forty-five minutes."

"We know," Thomas said. "We just wanted to make sure we got a seat. Didn't know if it was going to be crowded or not."

The guard peered at the small bulletin board next to the door. "Oh, it's the murder trial. Well, there will be more people than normal here. We don't get a lot of those. This courtroom hasn't been really packed since the Mayor's wife was on trial for shooting the Mayor and the young man he was with. Now that was a trial." He looked Zack up and down. "Tell you what. There are a few people in there getting everything set up, but if you can be quiet, I'll let you in now, so you can find a seat."

"Deal!" Thomas said.

Two minutes later, they were settled in a middle row all the way to the left of the courtroom, so Zack's cast was safely against the wall.

They spent the next half hour sitting quietly amid the setting and ritual tools of justice: the immense desk high at the front of the room, the gold-fringed flags of the United States and Oregon, the small desk where the court reporter would sit, the witness box.

As they waited, Thomas thought of Carrie.

She's been gone almost a year now, but I think of her every day. This brings her back. Can I feel her spirit here?

No. She's gone. Been gone since the moment Michael killed her. Hope you're happy wherever you are, Carrie Copeland. You were a sweet, intelligent girl. You deserved better endings than a dozen-plus suicides and one murder.

Thomas closed his eyes and a memory flooded in. He and Carrie sitting for the first time in the church, lit by a single small candle. She was singing *Amazing Grace*. Thomas's throat grew thick. *Thank you, Carrie. I do remember.*

Two bailiffs brought Michael Hollister in through a side door, wearing a dark suit and tie, eyes cast down. He didn't seem to notice Thomas. The bailiffs guided him to the left-hand table and sat him down amidst a squad of attorneys. There was Mr. Radishaw, but today he was lower on the legal food chain; he sat at the far end, next to a wall. Three other attorneys surrounded Michael and occasionally consulted with three other younger attorneys who couldn't get a space at the table, but instead sat in the front row of spectator seats.

Of course. The best defense money can buy.

Well, not quite. The best defense is innocence, but I know he doesn't have that on his side.

At 9:45, the double doors at the rear of the courtroom opened with a clang. A line of people filed in. The first person in the door was Gerald Copeland, looking thinner and grayer than he had a year earlier.

Losing both your wife and daughter in a short period of time will do that for you.

Mr. Copeland made eye contact with Thomas, then took a seat directly behind the prosecution table. He turned his head slightly toward the back of Michael's head and kept it there for long minutes.

A respectable crowd filtered into the rest of the dozen rows of seats. There were a fair number of people, but it wasn't overflowing. A rich kid murdering some unknown girl was interesting, but not in the same class as a mayor's wife shooting His Honor and His Lover. The proceedings didn't start right on time. A few minutes after ten o'clock, a bailiff said, "All rise, for the Honorable Judge Harrison Galvan."

Having readied his crutches, Zack stood with the rest. A trim, grey-haired, grey-bearded man in his sixties entered the room, wearing the traditional robes of the judiciary. Judge

Galvan climbed up behind the desk and sat down. "Please be seated."

The first half hour was all procedural—the judge instructing the jury, going over the schedule, and warning the crowd against any verbal outbreaks.

Michael's attorneys got first crack at the opening statement. His lead attorney was tall, tan, and exuded an air of confidence.

No way he comes from Middle Falls. Nobody around here looks like that. They must have brought him down from Portland, or up from San Francisco. It's good to be rich.

"Ladies and gentlemen of the jury, my name is Harvey Belk. I represent Mr. Hollister. First, I would like to thank you for your service today. I won't take up a lot of your time with my opening statement. Frankly, I hope the entire trial won't take too much of your time. At the same time, we have to remember the seriousness of the proceedings. A young man's life is in your hands."

He looks like Gordon Gekko, but he talks like he's one of the locals.

Mr. Belk's opening statement, lasting less than fifteen minutes, was long on indignity that an innocent young high-achieving scholar had been locked up in the county jail for nearly a year. He failed to mention that those delays had resulted from his own numerous pretrial motions.

The prosecution's statement wasn't as showy, but Thomas was finally able to get a good idea what evidence they really did have, a year's worth of rumors aside.

The lead prosecutor, George Jameson, was a paunchy fortysomething with a bad spine and a suit that screamed "public servant." His still-red hair had a cowlick. When he looked at the jury, he squinted through thick glasses.

A contrast in styles, to say the very least.

Mr. Jameson didn't have an ounce of showboat in him, but he was prepared. He laid out the state's case slowly, point by point. He started with the letter, told how it led the police to Michael Hollister. Thomas watched Michael shake his head vehemently and scribble a note to his attorney when the letter was mentioned.

Still haven't figured that part out, have you, asshole?

The prosecutor listed the evidence they found when they executed the search warrant on his home and automobile. They had found a number of hairs and a dot of blood in the Karmann Ghia's trunk, both matching Carrie's types. Upon searching Michael's room, they had found a small hidey-hole holding Carrie's necklace and her church key. The prosecutor said he would produce a witness who would testify that a mark on Carrie's shoulder matched Michael Hollister's bite pattern.

A bite mark. Son of a bitch. I'd like you to get off, so I can take another shot at killing you. If you do, this time I'll make sure nothing and no one stops me. To go by the expression on Mr. Copeland's face, he was thinking along the same lines.

Given what I said to Michael's dad in the principal's office, I wonder why no one summoned me to testify. I guess the only person in that room who would have said anything was Mr. Vincent, and he decided not to escalate conflict with C. Moneybags Hollister. Or if Mr. Vincent did say anything, maybe the firm of Letta, Crook, and Skaate got it thrown out as 'prejudicial to my client.'

Thomas remembered high-profile murder trials stretching on for days, weeks, and months. Judge Galvan was going to have none of that. Before adjourning for the day, he laid out the schedule for the next day. The last witness would be heard before lunch, final arguments would be in the afternoon, and the case would be in the jury's hands before dinner.

Thomas and Zack waited all day to see if Michael might turn around and notice them, but he didn't. As they worked their way out of the courtroom, Thomas said, "Wait. Did you see his mom or dad there?"

"I wouldn't know 'em if they were sitting right next to us. Would you?"

"Yeah. They came in to the office and tried to get me arrested the day I did my best to choke him out."

"Slightly ironic."

"Yeah. They weren't there today. Odd. Maybe they are embarrassed?"

"Or maybe they want to wait until they know if they have a convicted murderer in the family before they are seen with him again."

"His stock has gone down and cut its dividend. Time for Hollister Inc. to sell shares in Michael."

"Cut their losses."

Chapter Fifty-Nine

The next day, they arrived early again. Again, the same guard let them in early to reclaim their seats.

The prosecution wrapped up the People's case early in the morning. All of the trial was difficult to watch, but the testimony of the bite mark expert was hardest. Seeing pictures of not one, but a number of pictures of different bites blown up and projected onto a screen was almost too much for Thomas to bear.

The defense only had a handful of witnesses, but they were impressive. One witness disagreed with the State's expert on the bite marks. The State's expert came from the state crime lab. The defense's was a criminology professor from Stanford. Another testified as to the sketchiness and difficulty in identifying specific people via hair strands. Finally, Harvey Belk called one of the policemen who served the warrant.

"Sir," Belk asked, "Does this appear to be the necklace you claim to have found in the Hollister bedroom?"

A titter ran through the courtroom as the fifty-something police officer retrieved a pair of reading glasses from his pocket. He stared through them, then said, "I guess so. Looks like it to me."

"Good. Thank you." Belk reached into his pocket and pulled another, identical necklace out. "Then how about this one?" He looked at the jury. "Or, how about any of these?" He pulled out a handful of identical necklaces.

Jameson jumped out of his chair like his hair was on fire. "Objection. Your Honor, please. The defense is presenting evidence that was not entered into the court's log."

"Sustained. Mr. Belk, these theatrics may work elsewhere, but I advise you to follow my rules while you are in my court, or I will find you in contempt."

As if astonished, Belk returned the necklaces to his pocket. He seemed to wink at the jury as he returned to his place at the table. "No more questions, Your Honor. The defense rests."

The judge looked at the large clock at the back of the room. "Ladies and gentlemen of the jury, it is 3:45. You may retire to the jury room and elect a foreman. You are to consider only evidence heard in this courtroom over the last two days. If you haven't reached a verdict by 5:00, you may return to your homes, in which case you must be back here at 10 AM tomorrow to reconvene."

The jury stood and filed out. Thomas looked at Zack. "Okay, ready to head out?"

"Hell no! I think they're gonna fry his ass, and I want to be here to see it."

"They can't fry his ass, genius. We haven't had the death penalty for over ten years, so the most they can do is lock him up for life. They probably won't come to any kind of a verdict today, then we'll just be sitting here for another hour for nothing. How's your leg?"

Zack shrugged. "It hurts, but you know what? I haven't thought about that all day, and that's more than I can say when I'm home laying on the couch."

Gerald Copeland approached. Thomas stood. "Hello, Mr. Copeland."

"Hello, Tommy. I've seen you here the last few days. I wanted to let you know I appreciate it. I know Carrie would have too."

"Mr. Copeland, I've been meaning to stop by to talk to you. I..." Thomas looked at the front of the courtroom, where Michael was being led away. "I've felt guilty about what happened that night. If I had been there when I was supposed to, or if I hadn't started things with Michael to begin with—"

"Stop." Gently, but firmly. "Just stop. There's nothing good down that road, and it doesn't do either of us any good to think about it, although I have a hunch we've both lost a lot of sleep doing just that."

"Yes, sir."

"All right, then. Just wanted to tell you that." He turned and walked back to his seat, where he would have a perfect view of Michael if he were led in to hear the verdict.

At 4:55, while Thomas and Zack were getting restless, the bailiff came back in the room. "All rise."

Judge Galvan entered. "Be seated."

The jury filed silently back into their seats. The spectator section was nearly empty. Finally, the bailiffs led Michael Hollister back in. They escorted him to his seat amongst his defense team. His usual arrogance was gone. He looked tired and scared.

The judge banged his gavel. "Members of the jury, have you reached a verdict?"

A matronly, grey-haired woman stood up. "We have, Your Honor." She handed a slip of paper to a bailiff, who passed it up to the judge.

"Very well. I'll read the verdict." Judge Galvan paused. "We the jury, in the case of The State of Oregon versus Michael Hollister, Case #736-452, find the defendant, Michael Hollister, guilty of murder in the second degree."

Thomas looked from Michael Hollister to Gerald Copeland. Both hung their heads at that exact moment.

"Ho-lee shit," Zack whispered. "They got him."

Chapter Sixty

Thomas wasn't able to attend Michael's sentencing hearing. At that moment the sentence was handed down, he was struggling through a Plane Geometry test. He read about it in the next day's paper: "Michael Jepson Hollister, 18, of Middle Falls, was sentenced to twenty-six years in prison for the killing of fifteen year old Carrie Copeland last May. He will serve his sentence at the Oregon State Prison in Salem."

That's it, then. I've done what I can to stop that maniac. I'm done with him. I can let him go.

Thomas dropped the paper into his lap. He thought back to the list he had written, laying on his bed, what felt like so long ago.

Don't kill Zack. I got that one done.

Stop Michael from killing people. I failed that one, but I've made it as right as I can.

Help Carrie Copeland. She didn't need any help, but she sure helped me, and I let her down.

Help Ben be who he really is. That was a joke. Ben will always be who he is. He's my friend, now, and that's all I could ever ask.

You'd think with a chance to do everything over, I could do better than that, but life is still life. It still happens when you're not paying attention.

Postscript
July 4th, 1986

Thomas Weaver dropped a final six-pack of pop into the cooler as the doorbell rang. He jogged from the back yard through to the front of the house. "Got it, Mom!"

Ben and Simon were at the door. Ben was holding a Pyrex casserole dish covered in foil.

"Oh, it's just you two."

"A fine greeting for your oldest, dearest, and hippest best friends. Look, I brought a little culture into your intellectual wasteland." Simon produced a CD, Madonna's *True Blue*. "It just came out this week. You're welcome."

"No, I meant, you two know you don't need to ring the doorbell. Oh, hell, never mind. You knew what I meant. Shannon will love the CD, Simon. She's really into Madonna." *Ten years in, I still haven't gotten used to oldies being new again.* "Come on in. Ben, let's put the casserole in the kitchen for right now. I'm just getting the barbecue fired up."

On the way to the kitchen, Ben said, "We don't mind just barging in on you in your place, but since your mom moved into the country club, we figured we'd better find our manners."

"Come on outside. Zack and Jennifer and the girls should be here any second. Shannon just ran to the store to get more buns. Ben, maybe you can set up the badminton net while I get the burgers and dogs on the grill. Or would you rather do croquet?"

Ben looked at Simon, whose growth had topped out one inch below five feet. "How about croquet. Simon will have an advantage, since he can walk under the wickets."

"Ass," Simon said.

A hurricane of brown hair, pigtails, and bright holiday dresses blew through the front door. "Uncle Tommy, Uncle Tommy!"

Thomas bent down and scooped up Zack's identical twin girls, Mindy and Mandy, both of whom were pleading high-pitched cases about how the other had cheated at Aggravation that morning. Thomas laughed and hugged them both. He then set them down, patted them both on their bottoms and said, "Scoot. Lunch will be ready in a few. I'll bet Grandma has a copy of *101 Dalmatians* all queued up and ready for you two."

They ran off, still chattering, bouncing off their parents, ignoring the latter's commands to slow down. Zack was dressed in tan shorts, a polo shirt, and a Middle Falls Track & Field baseball hat. If a few pounds heavier than when he established the school's still-standing record time in the 880, Zack looked every bit the young PE teacher and track coach he was. Jennifer, belly slightly swollen with baby #3, hugged Thomas. "Where's your mom?"

"She and Paul were in the garage, trying to find the briquettes so I can get this barbecue underway."

"And here we are, right on schedule," Anne said. Ten years older, yes, but lovelier than ever. She and Paul Taylor, an ER doctor from the hospital, had been married for five years and it obviously agreed with her.

Paul, ten years older than Anne but in better shape than Thomas would ever be, handed the charcoal to Thomas. "I think my job here is done. It's all yours now, Thomas."

"Thank you, sir," Thomas said. He spread the briquettes out in a heap, sprayed lighter fluid all over them, and tossing in a match. The fluid whooshed into flame. "And now, we wait."

"Seems like I'm always waiting on you, Thomas." Shannon emerged onto the patio, carrying a paper bag filled with hot dog and hamburger buns. She kissed Thomas lightly, then hugged Anne. "Sorry I'm a little late."

"My fault. I forgot the buns."

"Beer and pop are in the cooler," Thomas said. "What's everybody want?"

Thomas acted as bartender, delivering wine coolers to Anne and Shannon, a sparkling water to Jennifer, and Rainier beer bottles to Paul, Simon, and Ben.

Thomas pointed to Zack's cap. "How's the team shaping up for next year, Coach?"

"Not bad. We're not going to set the world on fire, but we shouldn't embarrass ourselves. What I could really use is a couple of young Zack Weavers."

"There are times I could use a young Zack Weaver," Jennifer said.

Everyone laughed. "Looks like you've found someone who can keep you in line, brother," said Thomas.

"That," said Zack, "is not a problem."

Thomas grabbed a Coke from the cooler, then sat down with everyone else around the patio. He heard the happy chatter of his nieces from inside the house. Anne and Paul sat close together in the shade of the umbrella. Zack and Jennifer were whispering something to each other and giggling. Ben and Simon were in the yard, pushing the last of the wickets in for croquet. Simon swung his mallet mightily, shooting his ball off the grass and skittering across the patio to land in the pool. "It's not golf. Can't you tell the difference?" asked Ben through gales of laughter.

"There's that cunning legal mind at work, drawing unimportant distinctions," said Simon. He was trying to fish the croquet ball out with a pool skimmer net, not very successfully.

Thomas looked at Shannon and smiled. *It's so tough, dating someone when you know you're probably forty years older than they are. It's getting a little less weird the longer I'm here, and the older I get, though. The question is, how do I marry someone who doesn't know the truth about me? What do I do when I don't know any way to convince her of the truth?* "I know, Shannon, it sounds crazy, but ask my Mom. She'll vouch for me." *I don't think that will fly.*

Well, a problem for a different day. For now, this is good.

No. That's not right. Not just for now. For any time, this is good.

Postscript Two
August, 1977

Michael Hollister pushed his face against the bars of his cell. He was alone for a moment, a brief reprieve in an existence he could never have imagined. Beatings. Rape in its many varieties. More beatings. More rapes. An endless cycle of horror and ignominy. He wasn't strong enough to fight off even a single hardened thug, much less a pack of them. The inmates of C Block found such a fresh young prisoner an unusual treat to groom.

Michael removed the sheet from his bed and twisted it. If he missed this opportunity, they would put him on suicide watch. That might make this much harder.

Now that the moment was here, he didn't consider whether or not he really wanted to end his life. It was all he had thought about since his arrival, weeks ago. It had gotten him through ongoing cycles of physical and sexual assault, and now came his chance. He twisted the other end of the sheet, fixing it around the metal rung at the top of the bunk. There was nowhere to tie it at ceiling height, so he had to make do—and to make haste.

He tied the other end around his throat, paused for just a moment to remember the feeling of his hands around Carrie

Copeland's neck, and smiled for the last time. He jumped slightly and let himself fall, hoping to break his neck.

It did not. The sheet tightened and choked him. His bare feet beat a staccato tattoo against the concrete floor. His last thought before consciousness deserted him was, "Will this never end?"

Eventually it did.

Postscript Three
1963

Michael Hollister opened his eyes.

His childhood room was mostly dark, but he recognized it even so. He held his hand in front of his face. His long, thin fingers were gone, replaced by short, slightly chubby ones. He pushed his tongue forward and found his front teeth missing. He tried to get out of bed, but fell face first to the floor. It was much further down than he had anticipated. His bed seemed enormous.

He crept down the hall to where he remembered the bathroom was, closing the door behind him. He flicked on the light and blinked back the brightness. When his vision cleared, he gazed into the bathroom mirror.

Michael looked into his five-year-old face.

Coming Soon:

The Redemption of Michael Hollister

About the Author

Some stories come from an author's imagination. Some come from our lives. *The Unusual Second Life of Thomas Weaver* came from both. In 2014, I released my Rock 'n Roll Fantasy, *Rock 'n Roll Heaven*, and I was trying to decide on my next project. I always have a number of ideas bubbling just under the surface, waiting their turn to make it onto the page.

I thought of my wife, Dawn, whom I had loved since I was fifteen years old. We had been separated in 1979 and didn't really see each other again for thirty years. I thought back on our early years and wondered, "If I could go back and do it all again, what would I do differently? Could I find a way to change things so that we were never separated all those years?"

That was the beginning. I took this small wisp of an idea to Jonathan Kelley, who I fondly call my *Editor For Life*. To say he was not thrilled with the idea of me writing a third book about Dawn and I (*Feels Like the First Time* and *Both Sides Now* being the first two) is a vast understatement. He did everything he could to throw his body on the grenade that was that idea. I respect Jonathan's opinion, so I put the idea to rest for a few months.

Eventually, I thought of writing about my sister and nephew, who were never far from my thoughts. They had died within a few days of each other in late 2008. I knew that someday I wanted to write about them. My nephew, also Thomas, had died of alcohol abuse. His mother, my sister Terri, had died of a heart attack two days later. They were my two closest confidants. When they died, I was bereft. The idea that I could write a book about them and spend a year or so living with them again was intoxicating.

I knew the things that had caused my Tommy to turn to alcohol, but those were his reasons, and I wanted to leave them with him. I knew I needed something else. I turned to another piece of family history for the inciting incident of the book. When I was very young, I had two cousins, Carl and Eric. Carl was much like Zack Weaver—bright, athletic, a golden child. Eric grew up a bit in Carl's shadow. I loved them both.

In the early sixties, they went skiing. On the way home, for reasons I never knew, Carl asked Eric to drive them down the mountain. Eric was quite a few years younger than Carl. I don't know if he even had his full driver's license. On the trip home, there was an accident. Carl died, Eric lived. Eric was haunted by that accident for the rest of his life.

Ultimately, I combined these two bits of family history, fictionalized them, and *The Unusual Second Life of Thomas Weaver* was born.

Of course, Michael Hollister is a completely fictional character. As far as I know, I have no serial killers among my friends and acquaintances.

It's been a wonderful experience, spending time with Thomas and Anne, echoes of Terri and Tommy. In many ways, I am sad that it is over. Thus, the short tease at the end of the book that will eventually be the beginning of a new book also set in Middle Falls, Oregon: *The Redemption of Michael Hollister*. At some point, I also look forward to telling additional stories in this world. I'd like to know what happened to Emillion/Emily after she was recycled, and Simon is a character who is fascinating to me, even though he is just a small player in this story.

If you enjoyed this story and would like to know when more *Middle Falls* stories are available, I would love it if you would join my New Release Alert List. If you join, I'll send you an ebook copy of *Rock 'n Roll Heaven* absolutely free, no strings attached. Of course, I value your privacy as I value my own, and I will never sell or give away your email address.

Writing a book is very much a team effort.

As I mentioned earlier, Jonathan Kelley served as both developmental and substantive editor. That means that we discussed the book in advance, dissected each plot turn and character development and generally vetted the book before I even wrote it. Then, once I did write it, he took my prose and made me look like a better writer than I am. I will never ask for more than that. He is also my friend, and I thank him sincerely for his literary lessons, guidance, and invaluable advice.

The haunting cover for the book was designed by Maria Novillo Saravia of beauteBOOK. She took a small idea I had—the face of a young boy in transition to represent Thomas Weaver—and presented me with this cover. I loved it instantly. Maria also designed the new covers for *Feels Like the First Time* and *Both Sides Now*. She is an incredibly talented artist, and I know I am fortunate to work with her.

Prior to being released as a novel, I released *Thomas Weaver* as a six-part serial. The covers for those serial episodes were designed by Linda Boulanger of TreasureLine Books. Those covers were also wonderful and managed to catch the dichotomy of a fifty-four year old man living in a teenage body. I've been working with Linda since my very first book and look forward to creating many more projects with her.

Debra Galvan has served as my proofreader for my last few projects, and I never cease to be amazed by her work. She is thorough, sharp-eyed, and works so quickly that I honestly don't know how she does it. Thank you, Deb!

I had a number of early readers on this book. My monthly writer's group, including John Draper, Dianne Bunnell, and Dan Post, gave me many helpful suggestions and helped me shape this into the book it became. Likewise, the Meet and Critique group led by Michel King was exceptionally helpful in shaping the early chapters of the book. In addition to my groups, I need to thank my individual alpha readers: Zack Lester, my cousin Gene Inmon, Karen Lichtenwalter, Laura Heilman and my long-time friend Jeff Hunter. Many thanks to all of you for helping me knock off the rough edges of the story.

Ultimately, I am thankful to you as a reader. Without you, I wouldn't write. Thank you for sharing my stories and helping me bring them to life.

Shawn Inmon
Orting, Washington
July, 2016

More by Shawn Inmon

Feels Like the First Time

Both Sides Now

Rock 'n Roll Heaven

Second Chance Love

Lucky Man

Christmas Town

Chad Stinson Goes for a Walk

Printed in Great Britain
by Amazon